Meadow Grass

Alice Brown

Contents

MEADOW GRASS

BY

Alice Brown

TO M.G.R.
LOVER OF WOODS AND FIELD AND SEA.

NUMBER FIVE.

We who are Tiverton born, though false ambition may have ridden us to market, or the world's voice incited us to kindred clamoring, have a way of shutting our eyes, now and then, to present changes, and seeing things as they were once, as they are still, in a certain sleepy yet altogether individual corner of country life. And especially do we delight in one bit of fine mental tracery, etched carelessly, yet for all time, so far as our own' short span is concerned, by the unerring stylus of youth: the outline of a little red schoolhouse, distinguished from the other similar structures within Tiverton bounds by "District No. V.," painted on a shingle, in primitive black letters, and nailed aloft over the door. Up to the very hollow which made its playground and weedy garden, the road was elm-bordered and lined with fair meadows, skirted in the background by shadowy pines, so soft they did not even wave; they only seemed to breathe. The treasures of the road! On either side, the way was plumed and paved with beauties so rare that now, disheartened dwellers in city streets, we covetously con over in memory that roaming walk to school and home again. We know it now for what it was, a daily progress of delight. We see again the old watering-trough, decayed into the mellow loveliness of gray lichen and greenest moss. Here beside the ditch whence the water flowed, grew the pale forget-me-not and sticky star-blossomed cleavers. A step farther, beyond the nook where the spring bubbled first, were the riches of the common roadway; and over the gray, lichen-bearded fence, the growth of stubbly upland pasture. Everywhere, in road and pasture too, thronged milkweed, odorous haunt of the bee and those frailest butterflies of the year, born of one family with drifting blossoms; and straightly tall, the solitary mullein, dust-covered but crowned with a gold softer and more to be desired than the pride of kings. Perhaps the carriage folk from the outer world, who sometimes penetrate Tiverton's leafy quiet, may wonder at the queer little enclosures of sticks and pebbles on many a bare, tree-shaded slope along the road. "Left there from some game!" they say to one another, and drive on, satisfied. But these are no mere discarded playthings, dear ignorant travellers! They are tokens of the mimic earnest with which child-life is ever seeking to sober itself, and rushing unsummoned into the workaday fields of an aimlessly frantic world. They are houses, and the stone boundaries are walls. This tree stump is an armchair, this board a velvet sofa. Not more truly is "this thorn-bush, my thorn-bush; and this dog, my dog."

Across the road, at easy running distance from the schoolhouse at noontime or recess, crawled the little river, with its inevitable "hole," which each mother's son was warned to avoid in swimming, lest he be seized with cramp there where the pool was bottomless. What eerie wonders lurked within the mirror of those shallow brown waters! Long black hairs cleaved and clung in their limpid flowing. To this day, I know not whether they were horse-hairs, far from home, or swaying willow roots; the boys said they were "truly" hairs of the kind destined to become snakes in their last estate; and the girls, listening, shivered with all Mother Eve's premonitory thrill along the backbone. Wish-bugs, too, were here, skimming and darting. The peculiarity of a wish-bug is that he will bestow upon you your heart's desire, if only you hold him in the hand and wish. But the impossible premise defeats the conclusion. You never do hold him long enough, simply because you can't catch him in the first place. Yet the fascinating possibility is like a taste for drink, or the glamour of cards. Does the committee-man drive past to Sudleigh market, suggesting the prospect of a leisurely return that afternoon, and consequent dropping in to hear the geography class? Then do the laziest and most optimistic boys betake them hastily from their dinner-pails to the river, and spend their precious nooning in quest of the potent bug, through whose spell the unwelcome visit may be averted. The time so squandered in riotous gaming might have, fixed the afternoon's "North Poles and Equators" triumphantly in mind, to the everlasting defiance of all alien questioning; but no! for human delight lies ever in the unattainable. The committee-man comes like Nemesis, *aequo pede*, the lesson is unlearned, and the stern-fibred little teacher orders out the rack known as staying after school. But what durance beyond hours in the indescribably desolate schoolroom ever taught mortal boy to shun the delusive insect created for his special undoing? So long as the heart has woes of its own breeding, so long also will it dodge the discipline of labor, and grasp at the flicker of an easy success.

On either side the little bridge (over which horses pounded with an ominous thunder and a rain of dust on the head of him who lingered beneath the sleepers, in a fearsome joy), the meadows were pranked with purple iris and whispering rushes, mingling each its sweetness with the good, rank smell of mud below. Here were the treasures of the water-course, close hidden, or blowing in the light of day. The pale, golden-hearted arrow-head neighbored the homespun pickerel-weed, and-- oh, mysterious glory from an oozy bed!--luscious, sun-golden cow-lilies rose sturdily triumphant, dripping with color, glowing in sheen. The button-bush hung out her balls, and white alder painted the air with faint perfume; willow-herb built her bowery arches, and the flags were ever glancing like swords of roistering knights. These flags, be it known to such as have grown up in grievous ignorance of the lore inseparable from "deestrick school," hold the most practical significance in the mind of boy and girl; for they bring forth (I know we thought for our delight alone!) a delicacy known as flag-buds, everlastingly dear to the childish palate. These were devoured by the wholesale in their season, and little mouths grew oozy-green as those of happy beasties in June, from much champing and chewing. Did we lose our appetite for the delectable dinner-pail through such literal going to pasture? I think not. Tastes were elastic, in those days; and Nature, so bullied, durst seldom revolt.

On one side, the nearest neighbor to the school lived at least a mile away; but on the other, the first house of all owned treasures manifold for the little squad who, though the day were wet or dry, fair or frowning, trotted thither at noon. Here were trees under which lay, in happy season, over-ripe Bartlett pears; here, too, was one mulberry-tree, whereof the suggestion was strange and wonderful, and the fruit less appealing to taste than to a mystical fancy. But outside the bank wall grew the balm-of-Gileads, in a stately, benevolent row,--trees of healing, of fragrance and romantic charm. No child ever sought the old home to beg pears and mulberries, or to fill the school-house pail at its dark-bosomed well, without bearing away a few of the leaves in a covetous grasp. Sweet treasure-trove these, to be pressed to fresh young faces, and held and patted in hot little palms, till they grew flabby but evermore fragrant, still diffusing over the dusty schoolroom that warm odor, whispering to those who read no corner but their own New England, of the myrrh and balsams of the East.

We knew everything in those days, we aimless knights-errant with dinner-pail and slate; the dry, frosty hollow where gentians bloom when the pride of the field is over, the woody slopes of the hepatica's awakening, under coverlet of withered leaves, and the sunny banks where violets love to live with their good gossip, the trembling anemone. At noon, we roved abroad into solitudes so deep that even our unsuspecting hearts sometimes quaked with fear of dark and lonesomeness; and then we came trooping back at the sound of the bell, untamed, happy little savages, ready to settle, with a long breath, to the afternoon's drowsy routine. Arrant nonsense that! the boundary of British America and the conjugation of the verb *to be*! Who that might loll away the hours upon a bank in silken ease, needed aught even of computation or the tongues? He alone had inherited the earth.

All the little figures flitting through those tranquil early dramas are so sharply drawn, so brightly colored still! I meet Melissa Crane sometimes nowadays, a prosperous matron with space enough on her broad back for the very largest plaid ever woven; but her present identity is hazy and unreal. I see instead, with a sudden throb of memory, the little Melissa, who, one recess, accepted a sugared doughnut from me, and said, with a quaint imitation of old folks' manner,--

"I think your mother will be a real good cook, if she lives!"

I hear of Susie Marden, who went out West, married, and grew up with the country in great magnificence; but to me she is and ever will be the little girl who made seventy pies, one Thanksgiving time, thereby earning the somewhat stinted admiration of those among us who could not cook. Many a great deed, tacitly promised in that springtime, never came to pass; many a brilliant career ingloriously ended. There was Sam Marshall. He could do sums to the admiration of class and teacher, and, Cuvier-like, evolve an entire flock from Colburn's two geese and a half. His memory was prodigious. He could name the Presidents, bound the States and Territories, and rattle off the list of prepositions so fast that you could almost see the spark-shower from his rushing wheels of thought. It was an understood thing among us, when Sam was in his teens, that he should at least enter the Senate; perhaps he would even be President, and scatter offices, like halfpence, among his scampering townsmen. But to-day he patiently does his haying--by hand! and "goes sleddin'" in the winter. The Senate is as far from him as the Polar Star, and I question whether he could even bear the crucial test of two geese and a half. Yet I still look upon him with a thrill of awe, as the man selected by the popular vote to represent us in fame's Valhalla, and mysteriously defeated by some unexpected move of the "unseen hand at a game."

There were a couple of boys such good comrades as never to be happy save when together. They cared only for the games made for two; all their goods were tacitly held in common, and a tradition still lives that David, when a new teacher asked his exact age, claimed his comrade's birthday, and then wondered why everybody laughed. They had a way of wandering off together to the woods, on Saturday. mornings, when the routine of chores could be hurried through, and always they bore with them a store of eggs, apples, or sweet corn, to be cooked in happy seclusion. All this raw material was stolen from the respective haylofts and gardens at home, though, as the fathers owned, with an appreciative grin, the boys might have taken it openly for the asking. That, however, would so have alloyed the charm of gypsying that it was not to be thought of for a moment; and they crept about on their foraging expeditions with all the caution of a hostile tribe. Blessed fathers and mothers to wink at the escapade, and happy boys, wise chiefly in their longing to be free! We had a theory that Jonathan and David would go into business together. Perhaps we thought of them in the same country store, their chairs tilted on either side of the air-tight stove, telling stories, in the intervals of custom, as they apparently did in their earlier estate. For, shy as they were in general company, they chatted together with an intense earnestness all day long; and it was one of the stock questions in our neighborhood, when the social light burned low,--

"What under the sun do you s'pose Dave and Jont find to talk about?"

Alas! again the world had builded foolishly; for with early manhood, they fell in love with the same round-cheeked school-teacher. Jonathan married her, after what wrench of feeling I know not; and the other fled to the town, whence he never returned save for the briefest visit at Thanksgiving or Christmas time. The stay-at-home lad is a warm farmer, and the little school-teacher a mother whose unlined face shows the record of a placid life; but David cannot know even this, save by hearsay, for he never sees them. He is a moneyed man, and not a year ago, gave the town a new library. But is he happy? Or does the old wound still show a ragged edge? For that may be, they tell us, even "when you come to forty year."

Then, clad in brighter vestments of memory, there was the lad who earned unto himself much renown, even among his disapproving relatives, by running away from home, in quest of gold and glory. True, he was brought back at the end of three days, footsore and muddy, and with noble appetite for the griddle-cakes his mother cooked him in lieu of the traditional veal,--but all undaunted. He never tried it again, yet people say he has thrown away all his chances of a thrifty living by perpetual wandering in the woods with gun and fishing-rod, and that he is cursed with a deplorable indifference to the state of his fences and potato-patch. No one could call him an admirable citizen, but I am not sure that he has chosen the worser part; for who is so jovial and sympathetic on a winter evening, when the apples are passed, and even the shining cat purrs content before the blaze, or in the wood solitudes, familiar to him as his own house door?

"Pa'tridges' nests?" he said, one spring, with a cock of his eye calculated to show at once a humorous recognition of his genius and his delinquencies. "Sartain! I wish I was as sure where I keep my scythe sned!"

He has learned all the lore of the woods, the ways of "wild critters," and the most efficacious means both to woo and kill them. Prim spinsters eye him acridly, as a man given over to "shif'less" ways, and wives set him up, like a lurid guidepost, before husbands prone to lapse from domestic thrift; but the dogs smile at him, and children, for whom he is ever ready to make kite or dory, though all his hay should mildew, or to string thimbleberries on a grass spear while supper cools within, tumble merrily at his heels. Such as he should never assume domestic relations, to be fettered with requirements of time and place. Let them rather claim maintenance from a grateful public, and live, like troubadours of old, ministrant to the general joy.

Not all the memories of that early day are quite unspotted by remorse. Although we wore the mask of jocund faces and straightforward glance, we little people repeatedly proclaimed ourselves the victims of Adam's fall. Even then we needed to pray for deliverance from those passions which have since pursued us. There was the little bound girl who lived with a "selec'man's" wife, a woman with children of her own, but a hard taskmistress to the stranger within her gates. Poor little Polly! her clothes, made over from those of her mistress, were of dark, rough flannel, often in uncouth plaids and appalling stripes. Her petticoats were dyed of a sickly hue known as cudbar, and she wore heavy woollen stockings of the same shade. Polly got up early, to milk and drive the cows; she set the table, washed milkpans, and ran hither and thither on her sturdy cudbar legs, always willing, sometimes singing, and often with a mute, questioning look on her little freckled face, as if she had already begun to wonder why it has pleased God to set so many boundary lines over which the feeble may not pass. The selec'man's son--a heavy-faced, greedy boy--was a bully, and Polly became his butt; she did his tasks, hectored by him in private, and with a child's strange reticence, she never told even us how unbearable he made her life. We could see it, however; for not much remains hidden in that communistic atmosphere of the country neighborhood. But sometimes Polly revolted; her temper blazed up, a harmless flash in the pan, and then, it was said, Mis' Jeremiah took her to the shed-chamber and, trounced her soundly. I myself have seen her sitting at the little low window, when I trotted by, in the pride of young life, to "borry some emptin's," or the recipe for a new cake. Often she waved a timid hand to me; and I am glad to remember a certain sunny morning, illuminated now because I tossed her up a bright hollyhock in return. It was little to give out of a full and happy day; but Polly had nothing. Once she came near great good fortune,--and missed it! For a lady, who boarded a few weeks in the neighborhood, took a fancy to Polly, and was stirred to outspoken wrath by our tales of the severity of her life. She gave her a pretty pink cambric dress, and Polly wore it on "last day," at the end of the summer term. She was evidently absorbed in love of it, and sat, smoothing its shiny surface with her little cracked hand, so oblivious to the requirements of the occasion that she only looked up dazed when the teacher told her to describe the Amazon River, and unregretfully let the question pass. The lady meant to take Polly away with, her, but she fell sick with erysipelas in the face, and was hurried off to the city to be nursed, "a sight to behold," as everybody said. And whether she died, or whether she got well and forgot Polly, none of us ever heard. We only knew she did not return, bringing the odor of violets and the rustle of starched petticoats into our placid lives.

But all these thoughts of Polly would be less wearing, when they come in the night-time knocking at the heart, if I could only remember her as glowing under the sympathy and loving-kindness of her little mates. Alas! it was not so. We were senseless little brutes, who, never having learned the taste of misery ourselves, had no pity for the misfortunes of others. She was, indeed, ill-treated; but what were we, to translate the phrase? She was an under dog, and we had no mercy on her. We "plagued" her, God forgive us! And what the word means, in its full horror, only a child can compass. We laughed at her cudbar petticoats, her little "chopped hands;" and when she stumbled over the arithmetic lesson, because she had been up at four o'clock every morning since the first bluebirds came, we laughed at that. Life in general seems to have treated Polly in somewhat the same way. I hear that she did not marry well, and that her children had begun to "turn out bad," when she died, prematurely bent and old, not many weeks ago. But when I think of what we might have given and what we did withhold, when I realize that one drop of water from each of us would have filled her little cup to overflowing, there is one compensating thought, and I murmur, conscience-smitten, "I'm glad she had the pink dress!"

And now the little school is ever present with us, ours still for counsel or re-proof. Its long-closed sessions are open, by day and night; and I suppose, as time goes on, and we drop into the estate of those who sit by the fireside, oblivious to present scenes, yet acutely awake to such as

"Flash upon that inward eye   Which is the bliss of solitude,"

it will grow more and more lifelike and more near. Beside it, live all the joys of memory and many a long-past pain. For we who have walked in country ways, walk in them always, and with no divided love, even though brick pavements have been our chosen road this many a year. We follow the market, we buy and sell, and even run across the sea, to fit us with new armor for the soul, to guard it from the hurts of years; but ever do we keep the calendar of this one spring of life. Some unheard angelus summons us to days of feast and mourning; it may be the joy of the fresh-springing willow, or the nameless pain responsive to the croaking of frogs, in the month when twilights are misty, and waves of world-sorrow flood in upon the heart, we know not why. All those trembling half-thoughts of the sleep of the year and its awakening,--we have not escaped them by leaving the routine that brought them forth. We know when the first violets are blowing in the woods, and we paint for ourselves the tasselling of the alder and the red of maple-buds. We taste still the sting of checkerberry and woodsy flavor of the fragrant birch. When fields of corn are shimmering in the sun, we know exactly how it would seem to run through those dusty aisles, swept by that silken drapery, and counselled in whispers from the plumy tops so far above our heads. The ground-sparrow's nest is not strange to us; no, nor the partridge's hidden treasure within the wood. We can make pudding-bags of live-forever, dolls' bonnets, "trimmed up to the nines," out of the velvet mullein leaf, and from the ox-eyed daisies, round, cap-begirt faces, smiling as the sun. All the homely secrets of rural life are ours: the taste of pie, cinnamon-flavored, from the dinner-pails at noon; the smell of "pears a-b'ilin'," at that happiest hour when, in the early dusk, we tumble into the kitchen, to find the table set and the stove redolent of warmth and savor. "What you got for supper?" we cry,--question to be paralleled in the summer days by "What'd you have for dinner?" as, famished little bears, we rush to the dairy-wheel, to feed ravenously on the cold, delicious fragments of the meal eaten without us.

If time ever stood still, if we were condemned to the blank solitude of hospital nights or becalmed, mid-ocean days, and had hours for fruitless dreaming, I wonder what viands we should choose, in setting forth a banquet from that ambrosial past! Foods unknown to poetry and song: "cold b'iled dish," pan-dowdy, or rye drop-cakes dripping with butter! For these do we taste, in moments of retrospect; and perhaps we dwell the more on their homely savor because we dare not think what hands prepared them for our use, or, when the board was set, what faces smiled. We are too wise, with the cunning prudence of the years, to penetrate over-far beyond the rosy boundary of youth, lest we find also that bitter pool which is not Lethe, but the waters of a vain regret.

FARMER ELI'S VACATION

I t don't seem as if we'd really got round to it, does it, father?" asked Mrs. Pike. The west was paling, and the August insects stirred the air with their crooning chirp. Eli and his wife sat together on the washing-bench outside the back door, waiting for the milk to cool before it should be strained. She was a large, comfortable woman, with an unlined face, and smooth, fine auburn hair; he was spare and somewhat bent, with curly iron-gray locks, growing thin, and crow's-feet about his deep-set gray eyes. He had been smoking the pipe of twilight contentment, but now he took it out and laid it on the bench beside him, uncrossing his legs and straightening himself, with the air of a man to whom it falls, after long pondering, to take some decisive step.

"No; it don't seem as if 'twas goin' to happen," he owned. "It looked pretty dark to me, all last week. It's a good deal of an undertakin', come to think it all over. I dunno's I care about goin'."

"Why, father! After you've thought about it so many years, an' Sereno's got the tents strapped up, an' all! You must be crazy!"

"Well," said the farmer, gently, as he rose and went to carry the milk-pails into the pantry, calling coaxingly, as he did so, "Kitty! kitty! You had your milk? Don't you joggle, now!" For one eager tabby rose on her hind legs, in purring haste, and hit her nose against the foaming saucer.

Mrs. Pike came ponderously to her feet, and followed, with the heavy, swaying motion of one grown fleshy and rheumatic. She was not in the least concerned about Eli's change of mood. He was a gentle soul, and she had always been able to guide him in paths of her own choosing. Moreover, the present undertaking was one involving his own good fortune, and she meant to tolerate no foolish scruples which might interfere with its result. For Eli, though he had lived all his life within easy driving distance of the ocean, had never seen it, and ever since his boyhood he had cherished one darling plan,--some day he would go to the shore, and camp out there for a week. This, in his starved imagination, was like a dream of the Acropolis to an artist stricken blind, or as mountain outlines to the dweller in a lonely plain. But the years had flitted past, and the dream never seemed nearer completion. There were always planting, haying, and harvesting to be considered; and though he was fairly prosperous, excursions were foreign to his simple habit of life. But at last, his wife had stepped into the van, and organized an expedition, with all the valor of a Francis Drake.

"Now, don't you say one word, father," she had said. "We're goin' down to the beach, Sereno, an' Hattie, an' you an' me, an' we're goin' to camp out. It'll do us all good."

For days before the date of the excursion, Eli had been solemn and tremulous, as with joy; but now, on the eve of the great event, he shrank back from it, with an undefined notion that it was like death, and that he was not prepared. Next morning, however, when they all rose and took their early breakfast, preparatory to starting at five, he showed no sign of indecision, and even went about his outdoor tasks with an alacrity calculated, as his wife approvingly remarked, to "for'ard the v'y'ge." He had at last begun to see his way clear, and he looked well satisfied when his daughter Hattie and Sereno, her husband, drove into the yard, in a wagon cheerfully suggestive of a wandering life. The tents and a small hair-trunk were stored in the back, and the horse's pail swung below.

"Well, father," called Hattie, her rosy face like a flower under the large shade-hat she had trimmed for the occasion, "guess we're goin' to have a good day!"

He nodded from the window, where he was patiently holding his head high and undergoing strangulation, while his wife, breathing huskily with haste and importance, put on his stock.

"You come in, Hattie, an' help pack the doughnuts into that lard-pail on the table," she called. "I guess you'll have to take two pails. They ain't very big."

At length, the two teams were ready, and Eli mounted to his place, where he looked very slender beside his towering mate. The hired man stood leaning on the pump, chewing a bit of straw, and the cats rubbed against his legs, with tails like banners; they were all impressed by a sense of the unusual.

"Well, good-by, Luke," Mrs. Pike called, over her shoulder; and Eli gave the man a solemn nod, gathered up the reins, and drove out of the yard. Just outside the gate, he pulled up.

"Whoa!" he called, and Luke lounged forward. "Don't you forget them cats! Git up, Doll!" And this time, they were gone.

For the first ten miles of the way, familiar in being the road to market, Eli was placidly cheerful. The sense that he was going to do some strange deed, to step into an unknown country, dropped away from him, and he chatted, in his intermittent, serious fashion, of the crops and the lay of the land.

"Pretty bad job up along here, ain't it, father?" called Sereno, as they passed a sterile pasture where two plodding men and a yoke of oxen were redeeming the soil from its rocky fetters.

"There's a good deal o' pastur', in some places, that ain't fit for nothin' but to hold the world together," returned Eli; and then he was silent, his eyes fixed on Doll's eloquent ears, his mouth working a little. For this progress through a less desirable stratum of life caused him to cast a backward glance over his own smooth, middle-aged road.

"We've prospered, 'ain't we, Maria?" he said, at last; and his wife, unconsciously following his thoughts, in the manner of those who have lived long together, stroked her black silk *visite*, and answered, with a well-satisfied nod:

"I guess we 'ain't got no cause to complain."

The roadside was parched under an August sun; tansy was dust-covered, and ferns had grown ragged and gray. The jogging horses left behind their lazy feet a suffocating cloud.

"My land!" cried Mrs. Pike, "if that ain't goldenrod! I do b'lieve it comes earlier every year, or else the seasons are changin'. See them elderberries! Ain't they purple! You jest remember that bush, an' when we go back, we'll fill some pails. I dunno when I've made elderberry wine."

Like her husband, she was vaguely excited; she began to feel as if life would be all holidays. At noon, they stopped under the shadow of an elm-tree which, from its foothold in a field, completely arched the road; and there they ate a lunch of pie and doughnuts, while the horses, freed from their headstalls, placidly munched a generous feed of oats, near by. Hattie and her mother accepted this picnicking with an air of apologetic amusement; and when one or two passers-by looked at them, they smiled a little at vacancy, with the air of wishing it understood that they were by no means accustomed to such irregularities.

"I guess they think we're gypsies," said Hattie, as one carriage rolled past.

"Well, they needn't trouble themselves," returned her mother, rising with difficulty to brush the crumbs from her capacious lap. "I guess I've got as good an extension-table to home as any on 'em."

But Eli ate sparingly, and with a preoccupied and solemn look.

"Land, father!" exclaimed his wife, "you 'ain't eat no more'n a bird!

"I guess I'll go over to that well," said he, "an' git a drink o' water. I drink more'n I eat, if I ain't workin'." But when he came back, carefully bearing a tin pail brimming with cool, clear water, his face expressed strong disapprobation, and he smacked his lips scornfully.

"Terrible flat water!" he announced. "Tastes as if it come out o' the cistern." But the others could find no fault with it, and Sereno drained the pail.

"Pretty good, I call it," he said; and Mrs. Pike rejoined,--

"You always was pretty particular about water, father."

But Eli still shook his head, and ejaculated, "Brackish, brackish!" as he began to put the bit in Doll's patient mouth. He was thinking, with a passion of loyalty, of the clear, ice-cold water at home, which had never been shut out, by a pump, from the purifying airs of heaven, but lay where the splashing bucket and chain broke, every day, the image of moss and fern. His throat grew parched and dry with longing.

When they were within three miles of the sea, it seemed to them that they could taste the saltness of the incoming breeze; the road was ankle-deep in dust; the garden flowers were glaring in their brightness. It was a new world. And when at last they emerged from the marsh-bordered road upon a ridge of sand, and turned a sudden corner, Mrs. Pike faced her husband in triumph.

"There, father!" she cried. "There 'tis!"

But Eli's eyes were fixed on the dashboard in front of him. He looked pale.

"Why, father," said she, impatiently, "ain't you goin' to look? It's the sea!"

"Yes, yes," said Eli, quietly; "byme-by. I'm goin' to put the horses up fust."

"Well, I never!" said Mrs. Pike; and as they drew up on the sandy tract where

Sereno had previously arranged a place for their tents, she added, almost fretfully, turning to Hattie, "I dunno what's come over your father. There's the water, an' he won't even cast his eyes at it."

But Hattie understood her father, by some intuition of love, though not of likeness.

"Don't you bother him, ma," she said. "He'll make up his mind to it pretty soon. Here, le's lift out these little things, while they're unharnessin', and then they can get at the tents."

Mrs. Pike's mind was diverted by the exigencies of labor, and she said no more; but after the horses had been put up at a neighboring house, and Sereno, red-faced with exertion, had superintended the tent-raising, Hattie slipped her arm through her father's, and led him away.

"Come, pa," she said, in a whisper; "le's you and me climb over on them rocks."

Eli went; and when they had picked their way over sand and pools to a headland where the water thundered below, and salt spray dashed up in mist to their feet, he turned and looked at the sea. He faced it as a soul might face Almighty Greatness, only to be stricken blind thereafter; for his eyes filled painfully with slow, hot tears. Hattie did not look at him, but after a while she shouted in his ear, above the outcry of the surf,--

"Here, pa, take my handkerchief. I don't know how 'tis about you, but this spray gets in my eyes."

Eli took it obediently, but he did not speak; he only looked at the sea. The two sat there, chilled and quite content, until six o'clock, when Mrs. Pike came calling to them from the beach, with dramatic shouts, emphasized by the waving of her ample apron,--

"Supper's ready! Sereno's built a bum-fire, an' I've made some tea!"

Then they slowly made their way back to the tents, and sat down to the evening meal. Sereno seemed content, and Mrs. Pike was bustling and triumphant; the familiar act of preparing food had given her the feeling of home.

"Well, father, what think?" she asked, smiling exuberantly, as she passed him his mug of tea. "Does it come up to what you expected?"

Eli turned upon her his mild, dazed eyes.

"I guess it does," he said, gently.

That night, they sat upon the shore while the moon rose and laid in the water her majestic pathway of light. Eli was the last to leave the rocks, and he lay down on his hard couch in the tent, without speaking.

"I wouldn't say much to father," whispered Hattie to her mother, as they parted for the night. "He feels it more 'n we do."

"Well, I s'pose he is some tired," said Mrs. Pike, acquiescing, after a brief look of surprise. "It's a good deal of a jaunt, but I dunno but I feel paid a'ready. Should you take out your hair-pins, Hattie?"

She slept soundly and vocally, but her husband did not close his eyes. He looked, though he could see nothing, through the opening in the tent, in the direction where lay the sea, solemnly clamorous, eternally responsive to some infinite whisper from without his world. The tension of the hour was almost more than he could bear; he longed for morning, in sharp suspense, with a faint hope that the light might bring relief. Just as the stars faded, and one luminous line pencilled the east, he rose, smoothed his hair, and stepped softly out upon the beach. There he saw two shadowy figures, Sereno and Hattie. She hurried forward to meet him.

"You goin' to see the sunrise, too, father?" she asked. "I made Sereno come. He's awful mad at bein' waked up."

Eli grasped her arm.

"Hattie," he said, in a whisper, "don't you tell. I jest come out to see how 'twas here, before I go. I'm goin' home,--I'm goin' *now*."

"Why, father!" said Hattie; but she peered more closely into his face, and her tone changed. "All right," she added, cheerfully. "Sereno'll go and harness up."

"No; I'm goin' to walk."

"But, father--"

"I don't mean to breakup your stayin' here, nor your mother's. You tell her how 'twas. I'm goin' to walk."

Hattie turned and whispered to her husband for a moment. Then she took her father's hand.

"I'll slip into the tent and put you up somethin' for your breakfast and luncheon," she said. "Sereno's gone to harness; for, pa, you must take one horse, and you can send Luke back with it Friday, so's we can get the things home. What do we want of two horses down here, at two and ninepence a day? I guess I know!"

So Eli yielded; but before his wife appeared, he had turned his back on the sea, where the rose of dawn was fast unfolding. As he jogged homeward, the dusty roadsides bloomed with flowers of paradise, and the insects' dry chirp thrilled like the song of angels. He drove into the yard just at the turning of the day, when the fragrant smoke of many a crackling fire curls cheerily upward, in promise of the evening meal.

"What's busted?" asked Luke, swinging himself down from his load of fodder-corn, and beginning to unharness Doll.

"Oh, nothin'," said Eli, leaping, from the wagon as if twenty years had been taken from his bones. "I guess I'm too old for such jaunts. I hope you didn't forgit them cats."

AFTER ALL.

T he land o' gracious!" said Mrs. Lothrop Wilson, laying down her "drawing-in hook" on the rug stretched between two chairs in the middle of the kitchen, and getting up to look from the window. "If there ain't Lucindy comin' out o' the Pitmans' without a thing on her head, an' all them little curls a-flyin'! An' the old Judge ain't cold in his grave!"

"I guess the Judge won't be troubled with cold, any to speak of, arter this," said her husband from the window, where he sat eating his forenoon lunch of apple-pie and cheese. He was a cooper, and perhaps the pleasantest moment in his day was that when he slipped out of his shop, leaving a bit of paper tacked on the door to say he was "on errands," and walked soberly home for his bite and sup. "If he ain't good an' warm about now, then the Scriptur's ain't no more to be depended on than a last year's almanac."

"Late Wilson, I'm ashamed of you," retorted his wife, looking at him with such reproof that, albeit she had no flesh to spare, she made herself a double chin. "An' he your own uncle, too! Well, he *was* nigh, I'll say that for him; an' if he'd had his way, the sun'd ha' riz an' set when he said the word. But Lucindy's his only darter, an' if she don't so much as pretend to be a mourner, I guess there ain't nobody that will. There! don't you say no more! She's comin' in here!"

A light step sounded on the side piazza, and Lucindy came in, with a little delicate, swaying motion peculiar to her walk. She was a very slender woman, far past middle life, with a thin, smiling face, light blue eyes, shining with an eager brightness, and fine hair, which escaped from its tight twist in little spiral curls about the face.

"How do, Jane?" she said, in an even voice, stirred by a pleasant, reedy thrill. "How do, Lote?"

Lothrop pushed forward a chair, looking at her with an air of great kindliness. There was some slight resemblance between them, but the masculine type seemed entirely lacking in that bright alertness so apparent in her. Mrs. Wilson nodded, and went back to her drawing-in. She was making a very red rose with a pink middle.

"I dunno's I can say I'm surprised to see you, Lucindy," she began, with the duteous aspect of one forced to speak her disapproval, "for I ketched you comin' out o' the Pitmans' yard."

"Yes," said Lucindy, smiling, and plaiting her skirt between her nervous fingers. "Yes, I went in to see if they'd let me take Old Buckskin a spell to-morrow."

"What under the sun--" began Mrs. Wilson; but her husband looked at her, and she stopped. He had become so used to constituting himself Lucindy's champion in the old Judge's day, now just ended, that he kept an unremitting watch on any one who might threaten her peace. But Lucindy evidently guessed at the unspoken question.

"I should have come here, if I'd expected to drive," she said. "But I thought maybe your horse wa'n't much used to women, and I kind o' dreaded to be the first one to try him with a saddle."

Mrs. Wilson put down her hook again, and leaned back in her chair. She looked from her husband to Lucindy, without speaking. But Lucindy went on, with the innocent simplicity of a happy child.

"You know I was always possessed to ride horseback," she said, addressing herself to Lothrop, "and father never would let me. And now he ain't here, I mean to try it, and see if 'tain't full as nice as I thought."

"Lucindy!" burst forth Mrs. Wilson, explosively, "ain't you goin' to pay no respect to your father's memory?"

Lucindy turned to her, smiling still, but with a hint of quizzical shrewdness about her mouth.

"I guess I ain't called on to put myself out," she said, simply, yet not irreverently. "Father had his way in pretty much everything while he was alive. I always made up my mind if I should outlive him, I'd have all the things I wanted then, when young folks want the most. And you know then I couldn't get 'em."

"Well!" said Mrs. Wilson. Her tone spoke volumes of conflicting commentary.

"You got a saddle?" asked Lucindy, turning to her cousin. "I thought I remembered you had one laid away, up attic. I suppose you'd just as soon I'd take it?"

He was neither shocked nor amused. He had been looking at her very sadly, as one who read in every word the entire tragedy of a repressed and lonely life.

"Yes, we have, Lucindy," he said, gently, quieting his wife by a motion of the hand, "but 'tain't what you think. It's a man's saddle. You'd have to set straddle."

"Oh!" said Lucindy, a faint shade of disappointment clouding her face. "Well, no matter! I guess they've got one down to the Mardens'. Jane, should you just as soon come round this afternoon, and look over some bunnit trimmin's with me? I took two kinds of flowers home from Miss West's, and I can't for my life tell which to have."

"Ain't you goin' to wear black?" Mrs. Wilson spoke now in double italics.

"Oh, no! I don't feel called on to do that. I always liked bright colors, and I don't know's 'twould be real honest in me to put on mournin' when I didn't feel it."

"'Honor thy father'--" began Jane, in spite of her husband's warning hand; but Lucindy interrupted her, with some perplexity.

"I have, Jane, I have! I honored father all my life, just as much as ever I could. I done everything he ever told me, little and big! No, though, there's one thing I never fell in with. I did cheat him once. I don't know but I'm sorry for that, now it's all past and gone!"

Her cousin had been drumming absently on the window-sill, but he looked up with awakened interest. Mrs. Wilson, too, felt a wholesale curiosity, and she, at least, saw no reason for curbing it.

"What was it, Lucindy?" she asked. "The old hunks!" she repeated to herself, like an anathema.

Lucindy began her confession, with eyes down-dropped and a faltering voice.

"Father wanted I should have my hair done up tight and firm. So I pretended I done the best I could with it. I told him these curls round my face and down in my neck was too short, and I couldn't pin 'em up. But they wa'n't curls, and they wouldn't ha' been short if I hadn't cut 'em. For every night, and sometimes twice a day, I curled 'em on a pipe-stem."

"Ain't them curls nat'ral, Lucindy?" cried Mrs. Wilson. "Have you been fixin' 'em to blow round your face that way, all these years?"

"I begun when I was a little girl," said Lucindy, guiltily. "It did seem kind o' wrong, but I took real pleasure in it!"

Lothrop could bear no more. He wanted to wipe his eyes, but he chose instead to walk straight out of the room and down to his shop. His wife could only express a part of her amazement by demanding, in a futile sort of way,--

"Where'd you get the pipe?"

"I stole the first one from a hired man we had," said Lucindy, her cheeks growing pink. "Sometimes I had to use slate-pencils."

There was no one else to administer judgment, and Mrs. Wilson felt the necessity.

"Well," she began, "an' you can set there, tellin' that an' smilin'--"

"My smilin' don't mean any more'n some other folks' cryin', I guess," said Lucindy, smiling still more broadly. "I begun that more'n thirty years ago. I looked into the glass one day, and I see the corners of my mouth were goin' down. Sharper 'n, vinegar, I was! So I says to myself, 'I can smile, whether or no. Nobody can't help that!' And I did, and now I guess I don't know when I do it."

"Well!"

Lucindy rose suddenly and brushed her lap, as if she dusted away imaginary cares.

"There!" she exclaimed, "I've said more this mornin' than I have for forty year! Don't you lead me on to talk about what's past and gone! The only thing is, I mean to have a good time now, what there is left of it. Some things you can't get back, and some you can. Well, you step round this afternoon, won't you?"

"I dunno's I can. John's goin' to bring Claribel up, to spend the arternoon an' stay to supper."

"Why, dear heart! that needn't make no difference. I should admire to have her, too. I'll show her some shells and coral I found this mornin', up attic."

Lucindy had almost reached the street when she turned, as with a sudden resolution, and retraced her steps.

"Jane," she called, looking in at the kitchen window. "It's a real bright day, pretty as any 't ever I see. Don't you worry for fear o' my disturbin' them that's gone, if I do try to ketch at somethin' pleasant. If they're wiser now, I guess they'll be glad I had sense enough left to do it!"

That afternoon, Mrs. Wilson, in her best gingham and checked sunbonnet,

took her way along the village street to the old Judge Wilson house. It was a co-
lonial mansion, sitting austerely back in a square yard. In spite of its prosperity,
everything about it wore a dreary air, as if it were tired of being too well kept; for
houses are like people, and carry their own indefinable atmosphere with them. Mrs.
Wilson herself lived on a narrower and more secluded street, though it was said
that her husband, if he had not defied the old Judge in some crucial matter, might
have studied law with him, and possibly shared his speculations in wool. Then he,
too, might have risen to be one of the first men in the county, instead of working,
in his moderate fashion, for little more than day's wages. Claribel, a pale, dark-eyed
child, also dressed in her best gingham, walked seriously by her grandmother's side.
Lucindy was waiting for them at the door.

"I declare!" she called, delightedly. "I was 'most afraid you'd forgot to come!
Well, Claribel, if you 'ain't grown! They'll have to put a brick on your head, or
you'll be taller'n grandma."

Claribel submitted to be kissed, and they entered the large, cool sitting-room,
where they took off their things.

"You make yourself at home, Jane," said Lucindy, fluttering about, in pleasant
excitement. "I ain't goin' to pay you a mite of attention till I see Claribel fixed. Now,
Claribel, remember! you can go anywheres you're a mind to. And you can touch
anything there is. You won't find a thing a little girl can hurt. Here, you come here
where I be, and look across the entry. See that big lamp on the table? Well, if you
unhook them danglin' things and peek through 'em, you'll find the brightest colors!
My, how pretty they be! I've been lookin' through 'em this mornin'. I used to creep
in and do it when I was little," she continued, in an aside to Mrs. Wilson. "Once I
lost one." A strange look settled on her face; she was recalling a bitter experience.
"There!" she said, releasing Claribel with a little hug, "now run along! If you look
on the lower shelf of the what-not, you'll see some shells and coral I put there for
just such a little girl."

Claribel walked soberly away to her playing.

"Don't you hurt nothin'!" called Mrs. Wilson; and Claribel responded properly,--

"No, 'm."

"There!" said Lucindy, watching the precise little back across the hall, "Now le's talk a mite about vanity. You reach me that green box behind your chair. Here's the best flowers Miss West had for what I wanted. Here's my bunnit, too. You see what you think."

She set the untrimmed bonnet on her curls, and laid first a bunch of bright chrysanthemums against it, and then some strange lavender roses. The roses turned her complexion to an ivory whiteness, and her anxious, intent expression combined strangely with that undesirable effect.

"My soul, Lucindy!" cried Mrs. Wilson, startled into a more robust frankness than usual, "you do look like the Old Nick!"

A shade came over Miss Lucindy's honest face. It seemed, for a moment, as if she were going to cry.

"Don't you like 'em, Jane?" she asked, appealingly. "Won't neither of 'em do?"

Mrs. Wilson was not incapable of compunction, but she felt also the demands of the family honor.

"Well, Lucindy," she began, soothingly, "now 'tain't any use, is it, for us to say we ain't gettin' on in years? We be! You 're my age, an'--Why, look at Claribel in there! What should you say, if you see me settin' out to meetin' with red flowers on my bunnit? I should be nothin' but a laughin'-stock!"

Lucindy laid the flowers back in their box, with as much tenderness as if they held the living fragrance of a dream.

"Well!" she said, wistfully. Then she tried to smile.

"Here!" interposed Mrs. Wilson, not over-pleased with the part she felt called upon to play, "you give me your bunnit. Don't I see your old sheaf o'wheat in the box? Let me pin it on for you. There, now, don't that look more suitable?"

By the time she had laid it on, in conventional flatness, and held it up for inspection, every trace of rebellion had apparently been banished from Lucindy's mind.

"Here," said the victim of social rigor, "you hand me the box, and I'll set it away."

They had a cosey, old-fashioned chat, touching upon nothing in the least revolutionary, and Mrs. Wilson was glad to think Lucindy had forgotten all about the side-saddle. This last incident of the bonnet, she reflected, showed how much real influence she had over Lucindy. She must take care to exert it kindly but seriously now that the old Judge was gone.

"You goin' to keep your same help?" she asked, continuing the conversation.

"Oh, yes! I wouldn't part with Ann Toby for a good deal. She's goin' to have her younger sister come to live with us now. We shall be a passel o' women, sha'n't we?"

"I guess it's well for you Ann Toby's what she is, or she'd cheat you out o' your eye-teeth!"

"Well," answered Lucindy, easily, "I ain't goin' to worry about my eye-teeth. If I be cheated out of 'em, I guess I can get a new set."

At five o'clock, they had some cookies, ostensibly for Claribel, since Mrs. Wilson could not stay to tea; and then, when the little maid had taken hers out to the front steps, Lucindy broached a daring plan, that moment conceived.

"Say, Jane," she whispered, with great pretence of secrecy, "what do you think just come into my head? Do you s'pose Mattie would be put out, if I should give Claribel a hat?"

"Mercy sakes, no! all in the family so! But what set you out on that? She's got a good last year's one now, an' the ribbin's all pressed out an' turned, complete."

"I'll tell you," Said Lucindy, leaning nearer, and speaking as if she feared the very corners might hear. "You know I never was allowed to wear bright colors. And to this day, I see the hats the other girls had, blue on 'em, and pink. And if I could stand by and let a little girl pick out a hat for herself, without a word said to stop her, 'twould be real agreeable to me." Lucindy was shrewd enough to express herself somewhat moderately. She knew by experience how plainly Jane considered it a duty to discourage any overmastering emotion. But Jane Wilson was, at the same instant, feeling very keenly that Lucindy, faded and old as she was, needed to be indulged in all her riotous fancies. She repressed the temptation, however, at its birth.

"Why, I dunno's there's anything in the way of it," she said, soberly.

"Then, if you must go, I'll walk right along now. Claribel and I'll go down to Miss West's, and see what she's got. Nothin''s to be gained by waitin'!"

When they walked out through the hall together, Lucindy cast a quick and eager glance into the parlor. She almost hoped Claribel had unhooked the glass prisms from the lamp, and left them scattered on the floor, or that she had broken the precious shells, more than half a century old. She wanted to put her arms round her, and say fondly, "Never mind!" But the room was in perfect order, and little Claribel waited for them, conscious of a propriety unstained by guilt.

"Lucindy," said Mrs. Wilson, who also had used her eyes, "where's your father's canes? They al'ays stood right here in this corner."

Lucindy flushed.

"Jane," she whispered, "don't you tell, but I--I buried 'em! I felt somehow as if I couldn't--do the things I wanted to, if they set there just the same."

Jane could only look at her in silence.

"Well," she said, at length, "it takes all kinds o' people to make a world!"

That, at least, was non-committal.

She left the shoppers at her own gate, and they walked on together. Lucindy was the more excited of the two.

"Now, Claribel," she was saying, "you remember you can choose any hat you see, and have it trimmed just the way you like. What color do you set by most?"

"I don't know," said Claribel. "Blue, I guess."

"Well, there's a hat there all trimmed with it. I see it this mornin'. Real bright, pretty blue! I believe there was some little noddin' yellow flowers on it, too. But mind you don't take it unless you like it."

Miss West's shop occupied the front room of her house, a small yellow one on a side street. The upper part of the door was of glass, and it rang a bell as it opened. Lucindy had had very few occasions for going there, and she entered with some importance. The bell clanged; and Miss West, a portly woman, came in from the back room, whisking off her apron in haste.

"Oh, that you, Miss Lucindy?" she called. "I've just been fryin' some riz doughnuts. Well, how'd the flowers suit?"

"I haven't quite made up my mind," said Lucindy, trying to speak with the dignity befitting her quest. "I just come in with little Claribel here. She's goin' to have a new hat, and her grandma said she might come down with me to pick it out. You've got some all trimmed, I believe?"

Miss West opened a drawer in an old-fashioned bureau.

"Yes," she said, "I've got two my niece trimmed for me before she went to make her visit to Sudleigh. One's blue. I guess you've seen that. Then there's a nice white one. The 'Weekly' says white's all the go, this year."

She took out two little hats, and balanced them on either hand. The blue one was strongly accented. The ribbon was very broad and very bright, and its nodding cowslips gleamed in cheerful yellow.

"Ain't that a beauty?" whispered Lucindy close to the little girl's ear. "But there! Don't you have it unless you'd rather. There's lots of other colors, you know; pink, and all sorts.".

Claribel put out one little brown hand, and timidly touched the other hat.

"This one," she said.

It was very plain, and very pretty; yet there were no flowers, and the modest white ribbon lay smoothly about the crown. Miss Lucindy gave a little cry, as if some one had hurt her.

"O!" she exclaimed, "O Claribel! you sure?" Claribel was sure.

"She's got real good taste," put in Miss West. "Shall I wrop it up?"

"Yes," answered Lucindy, drearily. "We'll take it. But I suppose if she should change, her mind before she wore it--" she added, with some slight accession of hope.

"Oh, yes, bring it right back. I'll give her another choice."

But Claribel was not likely to change her mind. On the way home, she walked sedately, and carried her hat with the utmost care. At her grandmother's gate, she looked up shyly, and spoke of her own accord,--

"Thank you, ever so much!"

Then she fled up the path, her bundle waving before her. That, at least, looked like spontaneous joy, and the sight of it soothed Lucindy into a temporary resignation; yet she was very much disappointed.

The next afternoon, Tiverton saw a strange and wondrous sight. The Crane boy led Old Buckskin, under an ancient saddle, into Miss Lucindy's yard, and waited there before her door. The Crane boy had told all his mates, and they had told their fathers and mothers, so that a wild excitement flew through the village like stubble fire, stirring the inhabitants to futile action. "It's like the 'clipse," said one of the squad of children collected at the gate, "only they ain't no smoked glass." Some of the grown people "made an errand" for the sake of being in the street, but those who lived near-by simply mounted guard at their doors and windows. The horse had not waited long when Miss Lucindy appeared before the gaze of an eager world. Her face had wakened into a keen excitement.

"Here!" she called to the Crane boy's brother, who was lingering in the background grinding his toes on the gravel and then lifting them in sudden agony, "you take this kitchen chair and set it down side of him, so't I can climb up."

The chair was placed, and Miss Lucindy essayed to climb, but vainly.

"Ann!" she called, "you bring me that little cricket."

Ann Toby appeared unwillingly, the little cricket in her hand. She was a tall, red-haired woman, who bore the reputation of being willing to be "tore into inch pieces" for Miss Lucindy. Her freckled face burned red with shame and anger.

"For Heaven's sake, you come back into the house!" she whispered, with tragic meaning. "You jest give it up, an' I'll scatter them boys. Sassy little peeps! what are they starin' round here for, I'd like to know!"

But Lucindy had mounted the cricket with much agility, and seated herself on the horse's back. Once she slipped off; but the Crane boy had the address to mutter, "Put your leg over the horn!" and, owing to that timely advice, she remained. But he was to experience the gratitude of an unfeeling world; for Ann Toby, in the irritation of one tried beyond endurance, fell upon him and cuffed him soundly. And Mrs. Crane, passing the gate at that moment, did not blame her.

"My! it seems a proper high place to set," remarked Lucindy, adjusting herself. "Well, I guess I sha'n't come to no harm. I'll ride round to your place, boys, when I get through, and leave the horse there." She trotted out of the yard amid the silence of the crowd.

The spectacle was too awesome to be funny, even to the boys; it seemed to Tiverton strangely like the work of madness. Only one little boy recovered himself sufficiently to ran after her and hold up a switch he had been peeling.

"Here!" he piped up, daringly, "you want a whip."

Lucindy smiled upon him benignly.

"I never did believe in abusin' dumb creatur's," she said, "but I'm much obliged." She took the switch and rode on.

Now Mrs. Wilson had heard the rumor too late to admit of any interference on her part, and she was staying indoors, suffering an agony of shame, determined not to countenance the scandalous sight by her presence. But as she sat "hookingin," the window was darkened, and involuntarily she lifted her eyes. There was the huge bulk of a horse, and there was Lucindy. The horsewoman's cheeks were bright red with exercise and joy. She wore a black dress and black mitts. Her little curls were flying; and oh, most unbearable of all! they were surmounted by a bonnet bearing no modest sheaf of wheat, but blossoming brazenly out into lavender roses. The spectacle was too much for Mrs. Wilson. She dropped her hook, and flew to the door.

"Well, I've known a good deal, fust an' last, but I never see the beat o' this! Lucindy, where'd you git that long dress?"

"It's my cashmere," answered Lucindy, joyously. "I set up last night to lengthen it down."

"Well, I should think you did! Lothrop!"

Her husband had been taking a nap in the sitting-room, and he came out, rubbing his eyes. Mrs. Wilson could not speak for curiosity. She watched him with angry intentness. She wondered if he would take Lucindy's part now! But Lothrop only moved forward and felt at the girth.

"You know you want to pull him up if he stumbles," he said; "but I guess he won't. He was a stiddy horse, fifteen year ago."

"Lothrop," began his wife, "do you want to be made a laughin'-stock in this town--";

"I guess if I've lived in a place over sixty year an' hil' my own, I can yet," said Lothrop, quietly. "You don't want to ride too long, Lucindy. You'll be lame to-morrer."

"I didn't suppose 'twould jounce so," said Lucindy; "but it's proper nice. I don't know what 'twould be on a real high horse. Well, good-by!" She turned the horse about, and involuntarily struck him with her little switch. Old Buckskin broke into a really creditable trot, and they disappeared down the village street. Lothrop sensibly took his way down to the shop while his wife was recovering her powers of speech; and for that, Jane herself mentally commended him.

Lucindy kept on out of the village and along the country road. The orioles were singing in the elms, and the leaves still wore the gloss of last night's shower. The earth smiled like a new creation, very green and sweet, and the horse's hoofs made music in Lucindy's mind. It seemed to her that she had lost sight both of youth and crabbed age; the pendulum stood still in the jarring machinery of time, the hands pointing to a moment of joy. She was quite happy, as any of us may be who seek the fellowship of dancing leaves and strong, bright sun. She turned into a cross-road, hardly wider than a lane, and bordered with wild rose and fragrant raspberry. There was but one house here,--a little, time-stained cottage, where Tom McNeil lived with his wife and five children. Perhaps these were the happiest people in all Tiverton, though no one but themselves had ever found it out. Tom made shoes in a desultory fashion, and played the fiddle earnestly all winter, and in summer, ped-dled essences and medicines from a pack strapped over his shoulders. Sometimes in the warm summer weather Molly, his wife, and all the children tramped with him, so that the house was closed for weeks at a time,--a thing very trying to the conventional sensibilities of Tiverton. Tom might have had a "stiddy job o' work" with some of the farmers; Molly might have helped about the churning and ironing. But no! they were like the birds, nesting happily in summer, and drawing their feet under their feathers when the snow drifted in. The children--lank, wild-eyed crea-tures--each went to school a few months, and then stopped, unable to bear the cross of confinement within four dull walls. They could not write; it was even rumored that they had never learned to tell time. And, indeed, what good would it have done them when the clock was run down and stood always at the hour of noon? But they knew where thoroughwort grows, and the wholesome goldthread; they gathered cress and peppermint, and could tell the mushroom from its noisome kindred. Day after day, they roamed the woods for simples to be distilled by the father, and made into potent salves and ointments for man and the beasties he loved better.

When Lucindy came in sight of the house, she was glad to find it open. She had scarcely gone so far afield for years, and the reports concerning this strange people had reached her only by hearsay. She felt like a discoverer. In close neighborhood to the house stood a peculiar structure,--the half-finished dwelling McNeil had at-tempted, in a brief access of ambition, to build with his own hands. The chimney, slightly curving and very ragged at the top, stood foolishly above the unfinished lower story. Lucindy remembered hearing how Tom had begun the chimney first, and built the house round it. But the fulfilment of his worldly dream never came to pass; and perhaps it was quite as well, for thereby would the unity of his existence have been destroyed. He might have lived up to the house; he might even have grown into a proud man, and accumulated dollars. But the bent of birth was too much for him. A day dawned, warm and entrancing; he left his bricks and boards in the midst, and the whole family went joyfully off on a tramp. To Tiverton, the unfinished house continued to serve as an immortal joke, and Tom smiled as broadly as any. He always said he couldn't finish it; he had mislaid the plan.

A little flower-garden bloomed between the two houses, and on the grass, by one of its clove-pink borders, sat a woman, rocking back and forth in an ancient chair, and doing absolutely nothing. She was young, and seemed all brown; for her eyes were dark, and her skin had been tanned to the deep, rich tint sweeter to some eyes than pure roses and milk. Lucindy guided Buckskin up to the gate, and Molly McNeil looked up and smiled without moving.

"How do?" she said, in a soft, slow voice. "Won't you come in?"

Lucindy was delighted. It was long since she had met a stranger.

"Well, I would," she answered, "but I don't know as I can get down. This is new business to me."

"Ellen," called Mrs. McNeil, "you bring out somethin' to step on!"

A little girl appeared with a yellow kitchen chair. Mrs. McNeil rose, carried it outside the gate, and planted it by Buckskin's side.

"There!" she said, "you put your hand on my shoulder and step down. It won't tip. I've got my knee on it."

Lucindy alighted, with some difficulty, and drew a long breath.

"I'll hitch him," said Molly McNeil. "You go in and sit down in that chair, and Ellen'll bring you a drink of water."

Ellen was barelegged and barefooted. Her brown hair hung over her dark eyes in a pleasant tangle. Her even teeth were white, and her lips red. There was no fault nor blemish in her little face; and when she had brought the dipper full of water, and stood rubbing one foot against its neighboring leg, Lucindy thought she had never seen anything so absolutely bewitching. Molly had hitched the horse, in manly and knowing fashion, and then seated herself on the kitchen chair beside Lucindy; but the attitude seemed not to suit her, and presently she rose and lay quietly down at full length on the grass. She did it quite as a matter of course, and her visitor thought it looked very pleasant; possibly she would have tried it herself if she had not been so absorbed in another interest. She was watching the little girl, who was running into the house with the dipper.

"Ain't she complete!" she said. "Your oldest?"

"She ain't mine at 'all." Mrs. McNeil rose on one elbow, and began chewing a grass stem.

It was very restful to Lucindy to see some one who was too much interested in anything, however trivial, to be interested in her. "You know about the Italian that come round with the hand-organ last month? He was her father. Well, he died,-- fell off a mow one night,--and the town sold the hand-organ and kept Ellen awhile on the farm. But she run away, and my boys found her hidin' in the woods starved most to death. So I took her in, and the overseer said I was welcome to her. She's a nice little soul."

"She's proper good-lookin'!" Lucindy's eyes were sparkling.

"She don't look as well as common to-day, for the boys went off plummin' without her. She was asleep, and I didn't want to call her. She had a cryin' spell when she waked up, but I didn't know which way they'd gone."

Ellen came wandering round the side of the house, and Lucindy crooked a trembling finger at her.

"Come here!" she called. "You come here and see me!"

Ellen walked up to her with a steady step, and laid one little brown hand on Lucindy's knee. But the old Judge's daughter drew the child covetously to her lap.

"Look here," she said, "should you like to go home and spend a week with me?"

The little maid threw back her tangle of curls, and looked Lucindy squarely in the eyes.

"Yes," she answered.

Lucindy's grasp tightened round her.

"How should you like to live with me?"

The child touched her little breast inquiringly with one finger.

"Me?" She pointed over to Mrs. McNeil, who lay listening and stretching her limbs in lazy comfort. "Leave *her*?" And then, gravely, "No; she's good to me."

Lucindy's heart sank.

"You could come over to see her," she pleaded, "and I'd come too. We'd all go plummin' together. I should admire to! And we'd have parties, and ask 'em all over.

What say?"

The child sat straight and serious, one warm hand clinging to Lucindy's slender palm. But her eyes still sought the face of her older friend. Molly McNeil rose to a sitting posture. She took the straw from her mouth, and spoke with the happy frankness of those who have no fear because they demand nothing save earth and sky room.

"I know who you are," she said to Lucindy. "You're left well off, and I guess you could bring up a child, give you your way. We're as poor as poverty! You take her, if she'll go. Ellen, she's a nice lady; you better say 'yes.'"

Lucindy was trembling all over.

"You come, dear," she urged, piteously. "You come and live with me."

Ellen thought a moment more. Then she nodded.

"I'll come," said she.

Lucindy could not wait.

"I'll send a wagon over after her to-night." She had put Ellen down, and was rising tremblingly. "I won't stop to talk no more now, but you come and see me, won't you? Now, if you'll help me mount up--there! My! it's higher 'n 'twas before! Well, I'll see you again." She turned Old Buckskin's head away from the fence; then she pulled him fiercely round again. "Here!" she called, "what if she should jump up behind me and come now!"

Mrs. McNeil, being the thrall only of the earth, saw no reason, why a thing should not be done as one wanted it. She lifted; the child and set her on the horse behind Lucindy. And so, in this strange fashion, the two entered the high street of Tiverton.

A few weeks after this, Mrs. Wilson and Lucindy went together to the little millinery shop. Ellen trotted between them, taking excursions into the street, now and again, in pursuit of butterflies or thistledown. When they entered, Miss West, who had seen their approach from her position at the ironing-board, came forward with a gay little hat in her hand. It was trimmed with pink, and a wreath of tiny white flowers clung about the crown. She set it on Ellen's curls; and Ellen, her face quite radiant, looked up at Miss Lucindy for approval. But that lady was gazing anxiously at Mrs. Wilson.

"Now, there ain't anything unsuitable about that, is there?" she asked. "I know, it's gay, and I want it to be gay. I can tell about *that*! But is it all right? Is it such as you'd be willin' to have Claribel wear?"

"It's a real beauty!" Mrs. Wilson answered, cordially; but she could not refrain from adding, while Miss West was doing up the hat, and Ellen surreptitiously tried on a black poke bonnet, "Now, don't you spile her, Lucindy! She's a nice little girl as ever was, but you ain't no more fit to bring up a child than the cat!"

Lucindy did not hear. She was smiling at Ellen, and Ellen smiled back at her. They thought they knew.

TOLD IN THE POORHOUSE.

Le' me see," said old Sally Flint, "was it fifty year ago, or was it on'y forty? Some'er's betwixt 1825 an' '26 it must ha' been when they were married, an' 'twas in '41 he died."

The other old women in the Poorhouse sitting-room gathered about her. Old Mrs. Forbes, who dearly loved a story, unwound a length of yarn with peculiar satisfaction, and put her worn shoe up to the fire. Everybody knew when Sally Flint was disposed to open her unwritten book of folk-tales for the public entertainment; and to-day, having tied on a fresh apron and bound a new piece of red flannel about her wrist, she was, so to speak, in fighting trim. The other members of the Poorhouse had scanty faith in that red flannel. They were aware that Sally had broken her wrist, some twenty years before, and that the bandage was consequently donned on days when her "hand felt kind o' cold," or was "burnin' like fire embers;" but there was an unspoken suspicion that it really served as token of her inability to work whenever she felt bored by the prescribed routine of knitting and sweeping. No one had dared presume on that theory, however, since the day when an untactful overseer had mentioned it, to be met by such a stream of unpleasant reminiscence concerning his immediate ancestry that he had retreated in dismay, and for a week after, had served extra pieces of pie to his justly offended charge.

"They were married in June," continued Sally. "No, 'twa'n't; 'twas the last o' May. May thirty-fust--no, May 'ain't but thirty days, has it?"

"'Thirty days hath September,'" quoted Mrs. Giles, with importance. "That's about all I've got left o' my schoolin', Miss Flint. May's got thirty-one days, sure enough."

"Call it the thirty-fust, then. It's nigh enough, anyway. Well, Josh Marden an' Lyddy Ann Crane was married, an' for nine year they lived like two kittens. Old

Sperry Dyer, that wanted to git Lyddy himself, used to call 'em cup an' sasser, 'There they be,' he'd say, when he stood outside the meetin'-house door an' they drove up; 'there comes cup an' sasser.' Lyddy was a little mite of a thing, with great black eyes; an' if Josh hadn't been as tough as tripe, he'd ha' got all wore out waitin' on her. He even washed the potaters for her, made the fires, an' lugged water. Scairt to death if she was sick! She used to have sick headaches, an' one day he stopped choppin' pine limbs near the house 'cause the noise hurt Lyddy Ann's head. Another time, I recollect, she had erysipelas in her face, an' I went in to carry some elder-blows, an' found him readin' the Bible. 'Lord!' says I, 'Josh; that's on'y Genesis! 'twon't do the erysipelas a mite o' good for you to be settin' there reading the be'gats! You better turn to Revelation.' But 'twa'n't all on his side, nuther. 'Twas give an' take with them. It used to seem as if Lyddy Ann kind o' worshipped him. 'Josh' we all called him; but she used to say 'Joshuay,' an' look at him as if he was the Lord A'mighty."

"My! Sally!" said timid Mrs. Spenser, under her breath; but Sally gave no heed, and swept on in the stream of her recollections.

"Well, it went on for fifteen year, an' then 'Mandy Knowles, Josh's second cousin, come to help 'em with the work. 'Mandy was a queer creatur'. I've studied a good deal over her, an' I dunno's I've quite got to the bottom of her yit. She was one o' them sort o' slow women, with a fat face, an' she hadn't got over dressin' young, though Lyddy an' the rest of us that was over thirty was wearin' caps an' talkin' about false fronts. But she never'd had no beaux; an' when Josh begun to praise her an' say how nice 'twas to have her there, it tickled her e'en a'most to death. She'd lived alone with her mother an' two old-maid aunts, an' she didn't know nothin' about men-folks; I al'ays thought she felt they was different somehow,--kind o' cherubim an' seraphim,--an' you'd got to mind 'em as if you was the Childern of Isr'el an' they was Moses. Josh never meant a mite o' harm, I'll say that for him. He was jest man-like, that's all. There's lots o' different kinds,--here, Mis' Niles, you know; you've buried your third,--an' Josh was the kind that can't see more'n, one woman to a time. He looked at 'Mandy, an' he got over seein' Lyddy Ann, that's all. Things would ha' come out all right--as right as they be for most married folks--if Lyddy Ann hadn't been so high-sperited; but she set the world by Joshuay, an' there 'twas. 'Ain't it nice to have her here?' he kep' on sayin' over'n' over to Lyddy, an' she'd say 'Yes;' but byme-by, when she found he was al'ays on hand to bring a pail o' water for 'Mandy, or to throw away her suds, or even help hang out the clo'es--I see 'em hangin' out clo'es one day when I was goin' across their lot huckleberr'in', an' he did look like a great gump, an' so did she--well, then, Lyddy Ann got to seemin' kind o' worried, an' she had more sick headaches than ever. Twa'n't a year afore that, I'd been in one day when she had a headache, an' he says, as if he was perfessin' his faith in meetin', 'By gum! I wish I could have them headaches for her!' an' I thought o' speakin' of it, about now, when I run in to borrer some saleratus, an' he hollered into the bedroom: 'Lyddy Ann, you got another headache? If I had such a head as that, I'd cut it off!' An' all the time 'Mandy did act like the very Old Nick, jest as any old maid would that hadn't set her mind on menfolks till she was thirty-five. She bought a red-plaid bow an' pinned it on in front, an' one day I ketched her at the lookin'-glass pullin' out a gray hair.

"'Land, 'Mandy,' says I (I spoke right up), 'do you pull 'em out as fast as they come? That's why you ain't no grayer, I s'pose. I was sayin' the other day, "'Mandy Knowles is gittin' on, but she holds her own pretty well. I dunno how she manages it, whether she dyes or not,"' says I.

"An' afore she could stop herself, 'Mandy turned round, red as a beet, to look at Josh an' see if he heard. He stamped out into the wood-house, but Lyddy Ann never took her eyes off her work. Them little spiteful things didn't seem to make no impression on her. I've thought a good many times sence, she didn't care how handsome other women was, nor how scrawny she was herself, if she could on'y keep Josh. An' Josh he got kind o' fretful to her, an' she to him, an' 'Mandy was all honey an' cream. Nothin' would do but she must learn how to make the gingerbread he liked, an' iron his shirts; an' when Lyddy Ann found he seemed to praise things up jest as much as he had when she done 'em, she give 'em up, an' done the hard things herself, an' let 'Mandy see to Josh. She looked pretty pindlin' then, mark my words; but I never see two such eyes in anybody's head. I s'pose 'twas a change for Josh, anyway, to be with a woman like 'Mandy, that never said her soul's her own, for Lyddy'd al'ays had a quick way with her; but, land! you can't tell about men, what changes 'em or what don't. If you're tied to one, you've jest got to bear with him, an' be thankful if he don't run some kind of a rig an' make you town-talk."

There was a murmur from gentle Lucy Staples, who had been constant for fifty years to the lover who died in her youth; but no one took any notice of her, and

Sally Flint went on:

"It come spring, an' somehow or nuther 'Mandy found out the last o' March was Josh's birthday, an' nothin' would do but she must make him a present. So she walked over to Sudleigh, an' bought him a great long pocket-book that you could put your bills into without foldin' 'em, an' brought it home, tickled to death because she'd been so smart. Some o' this come out at the time, an' some wa'n't known till arterwards; the hired man told some, an' a good deal the neighbors see themselves. An' I'll be whipped if 'Mandy herself didn't tell the heft on't arter 'twas all over. She wa'n't more'n half baked in a good many things. It got round somehow that the pocket-book was comin', an' when, I see 'Mandy walkin' home that arternoon, I ketched up my shawl an' run in behind her, to borrer some yeast. Nobody thought anything o' birthdays in our neighborhood, an' mebbe that made it seem a good deal more 'n 'twas; but when I got in there, I vow I was sorry I come. There set Josh by the kitchen table, sort o' red an' pleased, with his old pocket-book open afore him, an' he was puttin' all his bills an' papers into the new one, an' sayin', every other word,--

"'Why, 'Mandy, I never see your beat! Ain't this a nice one, Lyddy?'

"An' 'Mandy was b'ilin' over with pride, an' she stood there takin' off her cloud; she'd been in such a hurry to give it to him she hadn't even got her things off fust. Lyddy stood by the cupboard, lookin' straight at the glass spoon-holder. I thought arterwards I didn't b'lieve she see it; an' if she did, I guess she never forgot it.

"'Yes, it's a real nice one,' says I.

"I had to say suthin', but in a minute, I was most scairt. Lyddy turned round, in a kind of a flash; her face blazed all over red, an' her eyes kind o' went through me. She stepped up to the table, an' took up the old pocket-book.

"'You've got a new one,' says she. 'May I have this?'

"'Course you may,' says he.

"He didn't look up to see her face, an' her voice was so soft an' still, I guess he never thought nothin' of it. Then she held the pocket-book up tight ag'inst her dress waist an' walked off into the bedroom. I al'ays thought she never knew I was there. An' arterwards it come out that that old pocket-book was one she'd bought for him afore they was married,--earned it bindin' shoes."

"'Twas kind o' hard," owned Mrs. Niles, bending forward, and, with hands clasped over her knees, peering into the coals for data regarding her own marital ex-periences. "But if 'twas all wore out--did you say 'twas wore?--well, then I dunno's you could expect him to set by it. An' 'twa'n't as if he'd give it away; they'd got it between 'em."

"I dunno; it's all dark to me," owned Sally Flint. "I guess 'twould puzzle a saint to explain men-folks, anyway, but I've al'ays thought they was sort o' numb about some things. Anyway, Josh Marden was. Well, things went on that way till the fust part o' the summer, an' then they come to a turnin'-p'int. I s'pose they'd got to, some time, an' it might jest as well ha' been fust as last. Lyddy Ann was pretty miserable, an' she'd been dosin' with thoroughwort an' what all when anybody told her to; but I al'ays thought she never cared a mite whether she lived to see another spring. The day I'm comin' to, she was standin' over the fire fryin' fish, an' 'Mandy was sort o' fiddlin' round, settin' the table, an' not doin' much of anything arter all. I dunno how she come to be so aggravatin', for she was al'ays ready to do her part, if she **had** come between husband an' wife. You know how hard it is to git a fish din-ner! Well, Lyddy Ann was tired enough, anyway. An' when Josh come in, 'Mandy she took a cinnamon-rose out of her dress, an' offered it to him.

"'Here's a flower for your button-hole,' says she, as if she wa'n't more 'n six-teen. An' then she set down in a chair, an' fanned herself with a newspaper.

"Now that chair happened to be Lyddy Ann's at the table, an' she see what was bein' done. She turned right round, with the fish-platter in her hand, an' says she, in an awful kind of a voice,--

"'You git up out o' my chair! You've took my husband away, but you sha'n't take my place at the table!'

"The hired man was there, washin' his hands at the sink, an' he told it to me jest as it happened. Well, I guess they all thought they was struck by lightnin', an' Lyddy Ann most of all. Josh he come to, fust. He walked over to Lyddy Ann.

"'You put down that platter!' says he. An' she begun to tremble, an' set it down.

"I guess they thought there was goin' to be murder done, for 'Mandy busted right out cryin' an' come runnin' over to me, an' the hired man took a step an' stood side o' Lyddy Ann. He was a little mite of a man, Cyrus was, but he wouldn't ha' stood no violence.

"Josh opened the door that went into the front entry, an' jest p'inted. 'You walk in there,' he says, 'an' you stay there. That's your half o' the house, an' this is mine. Don't you dast to darken my doors!'

"Lyddy Ann she walked through the entry an' into the fore-room, an' he shet the door."

"I wouldn't ha' done it!" snorted old Mrs. Page, who had spent all her property in lawsuits over a right of way. "Ketch me!"

"You would if you'd 'a' been Lyddy Ann!" said Sally Flint, with an emphatic nod. Then she continued: "I hadn't more'n heard 'Mandy's story afore I was over there; but jest as I put my foot on the door-sill, Josh he come for'ard to meet me.

"'What's wanted?' says he. An' I declare for't I was so scairt I jest turned round an' cut for home. An' there set 'Mandy, wringin' her hands.

"'What be I goin' to do?' says she, over 'n' over. 'Who ever'd ha' thought o' this?'

"'The thing for you to do,' says I, 'is to go, straight home to your mother, an' I'll harness up an' carry you. Don't you step your foot inside that house ag'in. Maybe ma'am will go over an' pack up your things. You've made mischief enough.' So we got her off that arter-noon, an' that was an end of *her*.

"I never could see what made Josh think so quick that day. We never thought he was brighter 'n common; but jest see how in that flash o' bein' mad with Lyddy Ann he'd planned out what would be most wormwood for her! He gi'n her the half o' the house she'd furnished herself with hair-cloth chairs an' a whatnot, but 'twa'n't the part that was fit to be lived in. She stayed pretty close for three or four days, an' I guess she never had nothin' to eat. It made me kind o' sick to think of her in there settin' on her hair-cloth sofy, an' lookin' at her wax flowers an' the coral on the what-not, an' thinkin' what end she'd made. It was of a Monday she was sent in there, an' Tuesday night I slipped over an' put some luncheon on the winder-sill; but 'twas there the next day, an' Cyrus see the old crower fly up an' git it. An' that same Tuesday mornin', Josh had a j'iner come an' begin a partition right straight through the house. It was all rough boards, like a high fence, an' it cut the front entry in two, an' went right through the kitchen--so't the kitchen stove was one side on't, an' the sink the other. Lyddy Ann's side had the stove. I was glad o' that, though I s'pose she 'most had a fit every day to think o' him tryin' to cook over the airtight in the settin'-room. Seemed kind o' queer to go to the front door, too, for you had to open it wide an' squeeze round the partition to git into Lyddy Ann's part, an' a little mite of a crack would let you into Josh's. But they didn't have many callers. It was a good long while afore anybody dared to say a word to her; an' as for Josh, there wa'n't nobody that cared about seein' him but the tax-collector an' pedlers.

"Well, the trouble Josh took to carry out that mad fit! He split wood an' laid it down at Lyddy Ann's door, an' he divided the eggs an' milk, an' shoved her half inside. He bought her a separate barrel o' flour, an' all the groceries he could think on; they said he laid money on her winder-sill. But, take it all together, he was so busy actin' like a crazed one that he never got his 'taters dug till 'most time for the frost. Lyddy Ann she never showed her head among the neighbors ag'in. When she see she'd got to stay there, she begun to cook for herself; but one day, one o' the neighbors heard her pleadin' with Josh, out in the cow-yard, while he was milkin'.

"'O Joshuay,' she kep' a-sayin' over 'n' over, 'you needn't take me back, if you'll on'y let me do your work! You needn't speak to me, an' I'll live in the other part; but I shall be crazy if you don't let me do your work. O Joshuay! O Joshuay!' She cried an' cried as if her heart would break, but Josh went on milkin', an' never said a word.

"I s'pose she thought he'd let her, the old hunks, for the next day, she baked some pies an' set 'em on the table in his part. She reached in through the winder to do it. But that night, when Josh come home, he hove 'em all out into the back yard, an' the biddies eat 'em up. The last time I was there, I see them very pieces o' pie-plate, white an' blue-edged, under the syringa bush. Then she kind o' give up hope. I guess--But no! I'm gittin' ahead o' my story. She did try him once more. Of course his rooms got to lookin' like a hog's nest--"

"My! I guess when she see him doin' his own washin', she thought the pocket-book was a small affair," interpolated Mrs. Niles.

"She used to go round peerin' into his winders when he wa'n't there, an' one day, arter he'd gone off to trade some steers, she jest spunked up courage an' went in an' cleaned all up. I see the bed airin', an' went over an' ketched her at it. She hadn't more'n got through an' stepped outside when Josh come home, an' what should he do but take the wheelbarrer an', beat out as he was drivin' oxen five mile, go down to the gravel-pit an' get a barrerful o' gravel. He wheeled it up to the side door, an' put a plank over the steps, an' wheeled it right in. An' then he dumped it in the middle o' his clean floor. That was the last o' her tryin' to do for him on the sly.

"I should ha' had some patience with him if 'twa'n't for one thing he done to spite her. Seemed as if he meant to shame her that way afore the whole neighborhood. He wouldn't speak to her himself, but he sent a painter by trade to tell her he was goin' to paint the house, an' to ask her what color she'd ruther have. The painter said she acted sort o' wild, she was so pleased. She told him yaller; an' Josh had him go right to work on't next day. But he had her half painted yaller, an' his a kind of a drab, I guess you'd call it. He sold a piece o' ma'sh to pay for't. Dr. Parks said you might as well kill a woman with a hatchet, as the man did down to Sudleigh, as put her through such treatment. My! ain't it growin' late? Here, let me set back by the winder. I want to see who goes by, to-day. An' I'll cut my story short.

"Well, they lived jest that way. Lyddy Ann she looked like an old woman, in a month or two. She looked every minute as old as you do, Mis' Gridley. Ain't you sixty-nine? Well, she wa'n't but thirty-six. Her hair turned gray, an' she was all stooped over. Sometimes I thought she wa'n't jest right. I used to go in to see if she'd go coltsfootin' with me, or plummin'; but she never'd make me no answer. I recollect two things she said. One day, she set rockin' back'ards an' for'ards in a straight chair, holdin' her hands round her knees, an' she says,--

"'I 'ain't got no pride, Sally Flint! I 'ain't got no pride!'

"An' once she looked up kind o' pitiful an' says, 'Ain't it queer I can't die?' But, poor creatur', I never thought she knew what she was sayin'. She'd ha' been the last one to own she wa'n't contented if she'd had any gover'ment over her words.

"Well, Josh he'd turned the hired man away because he couldn't do for him over the airtight stove, an' he got men to help him by days' works. An' through the winter, he jest set over the fire an' sucked his claws, an' thought how smart he was. But one day 'twas awful cold, an' we'd been tryin' out lard, an' the fat ketched fire, an' everything was all up in arms, anyway. Cyrus he was goin' by Josh's, an' he didn't see no smoke from the settin'-room stove. So he jest went to the side door an' walked in, an' there set Josh in the middle o' the room. Couldn't move hand nor foot! Cyrus didn't stop for no words, but he run over to our house, hollerin', 'Josh Harden's got a stroke!' An' ma'am left the stove all over fat an' run, an' I arter her, I guess Lyddy Ann must ha' seen us comin', for we hadn't more'n got into the settin'-room afore she was there. The place was cold as a barn, an' it looked like a hurrah's nest. Josh never moved, but his eyes follered her when she went into the bedroom to spread up the bed.

"'You help me, Cyrus,' says she, kind, o' twittery-like, but calm. 'We'll carry him in here. I can lift.'

"But our men-folks got there jest about as they was tryin' to plan how to take him, an' they h'isted him onto the bed. Cyrus harnessed up our horse an' went after Dr. Parks, an' by the time he come, we'd got the room so's to look decent. An'--if you'll b'lieve it! Lyddy Ann was in the bedroom tryin' to warm Josh up an' make him take some hot drink; but when I begun to sweep up, an' swop towards that gravel-pile in the middle o' the floor, she come hurryin' up, all out o' breath. She ketched the broom right out o' my hand.

"'I'll sweep, byme-by,' says she. 'Don't you touch that gravel, none on ye!' An' so the gravel laid there, an' we walked round it, watchers an' all.

"She wouldn't have no watcher in his bedroom, though; she was determined to do everything but turn him an' lift him herself, but there was al'ays one or two settin' round to keep the fires goin' an' make sure there was enough cooked up. I swan, I never see a woman so happy round a bed o' sickness as Lyddy Ann was! She never made no fuss when Josh was awake, but if he shet his eyes, she'd kind o' hang over the bed an' smooth the clo'es as if they was kittens, an' once I ketched her huggin' up the sleeve of his old barn coat that hung outside the door. If ever a woman made a fool of herself over a man that wa'n't wuth it, 'twas Lyddy Ann Marden!

"Well, Josh he hung on for a good while, an' we couldn't make out whether he had his senses or not. He kep' his eyes shet most o' the time; but when Lyddy Ann's back was turned, he seemed to know it somehow, an' he'd open 'em an' foller her all round the room. But he never spoke. I asked the doctor about it.

"'Can't he speak, doctor?' says I. 'He can move that hand a leetle to-day. Don't you s'pose he could speak, if he'd a mind to?'

"The doctor he squinted up his eyes--he al'ays done that when he didn't want to answer--an' he says,--

"'I guess he's thinkin' on't over.'

"But one day, Lyddy Ann found she was all beat out, an' she laid down in the best bedroom an' went to sleep. I set with Josh. I was narrerin' off, but when I looked up, he was beckonin' with his well hand. I got up, an' went to the bed.

"'Be you dry?' says I. He made a little motion, an' then he lifted his hand an' p'inted out into the settin'-room.

"Do you want Lyddy Ann?' says I. 'She's laid down.' No, he didn't want her. I went to the settin'-room door an' looked out, an'--I dunno how 'twas--it all come to me.

"'Is it that gravel-heap?' says I. 'Do you want it carried off, an' the floor swop up?' An' he made a motion to say 'Yes.' I called Cyrus, an' we made short work o' that gravel. When, I'd took up the last mite on't, I went back to the bed.

"'Josh Marden,' says I, 'can you speak, or can't you?' But he shet his eyes, an' wouldn't say a word.

"When Lyddy Ann come out, I told her what he'd done, an' then she did give way a little mite. Two tears come out o' her eyes, an' jest rolled down her cheeks, but she didn't give up to 'em.

"'Sally,' says she, sort o' peaceful, 'I guess I'll have a cup o' tea.'

"Well, there was times when we thought Josh would git round ag'in, if he didn't have another stroke. I dunno whether he did have another or not, but one night, he seemed to be sort o' sinkin' away. Lyddy Ann she begun to turn white, an' she set down by him an' rubbed his sick hand. He looked at her,--fust time he had, fair an' square,--an' then he begun to wobble his lips round an' make a queer noise with 'em. She put her head down, an' then she says, 'Yes, Joshuay! yes, dear!' An' she got up an' took the pocket-book 'Mandy had gi'n him off the top o' the bureau, an' laid it down on the bed where he could git it. But he shook his head, an' said the word ag'in, an' a queer look--as if she was scairt an' pleased--flashed over Lyddy Ann's face. She run into the parlor, an' come back with that old pocket-book he'd give up to her, an' she put it into his well hand. That was what he wanted. His fingers gripped it up, an' he shet his eyes. He never spoke ag'in. He died that night."

"I guess she died, too!" said Lucy Staples, under her breath, stealthily wiping a tear from her faded cheek.

"No, she didn't, either!" retorted Sally Flint, hastily, getting up to peer from the window down the country road. "She lived a good many year, right in that very room he'd drove her out on, an' she looked as if she owned the airth. I've studied on it consid'able, an' I al'ays s'posed 'twas because she'd got him, an' that was all she cared for. There's the hearse now, an' two carriages, step an' step."

"Land! who's dead?" exclaimed Mrs. Forbes, getting up in haste, while her ball rolled unhindered to the other end of the room.

"It's Lyddy Ann Marden," returned Sally Flint, with the triumphant quiet of one first at the goal. "I see it this mornin' in the 'County Democrat,' when I was doin' up my wrist, an' you was all so busy."

HEMAN'S MA.

It was half-past nine of a radiant winter's night, and the Widder Poll's tooth still ached, though she was chewing cloves, and had applied a cracker poultice to her cheek. She was walking back and forth through the great low-studded kitchen, where uncouth shadows lurked and brooded, still showing themselves ready to leap aloft with any slightest motion of the flames that lived behind the old black fire-dogs. At every trip across the room, she stopped to look from the window into the silver paradise without, and at every glance she groaned, as if groaning were a duty. The kitchen was unlighted save by the fire and one guttering candle; but even through such inadequate illumination the Widder Poll was a figure calculated to stir rich merriment in a satirical mind. Her contour was rather square than oblong, and she was very heavy. In fact, she had begun to announce that her ankles wouldn't bear her much longer, and she should "see the day when she'd have to set by, from mornin' to night, like old Anrutty Green that had the dropsy so many years afore she was laid away." Her face, also, was cut upon the broadest pattern in common use, and her small, dull eyes and closely shut mouth gave token of that firmness which, save in ourselves, we call obstinacy. To-night, however, her features were devoid of even their wonted dignity, compressed, as they had been, by the bandage encircling her face. She looked like a caricature of her unprepossessing self. On one of her uneasy journeys to the window, she caught the sound of sleigh-bells; and staying only to assure herself of their familiar ring, she hastily closed the shutter, and, going back to the fireplace, sank into a chair there, and huddled over the blaze. The sleigh drove slowly into the yard, and after the necessary delay of unharnessing, a man pushed open the side door, and entered the kitchen. He, too, was short and square of build, though he had no superfluous flesh. His ankles would doubtless continue to bear him for many a year to come. His face was but slightly accented; he had very thin eyebrows, light hair, and only a shaggy fringe of whisker beneath the chin. This was Heman Blaisdell, the Widder Poll's brother-in-law, for whom she had persistently kept house ever since the death of his wife, four years ago. He came in without speaking, and after shaking himself out of his great-coat, sat silently down in his armchair by the fire. The Widder Poll held both hands to her face, and groaned again. At length, curiosity overcame her, and, quite against her judgment, she spoke. She was always resolving that she would never again take the initiative; but every time her resolution went down before the certainty that if she did not talk, there would be no conversation at all,--for Heman had a staying power that was positively amazing.

"Well?" she began, interrogatively.

Heman only stirred slightly in his chair.

"Well! ain't you goin' to tell me what went on at the meetin'?"

Her quarry answered patiently, yet with a certain dogged resistance of her,--

"I dunno's there's anything to tell."

"How'd it go off?"

"'Bout as usual."

"Did you speak?"

"No."

"Lead in prayer?"

"No."

"Wa'n't you *asked*?"

"No."

"Well, my soul! Was Roxy Cole there?"

"Yes."

"Did you fetch her home?"

"No, I didn't!" Some mild exasperation animated his tone at last. The Widder detected it, and occupied herself with her tooth.

"My soul an' body! I wonder if it's goin' to grumble all night long!" she exclaimed, bending lower over the blaze. "I've tried everything but a roasted raisin, an' I b'lieve I shall come to that."

Heman rose, and opened the clock on the mantel; he drew forth the key from under the pendulum, and slowly wound up the time-worn machinery. In another instant, he would be on his way to bed; the Widder knew she must waste no time in hurt silence, if she meant to find out anything. She began hastily,--

"Did they say anything about the, church fair?"

"They ain't goin' to have it."

"Not have it! Well, how *be* they goin' to git the shinglin' paid for?"

"They've got up the idee of an Old Folks' Concert."

"Singin'?"

"Singin' an' playin'."

"Who's goin' to play?"

"Brad Freeman an' Jont Marshall agreed to play fust an' second fiddle." Heman paused a moment, and straightened himself with an air of conscious pride; then he added,--

"They've asked me to play the bass-viol."

The Widder had no special objections to this arrangement, but it did strike her as an innovation; and when she had no other reason for disapproval, she still believed in it on general principles. So altogether effective a weapon should never rust from infrequent use!

"Well!" she announced. "I never heard of such carryin's-on,--never!"

Heman was lighting a small kerosene lamp. The little circle of light seemed even brilliant in the dusky room; it affected him with a relief so sudden and manifest as to rouse also a temporary irritation at having endured the previous gloom even for a moment.

"'Ain't you got no oil in the house?" he exclaimed, testily. "I wish you'd light up, evenin's, an' not set here by one taller candle!"

He had ventured on this remonstrance before, the only one he permitted himself against his housekeeper's ways, and at the instant of making it, he realized its futility.

"The gre't lamp's all full," said the Widder, warming her apron and pressing it to her poulticed face. "You can light it, if you've got the heart to. That was poor Mary's lamp, an' hard as I've tried, I never could bring myself to put a match to that wick. How many evenin's I've seen her set by it, rockin' back'ards an' for'ards,--an' her needle goin' in an' out! She was a worker, if ever there was one, poor creatur'! At it all the time, jes' like a silk-worm."

Heman was perfectly familiar with this explanation; from long repetition, he had it quite by heart. Possibly that was why he did not wait for its conclusion, but tramped stolidly away to his bedroom, where he had begun to kick off his shoes by the time his sister-in-law reached a period.

The Widder had a fresh poultice waiting by the fire. She applied it to her cheek, did up her face in an old flannel petticoat, and then, having covered the fire, toiled up to bed. It was a wearisome journey, for she carried a heavy soapstone which showed a tendency to conflict with the candle, and she found it necessary to hold together most of her garments; these she had "loosened a mite by the fire," according to custom on cold nights, after Heman had left her the field.

Next day, Heman went away into the woods chopping, and carried his dinner of doughnuts and cheese, with a chunk of bean-porridge frozen into a ball, to be thawed out by his noontime fire. He returned much earlier than usual, and the Widder was at the window awaiting him. The swelling in her cheek had somewhat subsided; and the bandage, no longer distended by a poultice beneath, seemed, in comparison, a species of holiday device. She was very impatient. She watched Heman, as he went first to the barn; and even opened the back door a crack to listen for the rattling of chains, the signal of feeding or watering.

"What's he want to do that now for?" she muttered, closing the door again, as the cold struck her cheek. "He'll have to feed 'em ag'in, come night!"

But at last he came, and, according to his silent wont, crossed the kitchen to the sink, to wash his hands. He was an unobservant man, and it did not occur to him that the Widder had on her Tycoon rep, the gown she kept "for nice." Indeed, he was so unused to looking at her that he might well have forgotten her outward appearance. He was only sure of her size; he knew she cut off a good deal of light. One sign, however, he did recognize; she was very cheerful, with a hollow good-nature which had its meaning.

"I got your shavin'-water all ready," she began. "Don't you burn ye when ye turn it out."

It had once been said of the Widder Poll that if she could hold her tongue, the devil himself couldn't get ahead of her. But fortune had not gifted her with such endurance, and she always spoke too often and too soon.

"Brad Freeman's been up here," she continued, eying Heman, as she drew out the supper-table and put up the leaves. "I dunno's I ever knew anybody so took up as he is with that concert, an' goin' to the vestry to sing to-night, an' all. He said he'd call here an' ride 'long o' you, an' I told him there'd be plenty o' room, for you'd take the pung."

If Heman felt any surprise at her knowledge of his purpose, he did not betray it. He poured out his shaving-water, and looked about him for an old newspaper.

"I ain't goin' in the pung," he answered, without glancing at her. "The shoe's most off'n one o' the runners now."

The Widder Poll set a pie on the table with an emphasis unconsciously embodying her sense that now, indeed, had come the time for remedies.

"I dunno what you can take," she remarked, with that same foreboding liveliness. "Three on a seat, an' your bass-viol, too!"

Heman was lathering his cheeks before the mirror, where a sinuous Venus and a too-corpulent Cupid disported themselves in a green landscape above the glass. "There ain't goin' to be three," he said, patiently. "T'others are goin' by themselves."

The Widder took up her stand at a well-chosen angle, and looked at him in silence. He paid no attention to her, and it was she who, of necessity, broke into speech.

"Well! I've got no more to say. Do you mean to tell me you'd go off playin' on fiddles an' bass-viols, an' leave me, your own wife's sister, settin' here the whole evenin' long, all swelled up with the toothache?"

Heman often felt that he had reached a state of mind where nothing could surprise him, but this point of view was really unexpected. He decided, however, with some scorn, that the present misunderstanding might arise from a confusion of terms in the feminine mind.

"This ain't the concert," he replied, much as if she had proposed going to the polls. "It's the rehearsal. That means where you play the tunes over. The concert ain't comin' off for a month."

And now the Widder Poll spoke with the air of one injured almost beyond reparation.

"I'd like to know what difference that makes! If a man's goin' where he can't take his womenfolks, I say he'd better stay to home! an' if there's things goin' on there't you don't want me to git hold of, I tell you, Heman Blaisdell, you'd better by half stop shavin' you now, an' take yourself off to bed at seven o'clock! Traipsin' round playin' the fiddle at your age! Ain't I fond o' music?"

"No, you ain't!" burst forth Heman, roused to brief revolt where his beloved instrument was concerned. "You don't know Old Hunderd from Yankee Doodle!"

The Widder walked round the table and confronted him as he was turning away from the glass, shaving-mug in hand.

"You answer me one question! I know who's goin' to be there, an' set in the chorus an' sing alto. Brad Freeman told me, as innercent as a lamb. Heman Blaisdell, you answer me? Be you goin' to bring anybody here to this house, an' set her in poor Mary's place? If you be, I ought to be the fust one to know it."

Heman looked at the shaving-mug for a moment, as if he contemplated dashing it to the floor. Then he tightened his grasp on it, like one putting the devil behind him.

"No, I ain't," he said, doggedly, adding under his breath, "not unless I'm drove to 't."

"I dunno who could ha' done more," said the Widder, so patently with the air of continuing for an indefinite period that Heman reached up for his hat. "Where you goin'? Mercy sakes alive! don't you mean to eat no supper, now I've got it all ready?"

But Heman pushed his way past her and escaped, muttering something about "feedin' the critters." Perhaps the "critters" under his care were fed oftener than those on farms where the ingle-nook was at least as cosey as the barn.

These slight skirmishes always left Heman with an uneasy sense that somehow he also must be to blame, though he never got beyond wondering what could have been done to avert the squall. When he went back into the kitchen, however,-- the "critters" fed, and his own nerves soothed by pitchforking the haymow with the vigor of one who assaults a citadel,--he was much relieved at finding the at- mosphere as clear as usual; and as the early twilight drew on, he became almost happy at thought of; the vivid pleasure before him. Never, since his wife died, had he played his bass-viol in public; but he had long been in the habit of "slying off" upstairs to it, as to a tryst with lover or friend whom the world denied. The Widder Poll, though she heard it wailing and droning thence, never seriously objected to it;

the practice was undoubtedly "shaller," but it kept him in the house.

They ate supper in silence; and then, while she washed the dishes, Heman changed his clothes, and went to the barn to harness. He stood for a moment, ir-resolute, when the horse was ready, and then backed him into the old blue pung. A queer little smile lurked at the corners of his mouth.

"I guess the shoe'll go once more," he muttered. "No, I ain't goin' to marry ag'in! I said I ain't, an' I ain't. But I guess I can give a neighbor a lift, if I want to!"

Brad Freeman was waiting near the tack door when Heman led the horse out of the barn. He was lank and lean, and his thick red hair strayed low over the fore-head. His army overcoat was rent here and there beyond the salvation which lay in his wife's patient mending, and his old fur cap showed the skin in moth-eaten patches; yet Heman thought, with a wondering protest, how young he looked, how free from care.

"Hullo, Heman!" called Brad.

"How are ye?" responded Heman, with a cordiality Brad never failed to elicit from his brother man.

Heman left the horse standing, and opened the back door.

He stopped short. An awful vision confronted him,--the Widder Poll, clad not only in the Tycoon rep, but her best palm-leaf shawl, her fitch tippet, and pump-kin hood; her face was still bandaged, and her head-gear had been enwound by a green *barege* veil. She stepped forward with an alertness quite unusual in one so accustomed to remembering her weight of mortal flesh.

"Here!" she called, "you kind o' help me climb in. I ain't so spry as I was once. You better give me a real boost. But, land! I mustn't talk. I wouldn't git a mite of air into that tooth for a dollar bill."

Heman stepped into the house for his bass-viol, and brought it out with an extremity of tender care; he placed it, enveloped in its green baize covering, in the bottom of the pung. Some ludicrous association between the baize and the green *barege* veil struck Brad so forcibly that he gave vent to a chuckle, sliding cleverly into a cough. He tried to meet Heman's eye, but Heman only motioned him to get in, and took his own place without a word. Brad wondered if he could be ill; his face had grown yellowish in its pallor, and he seemed to breathe heavily.

Midway in their drive to the vestry, they passed a woman walking briskly along in the snowy track. She was carrying her singing-books under one arm, and holding her head high with that proud lift which had seemed, more than anything else, to keep alive her girlhood's charm.

"There's Roxy," said Brad. "Here, Heman, you let me jump out, an' you give her a lift." But Heman looked straight before him, and drove on.

By the time they entered Tiverton Street, the vestry was full of chattering groups. Heman was the last to arrive. He made a long job of covering the horse, inside the shed, resolved that nothing should tempt him to face the general mirth at the Widder's entrance. For he could not deceive himself as to the world's amused estimate of her guardianship and his submission. He had even withdrawn from the School Board, where he had once been proud to figure, because, entering the schoolroom one day at recess, he had seen, on a confiscated slate at the teacher's desk, a rough caricature representing "Heman and his Ma." The Ma was at least half the size of the slate, while Heman was microscopic; but, alas! his inflamed consciousness found in both a resemblance which would mightily have surprised the artist. He felt that if he ever saw another testimony of art to his unworthiness, he might commit murder.

When he did muster courage to push open the vestry door, the Widder Poll sat alone by the stove, still unwinding her voluminous wrappings, and the singers had very pointedly withdrawn by themselves. Brad and Jont had begun to tune their fiddles, and the first prelusive snapping of strings at once awakened Heman's nerves to a pleasant tingling; he was excited at the nearness of the coming joy. He drew a full breath when it struck home to him, with the warm certainty of a happy truth, that if he did not look at her, even the Widder Poll could hardly spoil his evening. Everybody greeted him with unusual kindliness, though some could not refrain from coupling their word with a meaning glance at the colossal figure near the stove. One even whispered,--

"She treed ye, didn't she, Heman?"

He did not trust himself to answer, but drew the covering from his own treasure, and began his part of the delicious snapping and screwing.

"Where's Roxy?" called Jont Marshall "Can't do without her alto. Anybody seen her?"

Roxy was really very late, and Heman could not help wondering whether she had delayed in starting because she had expected a friendly invitation to ride, "All right," he reflected, bitterly. "She must get used to it."

The door opened, and Roxy came in. She had been walking fast, and her color was high. Heman stole one glance at her, under cover of the saluting voices. She was forty years old, yet her hair had not one silver thread, and at that instant of happy animation, she looked strikingly like her elder sister, to whom Heman used to give lozenges when they were boy and girl together, and who died in India. Then Roxy took her place, and Heman bent over his bass-viol. The rehearsal began. Heman forgot all about his keeper sitting by the stove, as the old, familiar tunes swelled up in the little room, and one antique phrase after another awoke nerve-cells all unaccustomed nowadays to thrilling. He could remember just when he first learned The Mellow Horn, and how his uncle, the sailor, had used to sing it. "Fly like a youthful hart or roe!" Were there spices still left on the hills of life? Ah, but only for youth to smell and gather! Boldly, with a happy bravado, the choir sang,--

"The British yoke, the Gallic chain,　Were placed upon our necks in vain!"

And then came the pious climax of Coronation, America, and the Doxology. Above the tumult of voices following the end of rehearsal, some one announced the decision to meet on Wednesday night; and Heman, his bass-viol again in its case, awoke, and saw the Widder putting on her green veil. Rosa Tolman nudged her intimate friend, Laura Pettis, behind Heman's back, and whispered,--

"I wonder if she's had a good time! There 'ain't been a soul for her to speak to, the whole evenin' long!"

The other girl laughed, with a delicious sense of fun in the situation, and Heman recoiled; the sound was like a blow in the face.

"Say, Heman," said Brad, speaking in his ear. "I guess I'll walk home, so't you can take in Roxy."

But Heman had bent his head, and was moving along with the rest, like a man under a burden.

"No," said he, drearily. "I can't. You come along."

His tone was quite conclusive; and Brad, albeit wondering, said no more. The three packed themselves into the pung, and drove away. Heman was conscious of some dull relief in remembering that he need not pass Roxy again on the road, for he heard her voice ring out clearly from a group near the church. He wondered if anybody would go home with her, and whether she minded the dark "spell o' woods" by the river. No matter! It was of no use. She must get used to her own company.

The Widder was almost torpid from her long sojourn by the stove; but the tingling air roused her at last, and she spoke, though mumblingly, remembering her tooth,--

"Proper nice tunes, wa'n't they? Was most on 'em new?"

But Brad could not hear, and left it for Heman to answer; and Heman gave his head a little restive shake, and said, "No." At his own gate, he stopped.

"I guess I won't car' you down home," he said to Brad.

It was only a stone's-throw, Brad hesitated.

"No, I, didn't mean for ye to," answered he, "but I'll stop an' help unharness."

"No," said Heman, gently. "You better not. I'd ruther do it." Even a friendly voice had become unbearable in his ears.

So, Brad, stepped down, lifted out his fiddle-case, and said good-night. Heman drove into the yard, and stopped before the kitchen door. He took the reins in one hand, and held out the other to the Widder.

"You be a mite careful o' your feet," he said. "That bass-viol slipped a little for'ard when we come down Lamson's Hill."

She rose ponderously. She seemed to sway and hesitate; then she set one foot cautiously forward in the pung. There was a rending, crash. The Widder Poll had stepped into the bass-viol. She gave a little scream; and plunged forward.

"My foot's ketched!" she cried. "Can't you help me out?"

Heman dropped the reins; he put his hands on her arms, and pulled her forward. He never knew whether she reached the ground on her feet or her knees. Then he pushed past her, where she floundered, and lifted out his darling. He carried it into the kitchen, and lighted the candle, with trembling hands. He drew back the cover. The bass-viol had its mortal wound; he could have laid both fists into the hole. He groaned.

"My God Almighty!" he said aloud.

The Widder Poll had stumbled into the room. She threw back her green veil, and her face shone ivory white under its shadow; her small eyes were starting. She looked like a culprit whom direst vengeance had overtaken at last. At the sound of her step, Heman lifted his hurt treasure, carried it tenderly into his bedroom, and shut the door upon it. He turned about, and walked past her out of the house. The Widder Poll followed him, wringing her mittened hands.

"O Heman!" she cried, "don't you look like that! Oh, you'll do yourself some mischief, I know you will!"

But Heman had climbed into the pung, and given Old Gameleg a vicious cut. Swinging out of the yard they went; and the Widder Poll ran after until, just outside the gate, she reflected that she never could overtake him and that her ankles were weak; then she returned to the house, groaning.

Heman was conscious of one thought only: if any man had come home with Roxy, he should kill him with his own hands. He drove on, almost to the vestry, and found no trace of her. He turned about, and, retracing his way, stopped at her mother's gate, left Old Gameleg, and strode into the yard. There was no light in the kitchen, and only a glimmer in the chamber above. Heman went up to the kitchen door and knocked. The chamber window opened.

"Who is it?" asked Mrs. Cole. "Why, that you, Heman? Anybody sick?"

"Where's Roxy?" returned Heman, as if he demanded her at the point of the bayonet.

"Why, she's been abed as much as ten minutes. The Tuckers brought her home."

"You tell her to come here! I want to see her."

"What! down there? Law, Heman! you come in the mornin'. She'll ketch her death o' cold gittin' up an' dressin', now she's got all warmed through."

"What's he want, mother?" came Roxy's clear voice from within the room. "That's Heman Blaisdell's voice."

"Roxy, you come down here!" called Heman, masterfully.

There was a pause, during which Mrs. Cole was apparently pulled away from the window. Then Roxy, her head enveloped in a shawl, appeared in her mother's place.

"Well!" she said, impatiently. "What is it?"

Heman's voice found a pleading level.

"Roxy, will you marry me?"

"Why, Heman, you 're perfectly ridiculous! At this time o' night, too!"

"You answer me!" cried Heman, desperately. "I want you! Won't you have me, Roxy? Say?"

"Roxy!" came her mother's muffled voice from the bed. "You'll git your death o' cold. What's he want? Can't you give him an answer an' let him go?"

"Won't you, Roxy?" called Heman. "Oh, won't you?"

Roxy began to laugh hysterically. "Yes," she said, and shut the window.

When Heman had put up the horse, he walked into the kitchen, and straight up to the Widder Poll, who stood awaiting him, clinging to the table by one fat hand.

"Now, look here!" he said, good-naturedly, speaking to her with a direct address he had not been able to use for many a month, "You listen to me. I don't want any hard feelin', but to-morrer mornin' you've got to pick up your things an' go. You can have the house down to the Holler, or you can go out nussin', but you come here by your own invitation, an' you've got to leave by mine. I'm goin' to be married as soon as I can git a license." Then he walked to the bedroom, and shut himself in with his ruined bass-viol and the darkness.

And the Widder Poll did not speak.

*   *   *   *   *

There are very few cosey evenings when Heman and Roxy do not smile at each other across the glowing circle of their hearth, and ask, the one or the other, with a perplexity never to be allayed,--

"Do you s'pose she tumbled, or did she put her foot through it a-purpose?"

But Heman is sure to conclude the discussion with a glowing tribute to Brad Freeman, his genius and his kindliness.

"I never shall forgit that o' Brad," he announces. "There wa'n't another man in the State o' New Hampshire could ha' mended it as he did. Why, you never'd know there was a brack in it!"

HEARTSEASE.

"For as for heartsease, it groweth in a single night."

What be you doin' of, Mis' Lamson?" asked Mrs. Pettis, coming in from the kitchen, where she had been holding a long conversation with young Mrs. Lamson on the possibility of doing over sugar-barberry. Mrs. Pettis was a heavy woman, bent almost double with rheumatism, and she carried a baggy umbrella for a cane. She was always sighing over the difficulty of "gittin' round the house," but nevertheless she made more calls than any one else in the neighborhood. "It kind o' limbered her up," she said, "to take a walk after she had been bendin' over the dish-pan."

Mrs. Lamson looked up with an alert, bright glance. She was a little creature, and something still girlish lingered in her straight, slender figure and the poise of her head. "Old Lady Lamson" was over eighty, and she dressed with due deference to custom; but everything about her gained, in the wearing, an air of youth. Her aggressively brown front was rumpled a little, as if it had tried to crimp itself, only to be detected before the operation was well begun, and the purple ribbons of her cap flared rakishly aloft.

"I jest took up a garter," she said, with some apology in her tone. "Kind o' fiddlin' work, ain't it?"

"Last time I was here, you was knittin' mittins," continued Mrs. Pettis, seating herself laboriously on the lounge, and leaning forward upon the umbrella clutched steadily in two fat hands. "You're dretful forehanded. I remember I said so then. 'Samwel 'ain't got a mittin, to his name,' I says, 'nor he won't have 'fore November.'"

"Well, I guess David's pretty well on't for everything now," answered Mrs.

Lamson, with some pride. "He's got five pair o' new mittins, an' my little blue chist full o' stockin's. I knit 'em two-an'-two, an' two-an'-one, an' toed some on 'em off with white, an' some with red, so's to keep 'em in pairs. But Mary said I better not knit any more, for fear the moths'd git into 'em, an' so I stopped an' took up this garter. But *'tis* dretful fiddlin' work!"

A brief silence fell upon the two, while the sweet summer scents stole in at the window,--the breath of the cinnamon rose, of growing, grass and good brown earth. Mrs. Pettis pondered, looking vacantly before her, and Old Lady Lamson knit hastily on. Her needles clicked together, and she turned her work with a jerk in beginning a row. But neither was oppressed by lack of speech. They understood each other, and no more thought of "making talk" than of pulling up a seed to learn whether it had germinated. It was Mrs. Pettis who, after, a natural interval; felt moved to speak.

"Mary's master thoughtful of you, ain't she? 'Tain't many sons' wives would be so tender of, anybody, now is it?"

Mrs. Lamson looked up sharply, and then, with the same quick movement; bent her eyes on her work.

"Mary means to do jest what's right," she answered. "If she don't make out, it ain't for lack o' tryin'."

"So I says to Samwel this mornin'. 'Old Lady Lamson 'ain't one thing to concert herself with,' says I, 'but to git dressed an' set by the winder. When dinner-time comes, she's got nothin' to do but hitch up to the table; an' she don't have to touch her hand to a dish.' Now ain't that so, Mis' Lamson?"

"That's so," agreed Mrs. Lamson, with a little sigh, instantly suppressed. "It's different from what I thought to myself 'twould be when Mary come here. ''Tain't in natur' she'll have the feelin' for me she would for her own,' I says; but I b'lieve she has, an' more too. When she come for good, I made up my mind I'd put 'Up with everything, an' say 'twas all in the day's work; but law! I never had to. She an' David both act as if I was sugar or salt, I dunno which."

"Don't ye never help 'round, washin'-days?"

"Law, no! Mary won't hear to 't. She'd ruther have the dishes wait till everything's on the line; an' if I stir a step to go into the gardin to pick a 'mess o' beans, or kill a currant worm, she's right arter me. 'Mother, don't you fall!' she says, a dozen 'times a day. 'I dunno what David'd do to me, if I let anything happen to you.' An' 'David, he's ketched it, too. One night, 'long towards Thanksgivin' time, I kicked the soapstone out o' bed, an' he come runnin' up as if he was bewitched. 'Mother,' says he, 'did you fall? You 'ain't had a stroke, have ye?'"

Old Lady Lamson laughed huskily; her black eyes shone, and her cap ribbons nodded, and danced, but there was an ironical ring to her merriment.

"Do tell!" responded Mrs. Pettis, in her ruminating voice. "Well, things were different when we was young married folks, an' used to do our own spinnin' an' weavin'."

"I guess so!" Mrs. Lamson dropped her busy hands in her lap, and leaned back a moment, in eager retrospect. "Do you recollect that Friday we spun from four o'clock in the mornin' till six that evenin', because the men-folks had gone in the ma'sh, an' all we had to do was to stop an' feed the critters? An' Hiram Peasley come along with tinware, an' you says, 'If you're a mind to stop at my house, an' throw a colander an' a long-handled dipper over the fence, under the flowerin'-currant, an' wait till next time for your pay, I'll take 'em,' says you. 'But I ain't goin' to leave off spinnin' for anything less 'n Gabriel's trumpet,' says you. I remember your sayin' that, as if 'twas only yesterday; an' arter you said it, you kind o' drawed down your face an' looked scairt. An' I never thought on't ag'in till next Sabbath evenin', when Jim Bellows rose to speak, an' made some handle about the Day o' Judgment, an' then I tickled right out."

"How you do set by them days!" said Mrs. Pettis, striving to keep a steady face, though her heavy sides were shaking. "I guess you remember 'em better 'n your prayers!"

"Yes, I laughed out loud, an' you passed me a pep'mint over the pew, an' looked as if you was goin' to cry. 'Don't,' says you; an' it sort o' come over me you knew what I was laughin' at. Why, if there ain't John Freeman stoppin' here,--Mary's sister's brother-in-law, you know. Lives down to Bell P'int. Guess he's pullin' up to give the news."

Mrs. Pettis came slowly to her feet, and scanned the farmer, who was hitching his horse to the fence. When he had gone round to the back door, she turned, and grasped her umbrella with a firmer hand.

"Well, I guess 'twon't pay me to set down ag'in," she announced. "I'm goin' to take it easy on the way home. I dunno but I'll let down the bars, an' poke a little ways into the north pastur', an' see if I can't git a mite o' pennyr'yal. I'll be in ag'in to-morrer or next day."

"So do, so do," returned Mrs. Lamson.

"'Tain't no use to ask you to come down, I s'pose? You don't git, out so fur, nowadays."

"No," said the other, still with that latent touch of sarcasm in her voice. "If I should fall, there'd be a great hurrah, boys,--'fire on the mountain, run, boys, run!'"

Mrs. Pettis toiled out into the road; and Old Lady Lamson, laying her knitting on the table, bent forward, not to watch her out of sight, but to make sure whether she really would stop at the north pasture.

"No, she's goin' by," she said aloud, with evident relief. "No, she ain't either. I'll be whipped if she ain't lettin' down the bars! *'Twould* smell kind o' good, I declare!"

She was still peering forward, one slender hand on the window-sill, when Mary, a pretty young woman, with two nervous lines between her eyes, came hurrying in.

"Mother," she began, in that unnatural voice which is supposed to allay excitement in another, "I dunno what I'm goin' to do. Stella's sick."

"You don't say!" said Old Lady Lamson, turning away from the window. "What do they think 'tis?"

"Fever, John says. An' she's so full-blooded it'll be likely to go hard with her. They want me to go right down, an' David's got to carry me. John would, but he's gone to be referee in that land case, an' he won't be back for a day or two. It's a mercy David's just home from town, so he won't have to change his clo'es right through. Now, mother, if you should have little 'Liza Tolman come an' stay with you, do you think anything would happen, s'posin' we left you alone just one night?"

A little flush rose in the old lady's withered cheek. Her eyes gleamed brightly through her glasses.

"Don't you worry one mite about me," she replied, in an even voice. "You change your dress, an' git off afore it's dark. I shall be all right."

"David's harnessin' now," said Mary, beginning to untie her apron. "I sent John down to the lower barn to call him. But, mother, if anything should happen to you--"

"Lord-a-massy! nothin' 's goin' to!" the old lady broke forth, in momentary impatience. "Don't stan' here talkin'. You better have your mind on Stella. Fever's a quicker complaint than old age. It al'ays was, an' al'ays will be."

"Oh, I know it! I know it!" cried Mary, starting toward the door. "There ain't a thing for you to do. There's new bread an' preserves on the dairy-wheel, an' you have 'Liza Tolman pick you up some chips, an' build the fire for your tea; an' don't you wash the dishes, mother. Just leave 'em in the sink. An' for mercy sake, take a candle, an' not meddle with kerosene--"

"Come, come, ain't you ready?" came David's voice from the door. "I can't keep the horse stan'in' here till he's all eat up with flies."

Mary fled to her bedroom, unbuttoning her dress as she ran; and David came in, bringing an air of outdoor freshness into the little sitting-room, with his regal height, his broad shoulders, and tanned, fresh face.

"Well, mother," he said, putting a hand of clumsy kindliness on her shoulder, "if anything happens to you while we're gone, I shall wish we'd let the whole caboodle of 'em die in their tracks. Don't s'pose anything will, do ye?"

"Law, no, David!" exclaimed the old lady, looking at him with beaming pride. "You stan' still an' let me pick that mite o' lint off your arm. I shall be tickled to death to git rid on ye."

"Now, mother," counselled Mary, when she came but of the bedroom, hastily tying her bonnet strings, "you watch the school-children, an' ask 'Liza Tolman to stay with you, an' if she can't, to get one of the Daltons; an' tell her we'll give her some Bartlett pears when they're ripe."

"Yes, yes, I hear," answered the old lady, rising, and setting back her chair in its accustomed corner. "Now, do go along, or ye won't be down to Grapevine Run afore five o'clock."

She watched them while they drove out of the yard, shading her eyes with one nervous hand.

"Mother," called Mary, "don't you stan' there in that wind, with nothin' on your head!"

The old lady turned back into the house, and her face was alive with glee.

"Wind!" she ejaculated scornfully, and yet with the tolerance of one too happy for complaint. "Wind! I guess there wouldn't be so much, if some folks would save their breath to cool their porridge!"

She did not go back to the sitting-room and her peaceful knitting. She walked into the pantry, where she gave the shelves a critical survey, and then, returning to the kitchen, looked about her once more.

"If it's one day sence I've been down sullar," she said aloud, "it's two year." She 'was lighting a candle as she spoke. In another moment, she was taking sprightly steps down the stairs into the darkness below.

"Now, mother, don't you fall!" she chuckled, midway in the descent; and it was undeniable that the voice sounded much like Mary's in her anxious mood. "Now, ain't I a mean creatur' to stan' here laughin' at 'em!" she went on: "Well,' if she don't keep things nice! 'Taters all sprouted; an' the preserve cupboard never looked better in my day. Mary's been well brought up,--I'll say that for her."

Old Lady Lamson must have spent at least half an hour in the cellar, for when she ascended it was after four o'clock, and the school-children had passed the house on their way home. She heard their voices under the elms at the turn of the road.

"I ain't to blame if I can't ketch 'em," she remarked calmly, as she blew out her light. "I don't see's anybody could say I was to blame. An' I couldn't walk up to the Tolmans' to ask 'Liza. I might fall!"

She set about her preparations for supper. It was a favorite maxim in the household that the meal should be eaten early, "to get it out of the way;" and to-night this unaccustomed handmaid had additional reasons for haste. But the new bread and preserves were ignored. She built a rousing fire in the little kitchen stove; she brought out the moulding-board, and with trembling eagerness proceeded to mix cream-of-tartar biscuits. Not Cellini himself nor Jeannie Carlyle had awaited the results of passionate labor with a more strenuous eagerness; and when she drew out the panful of delicately browned biscuits, she set it down on the table, and looked at it in sheer delight.

"I'll be whipped if they ain't as good as if I'd made 'em every night for the last two year!" she cried. "I ain't got to git my hand in, an' that's truth an' fact!"

She brought out some "cold b'iled dish," made her strong green tea, and sat down to a banquet such as they taste who have reached the Delectable Mountains.

It held within it all the savor of a happy past; it satisfied her hungry soul.

After she had washed the supper dishes and scrupulously swept the hearth, she rested, for a moment's thought, in the old rocking-chair, and then took her way, candle in hand, to the attic. There was no further self-confidence on the stairs; she was too serious, now. Her hours were going fast. The attic, in spite of the open windows, lay hot under summer's touch upon the shingles outside, and odorous of the dried herbs hanging in bunches here and there.

"Wormwood--thoroughwort--spearmint," she mused, as she touched them, one after another, and inhaled their fragrance. "'Tain't so long ago I was out pickin' herbs an' dryin' 'em. Well, well, well!"

She made her way under the eaves, and pulled out a hair-trunk, studded with brass nails. A rush-bottomed chair stood near-by, and, setting her candle in it, she knelt before the trunk and began lifting out its contents: a brocaded satin waistcoat of a long-past day, a woolen comforter knit in stripes, a man's black broadcloth coat. She smoothed them, as she laid them by, and there was a wondering note in her lowered voice.

"My Lord!" she whispered reverently, as if speaking to One who would hear and understand, "it's over fifty year!"

A pile of yellowed linen lay in the bottom of the trunk, redolent of camphor from contact with its perishable neighbors. She lifted one shirt after another, looking at them in silence. Then she laid back the other clothes, took up her candle and the shirts, and went downstairs again. In hot haste, she rebuilt the kitchen fire, and set two large kettles of water on the stove. She dragged the washing-bench into the back kitchen from its corner in the shed, and on it placed her tubs; and when the water was heated, she put the garments into a tub, and rubbed with the vigor and ease of a woman well accustomed to such work. All the sounds of the night were loud about her, and the song of the whippoorwill came in at the open door. He was very near. His presence should have been a sign of approaching trouble, but Old Lady Lamson did not hear him. Her mind was reading the lettered scroll of a vanished year.

Perhaps the touch of the warm water on her hands recalled her to the present.

"Seems good to feel the suds," she said, happily, holding up one withered hand,

and letting the foam drip from her fingers, "I wish't I could dry outdoor! But when mornin' come, they'd be all of a sop."

She washed and rinsed the garments, and, opening a clothes-horse, spread them out to dry. Then she drew a long breath, put out her candle, and wandered to the door. The garden lay before her, unreal in the beauty of moonlight. Every bush seemed an enchanted wood. The old lady went forth, lingering at first, as one too rich for choosing; then with a firmer step. She closed the little gate, and walked out into the country road. She hurried along to the old signboard, and turned aside unerringly into a hollow, there, where she stooped and filled her hands with tansy, pulling it up in great bunches, and pressing it eagerly to her face.

"Seventy-four year ago!" she told the unseen listener of the night, with the same wonder in her voice. "Sir laid dead, an' they sent me down here to pick tansy to put round him. Seventy-four year ago!"

Still holding it; she rose, and went through the bars into the dewy lane. Down the wandering path, trodden daily by the cows, she walked, and came out in the broad pasture, irregular with its little hillocks, where, as she had been told from her babyhood, the Indians used to plant their corn. She entered the woods by a cart-path hidden from the moon, and went on with a light step, gathering a bit of green here and there,--now hemlock, now a needle from the sticky pine,--and inhaling its balsam on her hands. A sharp descent, and she had reached the spot where the brook ran fast, and where lay "Peggy's b'ilin' spring," named for a great-aunt she had never seen, but whose gold beads she had inherited, and who had consequently seemed to her a person of opulence and ease.

"I wish't I'd brought a cup," she said. "There ain't no such water within twenty mile."

She crouched beside the little black pool, where the moon glinted in mysterious, wavering, symbols to beckon the gaze upward, and, making a cup of her hand, drank eagerly. There was a sound near-by, as if some wood creature were stirring; she thought she heard a fox barking in the distance. Yet she was really conscious only of the wonder of time, the solemn record of the fleeting years.

When she made her way back through the woods, the moon was sinking, and the shadows had grown heavy. As she reached the bars again, on her homeward track, she stopped suddenly, and her face broke into smiling at the pungent fragrance rising from the bruised herbage beneath her feet. She stooped and gathered one telltale, homely weed, mixed as it was with the pasture grass. "Pennyr'yal," she said happily, and felt the richness of being.

When Old Lady Lamson had ironed her shirts and put them away again, all hot and sweet from the fire, it was five o'clock, and the birds had long been trying to drag creation up from sleep, to sing with them the wonders of the dawn. At six, she had her cup of tea, and when, at eight, her son drove into the yard, she came placidly to the side door to meet him, her knitting in her hands.

"Well, if I ain't glad!" called David. "I couldn't git it out o' my mind somethin' 'd happened to you. Stella's goin' to be all right, they think, but nothin' will do but Mary must stay a spell. Do you s'pose you an' I could keep house a week or so, if I do the heft o' the work?"

Old Lady Lamson's eyes took on the look which sometimes caused her son to inquire suspiciously, "Mother, what you laughin' at?"

"I guess we can, if we try hard enough," she said, soberly, rolling up her yarn. "Now you come in, an' I'll git you a bite o' somethin' t'eat."

MIS' WADLEIGH'S GUEST.

Cyrus Pendleton sat by the kitchen fire, his stockinged feet, in the oven, and his; hands stretched out toward the kettles, which were bubbling prosperously away, and puffing a cloud of steam, into his face. He was a meagre, sad-colored man, with mutton-chop whiskers so thin as to lie like a shadow on his fallen cheeks; and his glance, wherever it fell, Seemed to deprecate reproof. Thick layers of flannel swathed his throat, and from time to time, he coughed wheezingly, with the air of one who, having a cold, was determined to be conscientious about it. A voice from the buttery began pouring forth words only a little slower than the blackbird sings, and with no more reference to reply.

"Cyrus, don't you feel a mite better? Though I dunno how you could, expect to, arter such a night as you had on't, puffin' an' blowin'!" Mrs. Pendleton followed the voice. She seemed to be borne briskly in on its wings, and came scudding over the kitchen sill, carrying a pan of freshly sifted flour. She set it down on the table, and began "stirrin' up." "I dunno where you got such a cold, unless it's in the air," she continued. "Folks say they're round, nowadays, an' you ketch 'em, jest as you would the mumps. But there! nobody on your side or mine ever had the mumps, as long as I can remember. Except Elkanah, though! an' he ketched 'em down to Portsmouth, when he went off on that fool's arrant arter elwives. Do you s'pose you could eat a mite o' fish for dinner?"

"I was thinkin'--" interposed Cyrus, mildly; but his wife swept past him, and took the road.

"I dunno's there's any use in gittin' a real dinner, jest you an' me, an' you not workin' either. Folks say there's more danger of eatin' too much'n too little. Gilman Lane, though, he kep' eatin' less an' less, an' his stomach dried all up, till 'twa'n't no bigger'n a bladder. Look here, you! I shouldn't wonder a mite if you'd got some o' them stomach troubles along with your cold. You 'ain't acted as if you'd relished a meal o' victuals for nigh onto ten days. Soon as I git my hands out o' the flour, I'll look in the doctor's book, an' find out. My! how het up I be!" She wiped her hands on the roller towel, and unpinned the little plaid shawl drawn tightly across her shoulders, Its removal disclosed a green sontag, and under that manifold layers of jacket and waist. She was amply protected from the cold. "I dunno's I ought to ha' stirred up rye'n' Injun," she went on, returning to her vigorous tossing and mixing at the table. "Some might say the steam was bad for your lungs. Anyhow, the doctor's book holds to't you've got to pick out a dry climate, if you don't want to go into a decline. Le' me see! when your Aunt Mattie was took, how long was it afore she really gi'n up? Arter she begun to cough, I mean?"

Cyrus moved uneasily.

"I dunno," he said, hastily. "I never kep' the run o' such things."

But Mirandy, pouring her batter into the pan, heeded him no more than was her wont.

"I s'pose that was real gallopin' consumption," she said, with relish." I must ask Sister Sarah how long 'twas, next time I see her. She set it down with the births an' deaths."

Cyrus was moved to some remonstrance. He often felt the necessity of asserting himself, lest he should presently hear his own passing-bell and epitaph.

"I guess you needn't stop steamin' bread for me! I ain't half so stuffed up as I was yisterday!"

Mrs. Pendleton clapped the loaf into the pot, wrinkling her face over the cloud of steam that came puffing into it.

"There!" she exclaimed. "Now perhaps I can git a minute to se' down. I ain't bound a shoe to-day. My! who's that out this weather?"

The side door was pushed open, and then shut with a bang. A vigorous stamping of snow followed, and the inner door swung in to admit a woman, very short, very stout, with a round, apple-cheeked face, and twinkling eyes looking out from the enveloping folds of a gray cloud.

"Well!" she said, in a cheery voice, beginning at once to unwind the cloud, "here I be! Didn't think I'd rain down, did ye? I thought myself, one spell, I should freeze afore I fell!"

Mrs. Pendleton hurried forward, wiping her hands on her apron as she went.

"For the land's sake, Marthy Wadleigh!" she cried, laying hold of the new-comer by the shoulders, and giving her an ineffectual but wholly delighted shake. "Well, I never! Who brought you over? Though I dunno which way you come. I 'ain't looked out--"

"I walked from the corner," said Mrs. Wadleigh, who never felt any compunction about interrupting her old neighbor. She was unpinning her shawl composedly, as one sure of a welcome. "How do, Cyrus? Jim Thomas took me up jest beyond the depot, an' give me a lift on his sled; but I was all of a shiver, an' at the corner, I told him he better let me step down an' walk. So I come the rest o' the way afoot an' alone. You ain't goin' to use the oven, be ye? I'll jest stick my feet in a minute. No, Cyrus, don't you move! I'll take t'other side. I guess we sha'n't come to 'blows over it."

She seemed to have brought into the kitchen, with that freshness of outdoor air which the new-comer bears, like a balsam, in his garments, a breath of fuller life, and even of jollity. As she sat there in her good brown dress, with her worked collar, fastened by a large cameo, her gold beads just showing, and her plump hands folded on a capacious lap, she looked the picture of jovial content, quite able to take care of herself, and perhaps apply a sturdy shoulder to the lagging machinery of the world.

"Didn't you git word I was comin' this week?" she asked. "I sent you a line."

"No, we 'ain't been so fur's the post-office," answered Mirandy, absently. She was debating over her most feasible bill of fare, now that a "pick-up dinner" seemed no longer possible. Moreover, she had something on her mind, and she could not help thinking how unfortunate it was that Cyrus shared her secret. Who could tell at what moment he might broach it? She doubted his discretion. "The roads wa'n't broke out till day before yisterday."

"I shouldn't think they were!" said Mrs. Wadleigh, scornfully, testing the heat with a hand on her skirt, and then lifting the breadths back over her quilted petticoat. "I thought that would be the way on't, but I'd made up my mind to come, an' come I would. Cyrus, what's the matter o' you? Nothin' more'n a cold, is it?"

Cyrus had withdrawn from the stove, and was feeling his chin, uncertainly.

"Oh, no, I guess not," he said. "We've been kind o' peaked, for a week or two, all over the neighborhood; but I guess we shall come out on't, now we've got into the spring. Mirandy, you git me a mite o' hot water, an' I'll see if I can't shave."

Mirandy was vigorously washing potatoes at the sink, but she turned, in ever-ready remonstrance.

"Shave!" she ejaculated, "Well, I guess you won't shave, such a day as this, in that cold bedroom, with a stockin'-leg round your throat, an' all! You want to git your death? Why, 'twas only last night, Marthy, he had a hemlock sweat, an' all the ginger tea I could git down into him! An' then I didn't know--"

"Law! let him alone!" said Marthy, with a comfortable, throaty laugh. "He'll feel twice as well, git some o' them things off his neck. Here, Cyrus, you reach me down your mug--ain't them your shavin' things up there?--an' I'll fill it for you. You git him a piece o' flannel, Mirandy, to put on when he's washed up an' took all that stuff off his throat. Why, he's got enough wool round there, if 'twas all in yarn, to knit Old Tobe a pair o' mittins! An' they say one o' his thumbs was bigger'n the hand o' Providence. You don't want to try all the goodness out of him, do ye?"

Cyrus gave one swift glance at his wife. "There! you see!" it said plainly. "I am not without defenders." He took down his shaving-mug, with an air of some bravado. But Mirandy was no shrew; she was simply troubled about many things.

"Well," she said, compressing her lips, and wrinkling her forehead in resignation. "If folks want to kill themselves, I can't hender 'em! But when he's down ag'in, I shall be the one to take care of him, that's all. Here, Cyrus, don't you go into that cold bedroom. You shave you here, if you're determined to do it."

So Cyrus, after honing his razor, with the pleasure of a bored child provided at last with occupation, betook himself to the glass set in the lower part of the clock, and there, with much contortion of his thin visage, proceeded to shave. Mirandy put her potatoes on to boil, and set the fish on the stove to freshen; then She sat down by the window, with a great basket beside her, and began to bind shoes.

"Here," said Mrs. Wadleigh, coming to her feet and adjusting her skirt, "you give me a needle! I've got my thimble right here in my pocket. It's three months sence I've seen a shoe. I should admire to do a pair or two. I wish I could promise ye more, but somehow I'm bewitched to git over home right arter dinner!"

Mrs. Pendleton laid down her work, and leaned back in her chair. Cyrus turned, cleared his throat, and looked at her.

"Marthy," said the hostess, "you ain't goin' over there to that lonesome house, this cold snap?"

"Ain't I?" asked Mrs. Wadleigh, composedly, as she trimmed the top of her shoe preparatory to binding it. "Well, you see'f I ain't!"

"In the fust place," went on Mrs. Pendleton, nervously, "the cross-road ain't broke out, an' you can't git there. I dunno's a horse could plough through; an' s'posin' they could, Cyrus ain't no more fit to go out an' carry you over'n a fly."

"Don't you worry," said Mrs. Wadleigh, binding off one top. "While I've got my own legs, I don't mean to be beholden to nobody. I've had a proper nice time all winter, fust with Lucy an' then with Ann,--an' I tell ye 'tain't everybody that's got two darters married so well!--but for the last fortnight, I've been in a real tew to come home. They've kep' me till I wouldn't stay no longer, an' now I've got so near as this, I guess I ain't goin' to stop for nobody!"

Mrs. Pendleton looked despairingly at her husband; and he, absently wiping his razor on a bit of paper, looked at her.

"Marthy!" she burst forth. "No, Cyrus, don't you say one word! You can't go! There's somebody there!"

Mrs. Wadleigh, in turn, put down her work.

"Somebody there!" she ejaculated. "Where?"

"In your house!"

"In my house? What for?"

"I dunno," said Mirandy, unhappily.

"Dunno? Well, what are they doin' there?"

"I dunno that. We only know there's somebody there."

Here the brown-bread kettle boiled over, creating a diversion; and Mirandy gladly rose to set it further back. A slight heat had come into Mrs. Wadleigh's manner.

"Cyrus," said she, with emphasis, "I should like to have you speak. I left that house in your care. I left the key with you, an' I should like to know who you've been an' got in there."

Cyrus opened his mouth, and then closed it again without saying a word. He looked appealingly at his wife; and she took up the tale with some joy, now that the first plunge had been made.

"Well," she said, folding her hands in her apron, and beginning to rock back and forth, a little color coming into her cheeks, and her eyes snapping vigorously. "You see, this was the way 'twas. Cyrus, do let me speak!" Cyrus had ineffectually opened his mouth again. "Wa'n't it in November you went away? I thought so. Jest after that first sprinklin' o' snow, that looked as if 'twould lay all winter. Well, we took the key, an' hung it up inside the clock--an' there 'tis now!--an' once a week, reg'lar as the day come round, Cyrus went over, an' opened the winders, an' aired out the house."

Mrs. Wadleigh sat putting her thimble off and on.

"I know all about that," she interposed, "but who's in there now? That's what I want to find out."

"I'm comin' to that. I don't want to git ahead o' my story. An' so't went on till it come two weeks ago Friday, an' Cyrus went over jest the same as ever. An' when he hitched to the gate, he see smoke comin' out o' the chimbly, an' there was a man's face at one square o' glass." She paused, enjoying her climax.

"Well? Why don't you go ahead? Mirandy Jane Pendleton, I could shake you! You can talk fast enough when somebody else wants the floor! How'd he git in? What'd he say for himself?"

"Why, he never said anything! Cyrus didn't see him."

"Didn't see him? I thought he see him lookin' out the winder!"

"Why, yes! so he did, but he didn't see him to speak to. He jest nailed up the door, an' come away."

Mrs. Wadleigh turned squarely upon the delinquent Cyrus, who stood, half-shaven, absently honing his razor.

"Cyrus," said she, with an alarming decision, "will you open your head, an' tell me what you nailed up that door for? an' where you got your nails? I s'pose you don't carry 'em round with you, ready for any door't happens to need nailin' up?"

This fine sarcasm was not lost on Cyrus. He perceived that he had become the victim of a harsh and ruthless dealing.

"I had the key to the front door with me, an' I thought I'd jest step round an' nail up t'other one," he said, in the tone of one conscious of right. "There was some nails in the wood-shed. Then I heard somebody steppin' round inside, an' I come away."

"You come away!" repeated Mrs. Wadleigh, rising in noble wrath. "You nailed up the' door an' come away! Well, if you! ain't a weak sister! Mirandy, you hand me down that key, out o' the clock, while I git my things!"

She walked sturdily across to the bedroom, and Mirandy followed her, wringing her hands in futile entreaty.

"My soul, Marthy! you ain't goin' over there! You'll be killed, as sure as you step foot into the yard. Don't you remember how that hired man down to Sudleigh toled the whole fam'ly out into the barn, one arter another, an' chopped their heads off--"

"You gi' me t'other end o' my cloud," commanded Mrs. Wadleigh. "I'm glad I've got on stockin'-feet. Where's t'other mittin? Oh! there 'tis, down by the sto'-leg. Cyrus, if you knew how you looked with your face plastered over o' lather, you'd wipe it off, an' hand me down that key. Can't you move? Well, I guess I can reach it myself."

She dropped the house key carefully into her pocket, and opened the outer door; both Cyrus and his wife knew they were powerless to stop her.

"O Marthy, do come back!" wailed Mrs. Pendleton after her. You 'ain't had a mite o' dinner, an' you'll never git out o' that house alive!"

"I'd rather by half hitch up myself," began Cyrus; but his wife turned upon him, at the word, bundled him into the kitchen, and shut the door upon him. Then she went back to her post in the doorway, and peered after Mrs. Wadleigh's square figure on the dazzling road, with a melancholy determination to stand by her to the last. Only when it occurred to her that it was unlucky to watch a departing friend out of sight, did she shut the door hastily, and go in to reproach Cyrus and prepare his dinner.

Mrs. Wadleigh plodded steadily onward. Her face had lost its robustness of scorn, and expressed only a cheerful determination. Once or twice her mouth relaxed, in retrospective enjoyment of the scene behind her, and she gave vent to a scornful ejaculation.

"A man in my house!" she said once, aloud. "I guess we'll see!"

She turned into the cross-road, where stood her dear and lonely dwelling, with no neighbors on either side for half a mile, and stopped a moment to gaze about her. The road was almost untravelled, and the snow lay encrusted over the wide fields, sparkling on the heights and blue in the hollows. The brown bushes by a hidden stone-wall broke the sheen entrancingly; here and there a dry leaf fluttered, but only enough to show how still such winter stillness can be, and a flock of little brown birds rose, with a soft whirr, and settled further on. Mrs. Wadleigh pressed her lips together in a voiceless content, and her eyes took on a new brightness. She had lived quite long enough in the town. Rounding a sweeping bend, and ploughing sturdily along, though it was difficult here to find the roadway, she kept her eyes fixed on a patch of sky, over a low elm, where the chimney would first come into view. But just before it stepped forward to meet her, as she had seen it a thousand times, a telltale token forestalled it; a delicate blue haze crept out, in spiral rings, and tinged the sky.

"He's got a fire!" she exclaimed loudly. "He's there! My soul!" Until now the enormity of his offence had not penetrated her understanding. She had heard the fact without realizing it.

The house was ancient but trimly kept, and it stood within a spacious yard, now in billows and mounds of snow, under which lay the treasures inherited by the spring. The trellises on either side the door held the bare clinging arms of jessamine and rose, and the syringa and lilac bushes reached hardily above the snow. As Mrs. Wadleigh approached the door, she gave a rapid glance at the hop-pole in the garden, and wondered if its vine had stood the winter well. That was the third hop vine she'd had from Mirandy Pendleton! Mounting the front steps, she drew forth the key, and put it in the door. It turned readily enough, but though she gave more than one valiant push, the door itself did not yield. It was evidently barricaded.

"My soul!" said Mrs. Wadleigh.

She stepped back, to survey the possibilities of attack; but at that instant, glancing up at the window, she had Cyrus Pendleton's own alarming experience. A head looked out at her, and was quickly withdrawn. It was dark, unkempt, and the movement was stealthy.

"That's him!" said Mrs. Wadleigh, grimly, and returning to the charge, she knocked civilly at the door. No answer. Then she pushed again. It would not yield. She thought of the ladder in the barn, of the small cellar-window; vain hopes, both of them!

"Look here!" she called aloud. "You let me in! I'm the Widder Wadleigh! This is my own house, an' I'm real tried stan'in' round here, knockin' at my own front door. You le'me in, or I shall git my death o' cold!"

No answer; and then Mrs. Wadleigh, as she afterwards explained it, "got mad." She ploughed her way round the side of the house,--not the side where she had seen the face, but by the "best-room" windows,--and stepped softly up to the back door. Cyrus Pendleton's nail was no longer there. The man had easily pushed it out. She lifted the latch, and set her shoulder against the panel.

"If it's the same old button, it'll give," she thought. And it did give. She walked steadily across the kitchen toward the clock-room, where the man that moment turned to confront her. He made a little run forward; then, seeing but one woman, he restrained himself. He was not over thirty years old; a tall, well-built fellow, with very black eyes and black hair. His features were good, but just now his mouth was set, and he looked darkly defiant. Of this, however, Mrs. Wadleigh did not think, for she was in a hot rage.

"What under the sun do you mean, lockin' me out o' my own house?" she cried, stretching out her reddened hands to the fire. "An' potaters b'iled all over this good kitchen stove! I declare, this room's a real hog's nest, an' I left it as neat as wax!"

Perhaps no man was ever more amazed than this invader. He stood staring at her in silence.

"Can't you shet the door!" she inquired, fractiously, beginning to untie her cloud. "An' put a stick o' wood in the stove? If I don't git het through, I shall ketch my death!"

He obeyed, seemingly from the inertia of utter surprise. Midway in the act of lifting the stove-cover, he glanced at her in sharp, suspicion.

"Where's the rest?" he asked, savagely. "You ain't alone?"

"Well, I guess I'm alone!" returned Mrs. Wadleigh, drawing off her icy stocking-feet, "an' walked all the way from Cyrus Pendleton's! There ain't nobody likely to be round," she continued, with grim humor. "I never knew 'twas such a God-forsaken hole, till I'd been away an' come back to 't. No, you needn't be scairt! The road ain't broke out, an' if 'twas, we shouldn't have no callers to-day. It's got round there's a man here, an' I'll warrant the selec'men are all sick abed with colds. But there!" she added, presently, as the soothing warmth of her own kitchen stove began to penetrate, "I dunno's I oughter call it a Godforsaken place. I'm kind o' glad to git back."

There was silence for a few minutes, while she toasted her feet, and the man stood shambling from one foot to the other and furtively watching her and the road. Suddenly she rose, and lifted a pot-cover.

"What you got for dinner?" she inquired, genially. "I'm as holler's a horn!"

"I put some potatoes on," said he, gruffly.

"Got any pork? or have you used it all up?"

"I guess there's pork! I 'ain't touched it. I 'ain't eat anything but potatoes; an' I've chopped wood for them, an' for what I burnt."

"Do tell!" said Mrs. Wadleigh. She set the potatoes forward, where they would boil more vigorously. "Well, you go down sullar an' bring me up a little piece o' pork--streak o' fat an' streak o' lean--an' I'll fry it. I'll sweep up here a mite while you're gone. Why, I never see such a lookin' kitchen! What's your name?" she called after him, as he set his foot on the Upper stair.

He hesitated. "Joe!" he said, falteringly.

"All right, then, Joe, you fly round an' git the pork!" She took down the broom from its accustomed nail, and began sweeping joyously; the man, fishing in the pork-barrel, listened meanwhile to the regular sound above. Once it stopped, and he held his breath for a moment, and stood at bay, ready to dash up the stairs and past his pursuers, had she let them in. But it was only her own step, approaching the cellar door.

"Joe!" she called. "You bring up a dozen apples, Bald'ins. I'll fry them, too."

Something past one o'clock, they sat down together to as strange a meal as the little kitchen had ever seen. Bread and butter were lacking, but there was quince preserve, drawn from some hidden hoard, the apples and pork, and smoking tea. Mrs. Wadleigh's spirits rose. Home was even better than her dreams had pictured it. She told her strange guest all about her darter Lucy and her darter Ann's children; and he listened, quite dazed and utterly speechless.

"There!" she said at last, rising, "I dunno's I ever eat such a meal o' victuals in my life, but I guess it's better'n many a poor soldier used to have. Now, if you've got some wood to chop, you go an' do it, an' I'll clear up this kitchen; it's a real hurrah's nest, if ever there was one!"

All that afternoon, the stranger chopped wood, pausing, from time to time, to look from the shed door down the country road; and Mrs. Wadleigh, singing "Fly like a Youthful," "But O! their end, their dreadful end," and like melodies which had prevailed when she "set in the seats," flew round, indeed, and set the kitchen in immaculate order. Evidently her guest had seldom left that room. He had slept there on the lounge. He had eaten his potatoes there, and smoked his pipe.

When the early dusk set in, and Mrs. Wadleigh had cleared away their supper of baked potatoes and salt fish, again with libations of quince, she drew up before the shining stove, and put her feet on the hearth.

"Here!" she called to the man, who was sitting uncomfortably on one corner of the woodbox, and eying her with the same embarrassed watchfulness. "You draw up, too! It's the best time o' the day now, 'tween sunset an' dark."

"I guess I'd better be goin'," he returned, doggedly.

"Goin'? Where?"

"I don't know. But I'm goin'."

"Now look here," said Mrs. Wadleigh, with rigor. "You take that chair, an' draw up to the fire. You do as I tell you!"

He did it.

"Now, I can't hender your goin', but if you do go, I've got a word to say to you."

"You needn't say it! I don't want nobody's advice."

"Well, you've got to have it jest the same! When you bile potaters, don't you let 'em run over onto the stove. Now you remember! I've had to let the fire go down here, an' scrub till I could ha' cried. Don't you never do such a thing ag'in, wherever you be!"

He could only look at her. This sort of woman was entirely new to his experience.

"But I've got somethin' else to say," she continued, adjusting her feet more comfortably. "I ain't goin' to turn anybody out into the snow, such a night as this. You're welcome to stay, but I want to know what brought ye here. I ain't one o' them that meddles an' makes, an' if you 'ain't done nothin' out o' the way, an' I ain't called on for a witness, you needn't be afraid o' my tellin'."

"You will be called on!" he broke in, speaking from a desperation outside his own control. "It's murder! I've killed a man!" He turned upon her with a savage challenge in the motion; but her face was set, placidly forward, and the growing dusk had veiled its meaning.

"Well!" she remarked, at length, "ain't you ashamed to set there talkin' about it! You must have brass enough to line a kittle! Why 'ain't you been, like a man, an' gi'n yourself up, instid o' livin' here, turnin' my kitchen upside down? Now you tell me all about it! It'll do ye good."

"I'm goin'," said the man, breathing hard as he spoke, "I'm goin' away from here tonight. They never'll take me alive. It was this way. There was a man over where I lived that's most drunk himself under ground, but he ain't too fur gone to do mischief. He told a lie about me, an' lost me my place in the shoe shop. Then one night, I met him goin' home, an' we had words. I struck him. He fell like an ox. I killed him. I didn't go home no more. I didn't even see my wife. I couldn't tell her. I couldn't be took *there*. So I run away. An' when I got starved out, an' my feet were most froze walkin', I see this house, all shet up, an' I come here."

He paused; and the silence was broken only by the slow, cosey ticking of the liberated clock.

"Well!" said Mrs. Wadleigh, at last, in a ruminating tone. "Well! well! Be you a drinkin' man?"

"I never was till I lost my job," he answered, sullenly. "I had a little then. I had a little the night he sassed me."

"Well! well!" said Mrs. Wadleigh, again. And then she continued, musingly: "So I s'pose you're Joe Mellen, an' the man you struck was Solomon Ray?"

He came to his feet with a spring.

"How'd you know?" he shouted.

"Law! I've been visitin' over Hillside way!" said Mrs. Wadleigh, comfortably. "You couldn't ha' been very smart not to thought o' that when I mentioned my darter Lucy, an' where the childern went to school. No smarter'n you was to depend on that old wooden button! I know all about that drunken scrape. But the queerest part on't was--Solomon Ray didn't die!"

"Didn't die!" the words halted, and he dragged them forth. "Didn't die?"

"Law, no! you can't kill a Ray! They brought him to, an' fixed him up in good shape. I guess you mellered him some, but he's more scairt than hurt. He won't prosecute. You needn't be afraid. He said he dared you to it. There, there now! I wouldn't. My sake alive! le' me git a light!"

For the stranger sat with his head bowed on the table, and he trembled like a child.

Next morning at eight o'clock, Mrs. Wadleigh was standing at the door, in the sparkling light, giving her last motherly injunction to the departing guest.

"You know where the depot is? An' it's the nine o'clock train you've got to take. An' you remember what I said about hayin' time. If you don't have no work by the middle o' May, you drop me a line, an' perhaps I can take you an' your wife, too; Lucy's childern al'ays make a sight o' work. You keep that bill safe, an'--Here, wait a minute! You might stop at Cyrus Pendleton's--it's the fust house arter you pass; the corner--an' ask 'em to put a sparerib an' a pat o' butter into the sleigh, an' ride over here to dinner. You tell 'em I'm as much obleeged to 'em for sendin' over last night to see if I was alive, as if I hadn't been so dead with sleep I couldn't say so. Good-bye! Now, you mind you keep tight hold o' that bill, an', spend it prudent!"

"Is Kelup Rivers comin' over here to-night?" suddenly asked Aunt Melissa Adams, peering over her gold-bowed glasses, and fixing her small shrewd eyes sharply upon her niece.

Amanda did not look up from her fine hemming, but her thin hand trembled almost imperceptibly, and she gave a little start, as if such attacks were not altogether unexpected.

"I don't know," she answered, in a low tone.

"Dunno! why don't ye know?" said her aunt, beginning to sway back and forth in the old-fashioned rocking-chair, but not once dropping her eyes from Amanda's face. "Don't he come every Saturday night?"

Amanda took another length, of thread, and this time her hand really shook.

"I guess so," she answered.

"You guess so? Don't ye know? An' if he's come every Saturday night for fifteen year, ain't he comin' to-night? I dunno what makes you act as if you wa'n't sure whether your soul's your own, 'Mandy Green. My dander al'ays rises when I ask you a civil question an' you put on that look."

Amanda bent more closely over her sewing. She was a woman of thirty-five, with a pathetically slender figure, thin blond hair painstakingly crimped, and anxious blue eyes. Something deprecating lay in her expression; her days had been uncomplainingly sacrificed to the comfort of those she loved, and the desire of peace and good-will had crept into her face and stayed there. Her mother, who looked even slighter than she, and whose cheeks were puckered by wrinkles, sat by the window watching the two with a smile of empty content. Old Lady Green had lost her mind, said the neighbors; but she was sufficiently like her former self to be a source of unspeakable joy and comfort to Amanda, who nursed and petted her as if their positions were reversed, and protected her from the blunt criticism of the literal-tongued neighborhood with a reverential awe belonging to the old days when the fifth commandment was written and obeyed.

"Gold-bowed," said Mrs. Green, with a look of unalloyed delight, pointing to her sister-in-law's spectacles; and Aunt Melissa repeated indulgently,--

"Yes, yes, gold-bowed. I'll let you take 'em a spell, arter I've set my heel. It'll please her, poor creatur'!" she added, in an audible aside to Amanda. Since the time when Mrs. Green's wits had ceased to work normally, she had treated her sympathetically, but from a lofty eminence. Aunt Melissa was perhaps too prosperous. She sat there, swaying back and forth, in her thin black silk trimmed with narrow rows of velvet, her heavy chin sunk upon a broad collar, worked in her youth, and she seemed to Mrs. Green a vision of majesty and delight, but to Amanda a virtuous censor, necessarily to be obeyed, yet whose presence made the summer day intolerable. Even her purple cap-ribbons bespoke terror to the evil-doer, and her heavy face was set, as a judgment, toward the doom of the man who knew not how to account for his actions. She began speaking again, and Amanda involuntarily gave a little start, as at a lightning flash.

"I says to myself when I drove off, this mornin': 'I'll have a little talk with 'Mandy. I don' go there to spend a day more'n four times a year, an' like as not she'll be glad to have somebody to speak to, seen' 's her mother's how she is.'"

Amanda gave a quick look at Mrs. Green; but the old lady was busily pleating the hem of her apron and then smoothing it out again. Aunt Melissa rocked, and went on:--

"I says to myself: 'Here they let Kelup carry on the farm at the halves, an' go racin' an' trottin' from the other place over here day in an' day out. An' when his Uncle Nat died, two year ago, then was the time for him to come over here an' marry 'Mandy an' carry on the farm. But no, he'd rather hang round the old place, an' sleep in the ell-chamber, an' do their chores for his board, an' keep on a-runnin' over here.' An' when young Nat married, I says to myself, 'That'll make him speak.' But it didn't--an' you 're a laughin'-stock, 'Mandy Green, if ever there was one. Every time the neighbors see him steppin' by Saturday nights, all fixed up, with that brown coat on he's had sence the year one, they have suthin' to say, 'Goin' over to 'Mandy's,' that's what they say. An' on'y last Saturday one on 'em hollered out to me, when I was pickin' a mess o' pease for Sunday, 'Wonder what 'Mandy'll answer when he gits round to askin' of her?' I hadn't a word to say. 'You better go to *him*,' says I, at last."

Amanda had put down her sewing in her lap, and was looking steadfastly out of the window, with eyes brimmed by two angry tears. Once she wiped them with a furtive movement of the white garment in her lap; her cheeks were crimson. Aunt Melissa had lashed herself into a cumulative passion of words.

"An' I says to myself, 'If there ain't nobody else to speak to 'Mandy, I will,' I says, when I was combin' my hair this mornin'. 'She 'ain't got no mother,' I says, 'nor as good as none, an' if she 'ain't spunk enough to look out for herself, somebody's got to look out for her.' An' then it all come over me--I'd speak to Kelup himself, an' bein' Saturday night, I knew I should ketch him here."

"O Aunt Melissa!" gasped Amanda, "you wouldn't do that!"

"Yes, I would, too!" asserted Aunt Melissa, setting her firm lips. "You see if I don't, an' afore another night goes over my head!"

But while Amanda was looking at her, paralyzed with the certainty that no mortal aid could save her from this dire extremity, there came an unexpected diversion. Old Lady Green spoke out clearly and decidedly from her corner, in so rational a voice that it seemed like one calling from the dead.

"'Mandy, what be you cryin' for? You come here an' tell me what 'tis, an' I'll see to't. You'll spile your eyes, 'Mandy, if you take on so."

"There, there, ma'am! 'tain't anything," said Amanda, hurrying over to her chair and patting her on the shoulder. "We was just havin' a little spat,--Aunt Melissa an' me; but we've got all over it. Don't you want to knit on your garter a little while now?"

But the old lady kept her glazed eyes fixed on Amanda's face.

"Be you well to-day, 'Mandy?" she said, wistfully. "If you ain't well, you must take suthin'.''

"There, there! don't you make a to-do, an' she'll come round all right," said Aunt Melissa, moving her chair about so that it faced the old lady. "I'll tell her suthin' to take up her mind a little." And she continued, in the loud voice which was her concession to Mrs. Green's feebleness of intellect, "They've got a boarder over to the Blaisdells'."

Mrs. Green sat up straight in her chair, smoothed her apron, and looked at her sister with grateful appreciation.

"Do tell!" she said, primly.

"Yes, they have. Name's Chapman. They thought he was a book agent fust. But he's buyin' up old dishes an' all matter o' truck. He wanted my andirons, an' I told him if I hadn't got a son in a Boston store, he might ha' come round me, but I know the vally o' things now. You don't want to sell them blue coverlids o' yourn, do ye?"

Aunt Melissa sometimes asked the old lady questions from a sense of the requirements of conversation, and she was invariably startled when they elicited an answer.

"Them coverlids I wove myself, fifty-five years ago come next spring," said Mrs. Green, firmly. "Sally Ann Mason an' me used to set up till the clock struck twelve that year, spinnin' an' weavin'. Then we had a cup or two o' green tea, an' went to bed."

"Well, you wove 'em, an' you don't want to sell 'em," said Aunt Melissa, her eyes on her work. "If you do, 'Lijah he'll take 'em right up to Boston for you, an' I warrant he'll git you a new white spread for every one on 'em."

"That was the year afore I was married," continued Old Lady Green. "I had a set o' white chiny with lavender sprigs, an' my dress was changeable. He had a flowered weskit. 'Mandy, you go into the clo'es-press in my bedroom an' git out that weskit, an' some o' them quilts, an' my M's an' O's table-cloths."

Amanda rose and hurried into the bedroom, in spite of Aunt Melissa's whispered comment: "What makes you go to overhaulin' things? She'll forgit it in a minute."

While she was absent, a smart wagon drove up to the gate, and a young man alighted from it, hitched his horse, and knocked at the front door. Aunt Melissa saw him coming, and peered at him over her glasses with an unrecognizing stare.

"'Mandy!" she called, "'Mandy, here's a pedler or suthin'! If he's got any essences, you ask him for a little bottle o' pep'mint."

Amanda dropped the pile of coverlets on the sofa, and went to the front door. Presently she reappeared, and with her, smoothly talking her down, came the young man. His eyes lighted first on the coverlets, with a look of cheerful satisfaction.

"Got all ready for me, didn't you?" he asked, briskly. "Heard I was coming, I guess."

He was a man of an alert Yankee type, with waxed blond mustache and eye-glasses; he was evidently to be classed among those who have exchanged their country honesty for a veneer of city knowingness.

"For the land's sake!" ejaculated Aunt Melissa, as soon as she had him at short range, "you're the one down to Blaisdell's that's buyin' up all the old truck in the neighborhood. Well, you won't git my andirons!"

He had begun to unfold the blue coverlets and examine them with a practised eye, while Amanda stood by, painfully conscious that some decisive action might be required of her; and her mother sat watching the triumph of her quilts in pleased importance.

"They ain't worth much," he said, dropping them, with a conclusive air. "Fact is, they ain't worth anything, unless any body's got a fancy for such old stuff. I'll tell you what, I'll give you fifty cents apiece for the lot! How many are there here--four? Two dollars, then."

Amanda took a hasty step forward.

"But we don't want to sell our coverlids!" she said, indignantly, casting an appealing glance at Aunt Melissa.

"I guess they don't want to git rid on 'em," said that lady, "'specially at such a price. They're wuth more 'n that to cover up the squashes when the frost comes."

"Mother wove 'em herself," exclaimed Amanda, irrelevantly. It began to seem to her as if the invader might pack up her mother's treasures and walk off with them.

"Well, then, I s'pose they're hers to do as she likes with?" he said, pleasantly, tipping back, in his chair, and beginning to pare his nails with an air of nicety that fascinated Amanda into watching him. "They're hers, I s'pose?" he continued, looking suddenly and keenly up at her.

"Why, yes," she answered, "they're mother's, but she don't want to sell. She sets by 'em."

"Just like me, for all the world," owned the stranger, "Now there's plenty of folks that wouldn't care a Hannah Cook about such old truck, but it just hits me in the right spot. Mother's doughnuts, mother's mince-pies, I say! Can't improve on **them**! And when my wife and I bought our little place, I said to her, 'We'll have it all furnished with old-fashioned goods.' And here I am, taking, time away from my business, riding round the country, and paying good money for what's no use to anybody but me."

"What is your business?" interrupted Aunt Melissa.

"Oh, insurance--a little of everything--Jack-of-all-trades!" Then he turned to Old Mrs. Green, and asked, abruptly, "What'll you take for that clock?"

The old lady followed his alert forefinger until her eyes rested on the tall eight-day clock in the corner. She straightened herself in her chair, and spoke with pride:--

"That was Jonathan's gre't-uncle Samwell's. He wound it every Sunday night, reg'lar as the day come round. I've rubbed that case up till I sweat like rain. 'Mandy she rubs it now."

"Well, what'll you take?" persisted he, while Amanda, in wordless protest, stepped in front of the clock. "Five dollars?"

"Five dollars," repeated the old lady, lapsing into senseless iteration. "Yes, five dollars."

But Aunt Melissa came to the rescue.

"Five dollars for that clock?" she repeated, winding her ball, and running the needles into it with a conclusive stab. "Well, I guess there ain't any eight-day clocks goin' out o' **this** house for five dollars, if they go at all! 'Mandy, why don't you speak up, an' not stand there like a chicken with the pip?"

"Oh, all right, all right!" said the visitor, shutting his knife with a snap, and getting briskly on his feet. "I don't care much about buying. That ain't a particularly good style of clock, anyway. But I like old things. I may drop in again, just to take a look at 'em. I suppose you're always at home?" he said to Amanda, with his hand on the door.

"Yes; but sometimes I go to Sudleigh with butter. I go Monday afternoons most always, after washin'."

With a cheerful good-day he was gone, and Amanda drew a long breath of relief.

"Well, some folks have got enough brass to line a kittle," said Aunt Melissa, carefully folding her knitting-work in a large silk handkerchief. "'Mandy, you'll have to git supper a little earlier'n common for me. I told Hiram to come by half arter six. Do you s'pose Kelup'll be round by that time? I'll wait all night afore I'll give up seein' him."

"I don't know, Aunt Melissa," said Amanda, nervously clearing the table of its pile of snowy cloth, and taking a flying glance from the window. She looked like a harassed animal, hunted beyond its endurance; but suddenly a strange light of determination flashed into her face. "Should you just as lieves set the table," she asked, in a tone of guilty consciousness, "while I start the kitchen fire? You know where things are." Hardly waiting for an assent, she fled from the room, and once in the kitchen, laid the fire in haste, with a glance from the window to accompany every movement. Presently, by a little path through the field, came a stocky man in blue overalls and the upper garment known as a jumper. He was bound for the pigpen in the rear of the barn; and there Amanda flew to meet him, stopping only to throw an apron over her head. They met at the door. He was a fresh-colored man, with honest brown eyes and a ring of whiskers under the chin. He had a way of blushing, and when Amanda came upon him thus unannounced, he colored to the eyes.

"Why, you're all out o' breath!" he said, in slow alarms.

"O Caleb!" she cried, looking at him with imploring eyes. "I'll feed the pigs to-night."

Caleb regarded her in dull wonderment. Then he set down the pail he had taken.

"Ain't there any taters to bile?" he asked, solving the difficulty in his own way; "or 'ain't you skimmed the milk? I'd jest as soon wait."

"You better not wait," answered Amanda, almost passionately, her thin hair blowing about her temples. "You better go right back. I'd ruther do it myself; I'd a good deal ruther."

Caleb turned about. He took a few steps, then stopped, and called hesitatingly over his shoulder, "I thought maybe I'd come an' set a spell to-night."

Then, indeed, Amanda felt her resolution, crack and quiver. "I guess you better come some other night," she said, in a steady voice, though her face was wet with tears. And Caleb walked away, never once looking back. Amanda stayed only to wipe her eyes, saying meanwhile to her sorry self, "Oh, I dunno how I can get along! I dunno!" Then she hurried back to the house, to find the kettle merrily singing, and Aunt Melissa standing at the kitchen cupboard, looking critically up and down the shelves.

"If you've got two sets o' them little gem-pans, you might lend me one," she remarked; and Amanda agreed, not knowing what she gave.

The supper was eaten and the dishes were washed, Aunt Melissa meantime keeping a strict watch from the window.

"Is it time for Kelup?" she asked, again and again; and finally she confronted the guilty Amanda with the challenge, "Do you think Kelup ain't comin'?"

"I--guess not," quavered Amanda, her cheeks scarlet, and her small, pathetic hands trembling. She was not more used to *finesse* than to heroic action.

"Do you s'pose there's any on 'em sick down to young Nat's?" asked Aunt Melissa; and Amanda was obliged to take recourse again to her shielding "I guess not." But at length Uncle Hiram drove up in the comfortable carry-all; and though his determined spouse detained him more than three-quarters of an hour, sitting beside him like a portly Rhadamanthus, and scanning the horizon for the Caleb who never came, he finally rebelled, shook the reins, and drove off, Aunt Melissa meantime screaming over her shoulder certain vigorous declarations, which evidently began with the phrase, "You tell Kelup--"

Then Amanda went into the house, and sat down by the window in the gathering dusk, surveying the wreckage of her dream. The dream was even more precious in that it had grown so old. Caleb was a part of her every-day life, and for fifteen years Saturday had brought a little festival, wherein the commonplace man with brown eyes had been high-priest. He would not come to-night. Perhaps he never would come again. She knew what it was to feel widowed.

Sunday passed; and though Caleb fed the pigs and did the barn-work as usual, he spoke but briefly. Even in his customary salutation of "How dee?" Amanda detected a change of tone, and thereafter took flight whenever she heard his step at the kitchen door. So Monday forenoon passed; Caleb brought water for her tubs and put out her clothes-line, but they had hardly spoken. The intangible monster of a misunderstanding had crept between them. But when at noon he asked as usual, though without looking at her, "Goin' to Sudleigh with the butter to-day?" Amanda had reached the limit of her endurance. It seemed to her that she could no longer bear this formal travesty of their old relations, and she answered in haste,--

"No, I guess not."

"Then you don't want I should set with your mother?"

"No!" And again Caleb turned away, and plodded soberly off to young Nat's.

"I guess I must be crazy," groaned poor Amanda, as she changed her washing-dress for her brown cashmere. "The butter's got to go, an' now I shall have to harness, an' leave ma'am alone. Oh, I wish Aunt Melissa'd never darkened these doors!"

Everything went wrong with Amanda, that day. The old horse objected to the bits, and occupied twenty minutes in exasperating protest; the wheels had to be greased, and she lost a butter-napkin in the well. Finally, breathless with exertion, she went in to bid her mother good-by, and see that the matches were hidden and the cellar door fastened.

"Now, ma'am," she said, standing over the little old woman and speaking with great distinctness, "don't you touch the stove, will you? You jest set right here in your chair till I come back, an' I'll bring you a good parcel o' pep'-mints. Here's your garter to knit on, an' here's the almanac. Don't you stir now till I come."

And so, with many misgivings, she drove away.

When, Amanda came back, she did not stay to unharness, but hurried up to the kitchen door, and called, "You all right, ma'am?" There was no answer, and she stepped hastily across the floor. As she opened the sitting-room door, a low moaning struck her ear. The old lady sat huddled together in, her chair, groaning at intervals, and looking fixedly at the corner of the room.

"O ma'am, what is it? Where be you hurt?" cried Amanda, possessed by an anguish of self-reproach. But the old lady only continued her moaning; and then it was that Amanda noticed her shrivelled and shaking fingers tightly clasped upon a roll of money in her lap.

"Why, ma'am, what you got?" she cried; but even as she spoke, the explanation flashed upon her, and she looked up at the corner of the room. The eight-day clock was gone.

"Here, ma'am, you let me have it," she said, soothingly; and by dint of further coaxing, she pulled the money from the old lady's tense fingers. There were nine dollars in crisp new bills. Amanda sat looking at them in unbelief and misery.

"O my!" she whispered, at length, "what a world this is! Ma'am, did you tell him he might have 'em?"

"I dunno what Jonathan'll do without that clock," moaned the old lady. "I see it carried off myself."

"Did you tell him he might?" cried Amanda, loudly.

"I dunno but I did, but I never'd ha' thought he'd ha' done it. I dunno what time 'tis now;" and she continued her low-voiced lamenting.

"O my Lord!" uttered Amanda, under her breath. Then she roused herself to the present exigency of comfort. "You come an' set in the kitchen a spell," she said, coaxingly, "an' I'll go an' get the things back."

Old Lady Green looked at her with that unquestioning trust which was the most pathetic accompaniment of her state. "You'll git 'em back, 'Mandy, won't ye?" she repeated, smiling a little and wiping her eyes. "That's a good gal! So't we can tell what time 'tis."

Amanda led her into the kitchen, and established her by the window. She shut the door of the denuded sitting-room, and, giving her courage no time to cool, ran across lots to the Blaisdells', the hated money clasped tightly in her hand. The family was at supper, and the stranger with them, when she walked in at the kitchen door. She hurried up to her enemy, and laid the little roll of bills by his plate. Her cheeks were scarlet, her thin hair-flying.

"Here's your money," she said, in a strained, high voice, "an' I want our things. You hadn't ought to gone over there an' talked over an old lady that--that--"

There she stopped. Amanda had never yet acknowledged that her mother was not in her "perfect mind." Chapman took out a long pocket-book, and for a moment her courage stood at flood-tide; she thought he was about to accept the money and put it away. But no! He produced a slip of white paper and held it up before her. She bent forward and examined it,--a receipt signed by her mother's shaking hand.

"But it ain't right!" she cried, helpless in her dismay. "Cap'n Jabez, you speak to him! You know how 'tis about mother! She wouldn't any more ha' sold that clock than she'd ha' sold--me!"

Captain Jabez looked at his plate in uncomfortable silence. He was a just man, but he hated to interfere.

"Well, there!" he said, at length, pushing his chair back to leave the table. "It don't seem jestly right to me, but then he's got the resate, an' your mother signed it--an' there 'tis!"

"An' you won't do anything?" cried Amanda, passionately, turning back to the stranger. "You mean to keep them things?"

He was honestly sorry for her, as the business man for the sentimentalist, but he had made a good bargain, and he held it sacred.

"I declare, I wish it hadn't happened so," he said, good-naturedly. "But the old lady'll get over it. You buy her a nice bright little nickel clock that'll strike the half-hours, and she'll be tickled to death to watch it."

Amanda turned away and walked out of the house.

"Here," called Chapman, "come back and get your money!" But she hurried on. "Well, I'll leave it with Captain Jabez," he called again, "and you can come over and get it. I'm going in the morning, early."

Amanda was passing the barn, and there, through the open door, she saw the old clock pathetically loaded on the light wagon, protected by burlap, and tied with ropes. The coverlets lay beside it. A sob rose in her throat, but her eyes were dry, and she hurried across lots home. At the back door she found Caleb unharnessing the horse. She had forgotten their misunderstanding in the present practical emergency.

"O Caleb," she began, before she had reached him, "ma'am's sold the clock an' some coverlids, an' I can't get 'em back!"

"Cap'n Jabez said she had, this arternoon," said Caleb, slowly, tying a trace. "I dunno's the old lady's to blame. Seem's if she hadn't ought to be left alone."

"But how'm I goin' to get 'em back?" persisted Amanda, coming close to him, her poor little face pinched and eager. "He jest showed me the receipt, all signed. How'm I goin' to get the things, Caleb?"

"If he's got the receipt, an' the things an' all, an' she took the money, I dunno's you can get 'em," said Caleb, "unless you could prove in a court o' law that she wa'n't in her right mind. I dunno how that would work."

Amanda stood looking him in the face. For the first time in all her gentle life she was questioning masculine superiority, and its present embodiment in Caleb Rivers.

"Then you don't see's anything can be done?" she asked, steadily.

"Why, no," answered Caleb, still reflecting. "Not unless you should go to law."

"You'd better give the pigs some shorts," said Amanda, abruptly. "I sha'n't bile any taters, to-night."

She walked into the house; and as Caleb watched her, it crossed his mind that she looked very tall. He had always thought of her as a little body.

Amanda set her lips, and went about her work. From time to time, she smiled mechanically at her mother; and the old lady, forgetful of her grief now that she was no longer reproached by the empty space on, the wall, sat content and sleepy after her emotion. She was willing to go to bed early; and when Amanda heard her breathing peacefully, she sat down by the kitchen window to wait. The dusk came slowly, and the whippoorwill sang from the deep woods behind the house.

That night at ten o'clock, Caleb Rivers was walking stolidly along the country road, when his ear became aware of a strangely familiar sound,--a steadily recurrent creak. It was advancing, though intermittently. Sometimes it ceased altogether, as if the machinery stopped to rest, and again it began fast and shrill. He rounded a bend of the road, and came full upon a remarkable vision. Approaching him was a wheelbarrow, with a long object balanced across it, and, wheeling it, walked a woman. Caleb was nearly opposite her before his brain translated the scene. Then he stopped short and opened his lips.

"'Mandy," he cried, "what under the heavens be you a-doin'?"

But Amanda did not pause. Whatever emotion the meeting caused in her was swiftly vanquished, and she wheeled on. Caleb turned and walked by her side. When he had recovered sufficiently from his surprise, he laid a hand upon her wrist.

"You set it down, an' let me wheel a spell," he said.

But Amanda's small hands only grasped the handles more tightly, and she went on. Caleb had never in his life seen a necessity for passionate remonstrance, but now the moment had come.

"'Mandy," he kept repeating, at every step, "you give me holt o' them handles! Why, 'Mandy, I should think you was crazy!"

At length, Amanda dropped the handles with a jerk, and turning about, sat down on the edge of the wheelbarrow, evidently to keep the right of possession. Then she began to speak in a high, strained voice, that echoed sharply through the country stillness.

"If you've got to know, I'll tell you, an' you can be a witness, if you want to. It won't do no hurt in a court o' law, because I shall tell myself. I've gone an' got our clock an' our coverlids from where they were stored in the Blaisdells' barn. The man's got his money, an' I've took our things. That's all I've done, an' anybody can know it that's a mind to."

Then she rose, lifted the handles, and went on, panting. Caleb walked by her side.

"But you ain't afraid o' me, 'Mandy?" he said, imploringly. "Jest you let me wheel it, an' I won't say a word if I never set eyes on you ag'in. Jest you let me wheel, 'Mandy."

"There ain't anybody goin' to touch a finger to it but me," said Amanda, short-ly. "If anybody's got to be sent to jail for it, it'll be me. I can't talk no more. I 'ain't got any breath to spare."

But the silence of years had been broken, and Caleb kept on.

"Why, I was goin' over to Blaisdell's myself to buy 'em back. Here's my wallet an' my bank-book. Don't that prove it? I was goin' to pay any price he asked. I set an' mulled over it all the evenin'. It got late, an' then I started. It al'ays has took me a good long spell to make up my mind to things. I wa'n't to blame this arternoon because I couldn't tell what was best to do all of a whew!"

At the beginning of this revelation, Amanda's shoulders twitched eloquently, but she said nothing. She reached the gate of the farmyard, and wheeled in, panting painfully as she ascended the rise of the grassy driveway. She toiled round to the back door; and then Caleb saw that she had prepared for her return by leaving the doors of the cellar-case open, and laying down a board over the steps. She turned the wheelbarrow to descend; and Caleb, seeing his opportunity, ran before to hold back its weight. Amanda did not prevent him; she had no breath left for remonstrance. When the clock was safely in the cellar, she went up the steps again, hooked the bulkhead door, and turned, even in the darkness, unerringly to the flight of stairs.

"You wait till I open the door into the kitchen," she said. "There's a light up there."

And Caleb plodded up the stairs after her with his head down, amazed and sorrowful.

"You can stay here," said Amanda, opening the outside door without looking at him. "I'm goin' back to Cap'n Blaisdell's."

She hurried out into the moonlit path across lots, and Caleb followed. They entered the yard, and Amanda walked up to the window belonging to the best bedroom. It was wide open, and she rapped on it loudly, and then turned her back.

"Hello!" came a sleepy voice from within.

"I've got to speak to you," called Amanda. "You needn't get up. Be you awake?"

"I guess so," said the voice, this time several feet nearer the window. "What's up?"

"I've been over an' got our clock an' the rest of our things," said Amanda, steadily. "An', you've got your money. I've carried the things home an' fastened 'em up. They're down cellar under the arch, an' I'm goin' to set over 'em till I drop afore anybody lays a finger on 'em again. An' you can go to law if you're a mind to; *but I've got our things*!"

There was a silence. Amanda felt that the stranger's eyes were fastened upon her back, and she tried not to tremble. Caleb knew they were, for he and the man faced each other.

"Well, now, you know you've as good as stole my property," began Chapman; but at that instant, Caleb's voice broke roughly upon the air.

"You say that ag'in," said he, "an' I'll horsewhip you within an inch of your life. You touch them things ag'in, an' I'll break every bone in your body. I dunno whose they be, accordin' to rights, but by gum!--" and he stopped, for words will fail where a resolute heart need not.

There was again a silence, and the stranger spoke: "Well, well!" he said, good-naturedly. "I guess we'll have to call it square. I don't often do business this way; but if you'll let me alone, I'll let you alone. Good luck to you!"

Amanda's heart melted. "You're real good!" she cried, and turned impulsively;

but when she faced the white-shirted form at the window, she ejaculated, "Oh, my!" and fled precipitately round the corner of the house.

Side by side, the two took their way across lots again. Amanda was shaking all over, with weariness and emotion spent. Suddenly a strange sound at her side startled her into scrutiny of Caleb's face.

"Why, Caleb Rivers!" she exclaimed, in amazement, "you ain't cryin'?"

"I dunno what I'm doin'," said Caleb, brushing off two big tears with his jumper sleeve, "an' I don't much care. It ain't your harnessin' for yourself an' feedin' the pigs, an' my not comin' Saturday night, but it's seein' you wheelin' that great thing all alone. An' you're so little, 'Mandy! I never thought much o' myself, an' it al'ays seemed kind o' queer you could think anything *of* me; but I al'ays s'posed you'd let me do the heft o' the work, an' not cast me off!"

"I 'ain't cast you off, Caleb," said Amanda, faintly, and in spite of herself her slender figure turned slightly but still gratefully toward him. And that instant, for the first time in all their lives, Caleb's arms were upholding her, and Amanda had received her crown. Caleb had kissed her.

"Say, 'Mandy," said he, when they parted, an hour later, by the syringa bush at the back door, "the world won't come to an end if you don't iron of a Tuesday. I was thinkin' we could ketch Passon True about ten o'clock better'n we could in the arternoon."

JOINT OWNERS IN SPAIN.

The Old Ladies' Home, much to the sorrow of its inmates, "set back from the road." A long, box-bordered walk led from the great door down to the old turnpike, and thickly bowering lilac-bushes forced the eye to play an unsatisfied hide-and-seek with the view. The sequestered old ladies were quite unreconciled to their leaf-hung outlook; active life was presumably over for them, and all the more did they long to "see the passing" of the little world which had usurped their places. The house itself was very old, a stately, square structure, with pillars on either side of the door, and a fanlight above. It had remained unpainted now for many years, and had softened into a mellow lichen-gray, so harmonious and pleasing in the midst of summer's vital green, that the few artists who ever heard of Tiverton sought it out, to plant umbrella and easel in the garden, and sketch the stately relic; photographers, also, made it one of their accustomed haunts. Of the artists the old ladies disapproved, without a dissenting voice. It seemed a "shaller" proceeding to sit out there in the hot sun for no result save a wash of unreal colors on a white ground, or a few hasty lines indicating no solid reality; but the photographers were their constant delight, and they rejoiced in forming themselves into groups upon, the green, to be "took" and carried away with the house.

One royal winter's day, there was a directors' meeting in the great south room, the matron's parlor, a sprat bearing the happy charm of perfect loyalty to the past, with its great fireplace, iron dogs and crane, its settle and entrancing corner cupboards. The hard-working president of the board was speaking hastily and from a full heart, conscious that another instant's discussion might bring the tears to her eyes:--

"May I be allowed to say--it's irrelevant, I know, but I should like the satisfaction of saying it--that this is enough to make one vow never to have anything to do with an institution of any sort, from this time forth for evermore?"

For the moment had apparently come when a chronic annoyance must be recognized as unendurable. They had borne with the trial, inmates and directors, quite as cheerfully as most ordinary people accept the inevitable; but suddenly the tension had become too great, and the universal patience snapped. Two of the old ladies, Mrs. Blair and Miss Dyer, who were settled in the Home for life, and who, before going there, had shown no special waywardness of temper, had proved utterly incapable of living in peace with any available human being; and as the Home had insufficient accommodations, neither could be isolated to fight her "black butterflies" alone. No inmate, though she were cousin to Hercules, could be given a room to herself; and the effect of this dual system on these two, possibly the most eccentric of the number, had proved disastrous in the extreme. Each had, in her own favorite fashion, "kicked over the traces," as the matron's son said in town-meeting (much to the joy of the village fathers), and to such purpose that, to continue the light-minded simile, very little harness was left to guide them withal. Mrs. Blair, being "high sperited," like all the Coxes from whom she sprung, had now so tyrannized over the last of her series of room-mates, so browbeaten and intimidated her, that the latter had actually taken to her bed with a slow-fever of discouragement, announcing that "she'd rather go to the poor-farm and done with it than resk her life there another night; and she'd like to know what had become of that hunderd dollars her nephew Thomas paid down in bills to get her into the Home, for she'd be thankful to them that laid it away so antic to hand it back afore another night went over her head, so't she could board somewheres decent till 'twas gone, and then starve if she'd got to!"

If Miss Sarah Ann Dyer, known also as a disturber of the public peace, presented a less aggressive front to her kind, she was yet, in her own way, a cross and a hindrance to their spiritual growth. She, poor woman, lived in a scarcely varying state of hurt feeling; her tiny world seemed to her one close federation, existing for the sole purpose of infringing on her personal rights; and though she would not take the initiative in battle, she lifted up her voice in aggrieved lamentation over the tragic incidents decreed for her alone. She had perhaps never directly reproached her own unhappy room-mate for selecting a comfortable chair, for wearing squeaking shoes, or singing "Hearken, ye sprightly," somewhat early in the morning, but she chanted those ills through all her waking hours in a high, yet husky tone, broken by frequent sobs. And therefore, as a result of these domestic whirlwinds and too stagnant pools, came the directors' meeting, and the helpless protest of the exasperated president. The two cases were discussed for an hour longer, in the dreary fashion pertaining to a question which has long been supposed to have but one side; and then it remained for Mrs. Mitchell, the new director, to cut the knot with the energy of one to whom a difficulty is fresh.

"Has it ever occurred to you to put them together?" asked she. "They are impossible people; so, naturally, you have selected the very mildest and most Christian women to endure their nagging. They can't live with the saints of the earth. Experience has proved that. Put them into one room, and let them fight it out together."

The motion was passed with something of that awe ever attending a Napoleonic decree, and passed, too, with the utmost good-breeding; for nobody mentioned the Kilkenny cats. The matron compressed her lips and lifted her brows, but said nothing; having exhausted her own resources, she was the more willing to take the superior attitude of good-natured scepticism.

The moving was speedily accomplished; and at ten o'clock, one morning, Mrs. Blair was ushered into the room where her forced colleague sat by the window, knitting. There the two were left alone. Miss Dyer looked up, and then heaved a tempestuous sigh over her work, in the manner of one not entirely surprised by its advent, but willing to suppress it, if such alleviation might be. She was a thin, colorless woman, and infinitely passive, save at those times when her nervous system conflicted with the scheme of the universe. Not so Mrs. Blair. She had black eyes, "like live coals," said her awed associates; and her skin was soft and white, albeit wrinkled. One could even believe she had reigned a beauty, as the tradition of the house declared. This morning, she held her head higher than ever, and disdained expression except that of an occasional nasal snort. She regarded the room with the air of an impartial though exacting critic; two little beds covered with rising-sun quilts, two little pine bureaus, two washstands. The sunshine lay upon the floor, and in that radiant pathway Miss Dyer sat.

"If I'd ha' thought I should ha' come to this," began Mrs. Blair, in the voice of one who speaks perforce after long sufferance, "I'd ha' died in my tracks afore I'd left my comfortable home down in Tiverton Holler. Story-'n'-a-half house, a good sullar, an' woods nigh-by full o' sarsaparilla an' goldthread! I've moved more times in this God-forsaken place than a Methodist preacher, fust one room an' then another; an' bad is the best. It was poor pickin's enough afore, but this is the crowner!"

Miss Dyer said nothing, but two large tears rolled down and dropped on her work. Mrs. Blair followed their course with gleaming eyes endowed with such uncomfortable activity that they seemed to pounce with every glance.

"What under the sun be you carryin' on like that for?" she asked, giving the handle of the water-pitcher an emphatic twitch to make it even with the world. "You 'ain't lost nobody, have ye, sence I moved in here?"

Miss Dyer put aside her knitting with ostentatious abnegation, and began rocking herself back and forth in her chair, which seemed not of itself to sway fast enough, and Mrs. Blair's voice rose again, ever higher and more metallic:--

"I dunno what you've got to complain of more'n the rest of us. Look at that dress you've got on,--a good thick thibet, an' mine's a cheap, sleazy alpaca they palmed off on me because they knew my eyesight ain't what it was once. An' you're settin' right there in the sun, gittin' het through, an' it's cold as a barn over here by the door. My land! if it don't make me mad to see anybody without no more sperit than a wet rag! If you've lost anybody, why don't ye say so? An' if it's a mad fit, speak out an' say that! Give me anybody that's got a tongue in their head, *I* say!"

But Miss Dyer, with an unnecessary display of effort, was hitching her chair into the darkest corner of the room, the rockers hopelessly snarling her yarn at every move.

"I'm sure I wouldn't keep the sun off'n anybody," she said, tearfully. "It never come into my head to take it up, an' I don't claim no share of anything. I guess, if the truth was known, 'twould be seen I'd been used to a house lookin' south, an' the fore-room winders all of a glare o' light, day in an' day out, an' Madeira vines climbin' over 'em, an' a trellis by the front door; but that's all past an' gone, past an' gone! I never was one to take more 'n belonged to me; an' I don't care who says it, I never shall be. An' I'd hold to that, if 'twas the last word I had to speak!"

This negative sort of retort had an enfeebling effect upon Mrs. Blair.

"My land!" she exclaimed, helplessly. "Talk about my tongue! Vinegar's nothin' to cold molasses, if you've got to plough through it."

The other sighed, and leaned her head upon her hand in an attitude of extreme dejection. Mrs. Blair eyed her with the exasperation of one whose just challenge has been refused; she marched back and forth through the room, now smoothing a fold of the counterpane, with vicious care, and again pulling the braided rug to one side or the other, the while she sought new fuel for her rage. Without, the sun was lighting snowy knoll and hollow, and printing the fine-etched tracery of the trees against a crystal sky. The road was not usually much frequented in winter time, but just now it had been worn by the week's sledding into a shining track, and several sleighs went jingling up and down.

Tiverton was seizing the opportunity of a perfect day and the best of "going," and was taking its way to market. The trivial happenings of this far-away world had thus far elicited no more than a passing glance from Mrs. Blair; she was too absorbed in domestic warfare even to peer down through the leafless lilac-boughs, in futile wonderment as to whose bells they might be, ringing merrily past. On one journey about the room, however, some chance arrested her gaze. She stopped, transfixed.

"Forever!" she cried. Her nervous, blue-veined hands clutched at her apron and held it; she was motionless for a moment. Yet the picture without would have been quite devoid of interest to the casual eye; it could have borne little significance save to one who knew the inner life history of the Tiverton Home, and thus might guess what slight events wrought all its joy and pain. A young man had set up his camera at the end of the walk, and thrown the cloth over his head, preparatory to taking the usual view of the house. Mrs. Blair recovered from her temporary inaction. She rushed to the window, and threw up the sash. Her husky voice broke strenuously upon the stillness:--

"Here! you keep right where you be! I'm goin' to be took! You wait till I come!"

She pulled down the window, and went in haste to the closet, in the excess of her eagerness stumbling recklessly forward into its depths.

"Where's my bandbox?" Her voice came piercingly from her temporary seclusion. "Where'd they put it? It ain't here in sight! My soul! where's my bunnit?"

These were apostrophes thrown off in extremity of feeling; they were not questions, and no listener, even with the most friendly disposition in the world, need have assumed the necessity of answering. So, wrapped in oblivion to all earthly considerations save that of her Own inward gloom, the one person who might have responded merely swayed back and forth, in martyrized silence. But no such spiritual withdrawal could insure her safety. Mrs. Blair emerged from the closet, and darted across the room with the energy of one stung by a new despair. She seemed about to fall upon the neutral figure in the corner, but seized the chair-back instead, and shook it with such angry vigor that Miss Dyer cowered down in no simulated fright.

"Where's my green bandbox?'" The words were emphasized by cumulative shakes, "Anybody that's took that away from me ought to be b'iled in ile! Hangin''s too good for 'em, but le' me git my eye on 'em an' they shall swing for 't! Yes, they shall, higher 'n Gil'roy's kite!"

The victim put both trembling hands to her ears.

"I ain't deef!" she wailed.

"Deef? I don't care whether you're deef or dumb, or whether you're nummer'n a beetle! It's my bandbox I'm arter. Isr'el in Egypt! you might grind some folks in a mortar an' you couldn't make 'em speak!"

It was of no use. Intimidation had been worse than hopeless; even bodily force would not avail. She cast one lurid glance at the supine figure, and gave up the quest in that direction as sheer waste of time. With new determination, she again essayed the closet, tossing shoes and rubbers behind her in an unsightly heap, quite heedless of the confusion of rights and lefts. At last, in a dark corner, behind a blue chest, she came upon her treasure. Too hurried now for reproaches, she drew it forth, and with trembling fingers untied the strings. Casting aside the cover, she produced a huge scoop bonnet of a long-past date, and setting it on her head, with the same fevered haste, tied over it the long figured veil destined always to make an inseparable part of her state array. She snatched her stella shawl from the drawer, threw it over her shoulders, and ran out of the room.

Miss Dyer was left quite bewildered by these erratic proceedings, but she had no mind to question them; so many stories were rife in the Home of the eccentricities embodied in the charitable phrase "Mis' Blair's way" that she would scarcely have been amazed had her terrible room-mate chosen to drive a coach and four up the chimney, or saddle the broom for a midnight revel. She drew a long breath of relief at the bliss of solitude, closed her eyes, and strove to regain the lost peace, which, as she vaguely remembered, had belonged to her once in a shadowy past.

Silence had come, but not to reign. Back flew Mrs. Blair, like a whirlwind. Her cheeks wore each a little hectic spot; her eyes were flaming. The figured veil, swept rudely to one side, was borne backwards on the wind of her coming, and her thin hair, even in those few seconds, had become wildly disarranged.

"He's gone!" she announced, passionately. "He kep' right on while I was findin' my bunnit. He come to take the house, an' he'd ha' took me an' been glad. An' when I got that plaguy front door open, he was jest drivin' away; an' I might ha' hollered till I was black in the face, an' then I couldn't ha' made him hear."

"I dunno what to say, nor what not to," remarked Miss Dyer, to her corner. "If I speak, I'm to blame; an' so I be if I keep still."

The other old lady had thrown herself into a chair, and was looking wrathfully before her.

"It's the same man that come from Sudleigh last August," she said, bitterly. "He took the house then, an' said he wanted another view when the leaves was off; an' that time I was laid up with my stiff ankle, an' didn't git into it, an' to-day my bunnit was hid, an' I lost it ag'in."

Her voice changed. To the listener, it took on an awful meaning.

"An' I should like to know whose fault it was. If them that owns the winder, an' set by it till they see him comin', had spoke up an' said, 'Mis' Blair, there's the photograph man. Don't you want to be took?' it wouldn't ha' been too late! If anybody had answered a civil question, an' said, 'Your bunnit-box sets there behind my blue chist,' it wouldn't ha' been too late then! An' I 'ain't had my likeness took sence I was twenty year old, an' went to Sudleigh Fair in my changeable *visite* an' leghorn hat, an' Jonathan wore the brocaded weskit he stood up in, the next week Thursday. It's enough to make a minister swear!"

Miss Dyer rocked back and forth.

"Dear me!" she wailed. "Dear me suz!"

The dinner-bell rang, creating a blessed diversion. Miss Blair, rendered absent-minded by her grief, went to the table still in her bonnet and veil; and this dramatic entrance gave rise to such morbid though unexpressed curiosity that every one forbore, for a time, to wonder why Miss Dyer did not appear. Later, however, when a tray was prepared and sent up to her (according to the programme of her bad days), the general commotion reached an almost unruly point, stimulated as it was by the matron's son, who found an opportunity to whisper one garrulous old lady that Miss Dyer had received bodily injury at the hands of her roommate, and that Mrs. Blair had put on her bonnet to be ready for the sheriff when he should arrive. This report, judiciously started, ran like prairie fire; and the house was all the afternoon in a pleasant state of excitement. Possibly the matron will never know why so many of the old ladies promenaded the corridors from dinnertime until long after early candlelight, while a few kept faithful yet agitated watch from the windows. For interest was divided; some preferred to see the sheriff's advent, and others found zest in the possibility of counting the groans of the prostrate victim.

When Mrs. Blair returned to the stage of action, she was much refreshed by her abundant meal and the strong tea which three times daily heartened her for battle. She laid aside her bonnet, and carefully folded the veil. Then she looked about her, and, persistently ignoring all the empty chairs, fixed an annihilating gaze on one where the dinner-tray still remained.

"I s'pose there's no need o' my settin' down," she remarked, bitingly. "It's all in the day's work. Some folks are waited on; some ain't. Some have their victuals brought to 'em an' pushed under their noses, an' some has to go to the table; when they're there, they can take it or leave it. The quality can keep their waiters settin' round day in an' day out, fillin' up every chair in the room. For my part, I should think they'd have an extension table moved in, an' a snowdrop cloth over it!"

Miss Dyer had become comparatively placid, but now she gave way to tears.

"Anybody can move that waiter that's a mind to," she said, tremulously. "I would myself, if I had the stren'th; but I 'ain't got it. I ain't a well woman, an' I 'ain't been this twenty year. If old Dr. Parks was alive this day, he'd say so. 'You 'ain't never had a chance,' he says to me. 'You've been pull-hauled one way or another sence you was born.' An' he never knew the wust on't, for the wust hadn't come."

"Humph!" It was a royal and explosive note. It represented scorn for which Mrs. Blair could find no adequate utterance. She selected the straightest chair in the room, ostentatiously turned its back to her enemy, and seated herself. Then, taking out her knitting, she strove to keep silence; but that was too heavy a task, and at last she broke forth, with renewed bitterness,--

"To think of all the wood I've burnt up in my kitchen stove an' air-tight, an' never thought nothin' of it! To think of all the wood there is now, growin' an' rottin' from Dan to Beersheba, an' I can't lay my fingers on it!"

"I dunno what you want o' wood. I'm sure this room's warm enough."

"You don't? Well, I'll tell ye. I want some two-inch boards, to nail up a partition in the middle o' this room, same as Josh Marden done to spite his wife. I don't want more'n my own, but I want it mine."

Miss Dyer groaned, and drew an uncertain hand across her forehead.

"You wouldn't have no gre't of an outlay for boards," she said, drearily. "'Twouldn't have to be knee-high to keep me out. I'm no hand to go where I ain't wanted; an' if I ever was, I guess I'm cured on't now."

Mrs. Blair dropped her knitting in her lap. For an instant, she sat there motionless, in a growing rigidity; but light was dawning in her eyes. Suddenly she came to her feet, and tossed her knitting on the bed.

"Where's that piece o' chalk you had when you marked out your tumbler-quilt?" The words rang like a martial order.

Miss Dyer drew it forth from the ancient-looking bag, known as a cavo, which was ever at her side.

"Here 'tis," she said, in her forlornest quaver. "I hope you won't do nothin' out o' the way with it. I should hate to git into trouble here. I ain't that kind."

Mrs. Blair was too excited to hear or heed her. She was briefly, flashingly, taking in the possibilities of the room, her bright black eyes darting here and there with fiery insistence. Suddenly she went to the closet, and, diving to the bottom of a baggy pocket in her "t'other dress," drew forth a ball of twine. She chalked it, still in delighted haste, and forced one end upon her bewildered room-mate.

"You go out there to the middle square o' the front winder," she commanded, "an' hold your end o' the string down on the floor. I'll snap it."

Miss Dyer cast one despairing glance about her, and obeyed.

"Crazy!" she muttered. "Oh my land! she's crazy's a loon. I wisht Mis' Mitchell'd pitch her tent here a spell!"

But Mrs. Blair was following out her purpose in a manner exceedingly methodical. Drawing out one bed, so that it stood directly opposite her kneeling helper, she passed the cord about the leg of the bedstead and made it fast; then, returning to the middle of the room, she snapped the line triumphantly. A faint chalk-mark was left upon the floor.

"There!" she cried. "Leggo! Now, you gi' me the chalk, an' I'll go over it an' make it whiter."

She knelt and chalked with the utmost absorption, crawling along on her knees, quite heedless of the despised alpaca; and Miss Dyer, hovering in a corner, timorously watched her. Mrs. Blair staggered to her feet, entangled by her skirt, and pitching like a ship at sea.

"There!" she announced. "Now here's two rooms. The chalk-mark's the partition. You can have the mornin' sun, for I'd jest as soon live by a taller candle if I can have somethin' that's my own. I'll chalk a lane into the closet, an' we'll both keep a right o' way there. Now I'm to home, an' so be you. Don't you dast to speak a word to me unless you come an' knock here on my headboard,--that's the front door,--an' I won't to you. Well, if I ain't glad to be alone! I've hung my harp on a willer long enough!"

It was some time before the true meaning of the new arrangement penetrated Miss Dyer's slower intelligence; but presently she drew her chair nearer the window and thought a little, chuckling as she did so. She, too, was alone.

The sensation was new and very pleasant. Mrs. Blair went back and forth through the closet-lane, putting her clothes away, with high good humor. Once or twice she sang a little--Derby's Ram and Lord Lovel--in a cracked voice. She was in love with solitude.

Just before tea, Mrs. Mitchell, in some trepidation, knocked at the door, to see the fruits of contention present and to come. She had expected to hear loud words; and the silence quite terrified her, emphasizing, as it did, her own guilty sense of personal responsibility. Miss Dyer gave one appealing look at Mrs. Blair, and then, with some indecision, went to open the door, for the latch was in her house.

"Well, here you are, comfortably settled!" began Mrs. Mitchell. She had the unmistakable tone of professional kindliness; yet it rang clear and true. "May I come in?"

"Set right down here," answered Miss Dyer, drawing forward a chair. "I'm real pleased to see ye."

"And how are you this afternoon?" This was addressed to the occupant of the other house, who, quite oblivious to any alien presence, stood busily rubbing the chalk-marks from her dress.

Mrs. Blair made no answer. She might have been stone deaf, and as dumb as the hearthstone bricks. Mrs. Mitchell cast an alarmed glance at her entertainer.

"Isn't she well?" she said, softly.

"It's a real pretty day, ain't it?" responded Miss Dyer. "If 'twas summer time, I should think there'd be a sea turn afore night. I like a sea turn myself. It smells jest like Old Boar's Head."

"I have brought you down some fruit." Mrs. Mitchell was still anxiously observing the silent figure, now absorbed in an apparently futile search in a brocaded work-bag. "Mrs. Blair, do you ever cut up bananas and oranges together?"

No answer. The visitor rose, and unwittingly stepped across the dividing line.

"Mrs. Blair--" she began, but she got no further.

Her hostess turned upon her, in surprised welcome.

"Well, if it ain't Mis' Mitchell! I can't say I didn't expect you, for I see you goin' into Miss Dyer's house not more'n two minutes ago. Seems to me you make short calls. Now set right down here, where you can see out o' the winder. That square's cracked, but I guess the directors'll put in another."

Mrs. Mitchell was amazed, but entirely interested. It was many a long day since any person, official or private, had met with cordiality from this quarter.

"I hope you and our friend are going to enjoy your room together," she essayed, with a hollow cheerfulness.

"I expect to be as gay as a cricket," returned Mrs. Blair, innocently. "An' I do trust I've got good neighbors. I like to keep to myself, but if I've got a neighbor, I want her to be somebody you can depend upon."

"I'm sure Miss Dyer means to be very neighborly." The director turned, with a smile, to include that lady in the conversation. But the local deafness had engulfed her. She was sitting peacefully by the window, with the air of one retired within herself, to think her own very remote thoughts. The visitor mentally improvised a little theory, and it seemed to fit the occasion. They had quarrelled, she thought, and each was disturbed at any notice bestowed on the other.

"I have been wondering whether you would both like to go sleighing with me some afternoon?" she ventured, with the humility so prone to assail humankind in a frank and shrewish presence. "The roads are in wonderful condition, and I don't believe you'd take cold. Do you know, I found Grandmother Eaton's foot-warmers, the other day! I'll bring them along."

"Law! I'd go anywheres to git out o' here," said Mrs. Blair, ruthlessly. "I dunno when I've set behind a horse, either. I guess the last time was the day I rid up here for good, an' then I didn't feel much like lookin' at outdoor. Well, I guess you *be* a new director, or you never'd ha' thought on't!"

"How do you feel about it, Miss Dyer?" asked the visitor. "Will you go,--perhaps on, Wednesday?"

The other householder moved uneasily. Her hands twitched at their knitting; a flush came over her cheeks, and she cast a childishly appealing glance at her neighbor across the chalkline. Her eyes were filling fast with tears. "Save me!" her look seemed to entreat "Let me not lose this happy fortune!" Mrs. Blair interpreted the message, and rose to the occasion with the vigor of the intellectually great.

"Mis' Mitchell," she said, clearly, "I may be queer in my notions, but it makes me as nervous as a witch to have anybody hollerin' out o' my winders. I don't care whether it's company nor whether it's my own folks. If you want to speak to Miss Dyer, you come along here after me,--don't you hit the partition now!--right out o' my door an' into her'n. Here, I'll knock! Miss Dyer, be you to home?"

The little old lady came forward, fluttering and radiant in the excess of her relief.

"Yes, I guess I be," she said, "an' all alone, too! I see you go by the winder, an' I was in' hopes you'd come in!"

Then the situation dawned upon Mrs. Mitchell with an effect vastly surprising to the two old pensioners. She turned from one to the other, including them both in a look of warm loving-kindness. It was truly an illumination. Hitherto, they had thought chiefly of her winter cloak and nodding ostrich plume; now, at last, they saw her face, and read some part of its message.

"You poor souls!" she cried. "Do you care so much as that? 'O you poor souls!"

Miss Dyer fingered her apron and looked at the floor, but her companion turned brusquely away, even though she trod upon the partition in her haste.

"Law! it's nothin' to make such a handle of" she said. "Folks don't want to be under each other's noses all the time. I dunno's anybody could stan' it, unless 'twas an emmet. They seem to git along swarmin' round together."

Mrs. Mitchell left the room abruptly.

"Wednesday or Thursday, then!" she called over her shoulder.

The next forenoon, Mrs. Blair made her neighbor a long visit. Both old ladies had their knitting, and they sat peacefully swaying back and forth, recalling times past, and occasionally alluding to their happy Wednesday.

"What I really come in for," said Mrs. Blair, finally, "was to ask if you don't think both our settin'-rooms need new paper."

The other gave one bewildered glance about her.

"Why, 'tain't been on more 'n two weeks," she began; and then remembrance awoke in her, and she stopped. It was not the scene of their refuge and conflict that must be considered; it was the house of fancy built by each unto herself. Invention did not come easily to her as yet, and she spoke with some hesitation.

"I've had it in mind myself quite a spell, but somehow I 'ain't been able to fix on the right sort o' paper."

"What do you say to a kind of a straw color, all lit up with tulips?" inquired Mrs. Blair; triumphantly.

"Ain't that kind o' gay?"

"Gay? Well, you want it gay, don't ye? I dunno why folks seem to think they've got to live in a hearse because they expect to ride in one! What if we be gittin' on a little mite in years? We ain't underground yit, be we? I see a real good ninepenny paper once, all covered over with green brakes. I declare if 'twa'n't sweet pretty! Well, whether I paper or whether I don't, I've got some thoughts of a magenta sofy. I'm tired to death o' that old horsehair lounge that sets in my clock-room. Sometimes I wish the moths would tackle it, but I guess they've got more sense. I've al'ays said to myself I'd have a magenta sofy when I could git round to it, and I dunno's I shall be any nearer to it than I be now."

"Well, you *are* tasty," said Miss Dyer, in some awe. "I dunno how you come to think o' that!"

"Priest Rowe had one when I wa'n't more 'n twenty. Some o' his relations give it to him (he married into the quality), an' I remember as if 'twas yesterday what a tew there was over it. An' I said to myself then, if ever I was prospered I'd have a magenta sofy. I 'ain't got to it till now, but now I'll have it if I die for't." "Well, I guess you're in the right on't." Miss Dyer spoke absently, glancing from the window in growing trouble. "O Mis' Blair!" she continued, with a sudden burst of confidence, "you don't think there's a storm brewin', do you? If it snows Wednesday, I shall give up beat!"

Mrs. Blair, in her turn, peered at the smiling sky.

"I hope you ain't one o' them kind that thinks every fair day's a weather breeder," she said. "Law, no! I don't b'lieve it will storm; an' if it does, why, there's other Wednesdays comin'!"

AT SUDLEIGH FAIR.

Delilah Joyce was sitting on her front doorstone with a fine disregard of the fact that her little clock had struck eight of the morning, while her bed was still unmade. The Tiverton folk who disapproved of her shiftlessness in letting the golden hours, run thus to waste, did grudgingly commend her for airing well. Her bed might not even be spread up till sundown, but the sheets were always hanging from her little side window, in fine weather, flapping dazzlingly in the sun; and sometimes her feather-bed lay, the whole day long, on the green slope outside, called by Dilly her "spring," only because the snow melted first there on the freedom days of the year. The new editor of the Sudleigh "Star," seeing her slight, wiry figure struggling with the bed like a very little ant under a caterpillar all too large, was once on the point of drawing up his horse at her gate. He was a chivalrous fellow, and he wanted to help; but Brad Freeman, hulking by with his gun at the moment, stopped him.

"That's only Dilly wrastlin' with, her bed," he called back, in the act of stepping over the wall into the meadow. "'Twon't do no good to take holt once, unless you're round here every mornin' 'bout the same time. Dilly'll git the better on't. She al'ays does." So the editor laughed, put down another Tiverton custom in his mental notebook, and drove on.

Dilly was a very little woman, with abnormally long and sinewy arms. Her small, rather delicate face had a healthy coat of tan, and her iron-gray hair was braided with scrupulous care. She resembled her own house to a striking degree; she was fastidiously neat, but not in the least orderly. The Tiverton housekeepers could not appreciate this attitude in reference to the conventional world. It was all very well to keep the kitchen floor scrubbed, but they did believe, also, in seeing the table properly set, and in finishing the washing by eight o'clock on Monday morning. Now Dilly seldom felt inclined to set any table at all. She was far more likely to take her bread and milk under a tree; and as for washing, Thursday was as good a day as any, she was wont to declare. Moreover, the tradition of hanging garments on the line according to a severely classified system, did not in the least appeal to her.

"I guess a petticoat'll dry jest as quick if it's hung 'side of a nightgown," she told her critics, drily. "An' when you come to hangin' stockin's by the pair, better separate 'em, I say! Like man an' wife! Give 'em a vacation, once in a while, an' love'll live the longer!"

Dilly was thinking, this morning, of all the possibilities of the lovely, shining day. So many delights lay open to her! She could take her luncheon in her pocket, and go threading through the woods behind her house. She could walk over to Pine Hollow, to see how the cones were coming on, and perchance scrape together a basket of pine needles, to add to her winter's kindling; or she might, if the world and the desires thereof assailed her, visit Sudleigh Fair. Better still, she need account to nobody if she chose to sit there on the doorstone, and let the hours go unregretted by. Presently, her happy musing was broken by a ripple from the outer world. A girl came briskly round the corner where the stone-wall lay hidden under a wilderness of cinnamon rosebushes and blackberry vines,--Rosa Tolman, dressed in white *pique*, with a great leghorn hat over her curls. The girl came hurrying up the path, with a rustle of starched petticoats, and still Dilly kept her trance-like posture.

"I know who 'tis!" she announced, presently, in a declamatory voice. "It's Rosy Tolman, an' she's dressed in white, with red roses, all complete, an' she's goin' to Sudleigh Cattle-Show."

Rosa lost a shade of pink from her cheeks. Her round blue eyes widened, in an unmistakable terror quite piteous to see.

"O Dilly!" she quavered, "how do you know such things? Why, you 'ain't looked at me!"

Dilly opened her eyes, and chuckled in keen enjoyment.

"Bless ye!" she said, "I can't help imposin' on ye, no more 'n a cat could help ketchin' a mouse, if't made a nest down her throat. Why, I see ye comin' round the corner! But when folks thinks you're a witch, it ain't in human natur' not to fool 'em. I ***am*** a witch, ain't I, dear? Now, ain't I?"

Rosa's color had faltered back, but she still stood visibly in awe of her old neighbor.

"Well," she owned, "Elvin Drew says you can see in the dark, but I don't know's he means anything by it."

Again Dilly broke into laughter, rocking back and forth, in happy abandonment.

"I can!" she cried, gleefully. "You tell him I can! An' when I can't, folks are so neighborly they strike a light for me to see by. You tell him! Well, now, what is it? You've come to ask suthin'. Out with it!"

"Father told me to come over, and see if you can't tell something about our cows. They're all drying up, and he don't see any reason why."

Dilly nodded her head sagely.

"You'd better ha' come sooner," she announced. "You tell him he must drive 'em to pastur' himself, an' go arter 'em, too."

"Why?"

"An' you tell him to give Davie a Saturday, here an' there, to go fishin' in, an' not let him do so many chores. Now, you hear! Your father must drive the cows, an' he must give Davie time to play a little, or there'll be dark days comin', an' he won't be prepared for 'em."

"My!" exclaimed Rosa, blankly. "My! Ain't it queer! It kind o' scares me. But, Dilly,"--she turned about, so that only one flushed cheek remained visible,--"Dilly, 'ain't you got something to say to me? We're going to be married next Tuesday, Elvin and me. It's all right, ain't it?"

Dilly bent forward, and peered masterfully into her face. She took the girl's plump pink handy and drew her forward. Rosa, as if compelled by some unseen force, turned about, and allowed her frightened gaze to lie ensnared by the witch's great black eyes. Dilly began, in a deep intense voice, with the rhythm of the Methodist exhorter, though on a lower key,--

"Two years, that boy's been arter you. Two years, you trampled on him as if he'd been the dust under your feet. He was poor an' strugglin'. He was left with his mother to take care on, an' a mortgage to work off. An' then his house burnt down, an' he got his insurance money; an' that minute, you turned right round an' says, 'I'll have you.' An' now, you say, 'Is it all right?' *Is* it right, Rosy Tolman? You tell *me*!"

Rosa was sobbing hysterically.

"Oh, I wish you wouldn't scare me so!" she exclaimed, yet not for a moment attempting to withdraw her hand, or turn aside her terrified gaze. "I wish I never'd said one word!"

Dilly broke the spell as lightly as she had woven it. A smile passed over her face, like a charm, dispelling all its prophetic fervor.

"There! there!" she said, dropping the girl's hand. "I thought I'd scare ye! What's the use o' bein' a witch, if ye can't upset folks? Now don't cry, an' git your cheeks all blotched up afore Elvin calls to fetch ye, with that hired horse, an' take ye to the Cattle-Show! But don't ye forget what I say! You remember we ain't goin' to wait for the Day o' Judgment, none on us. It comes every hour. If Gabriel was tootin', should you turn fust to Elvin Drew, an' go up or down with him, wherever he was 'lected? That's what you've got to think on; not your new hat nor your white *pique*. (Didn't iron it under the overskirt, did ye? How'd I know? Law! how's a witch know anything?) Now, you 'ain't opened your bundle, dear, have ye? Raisin-cake in it, ain't there?"

Rosa bent suddenly forward, and placed the package in Dilly's lap. In spite of the bright daylight all about her, she was frightened; if a cloud had swept over, she must have screamed.

"I don't know how you found it out," she whispered, "but *'tis* raisin-cake. Mother sent it. She knew I was going to ask you about the cows. She said I was to tell you, too, there's some sickness over to Sudleigh, and she thought you could go over there nussing, if you wanted to."

"I 'ain't got time," said Dilly, placidly. "I give up nussin', two year ago. I 'ain't got any time at all! Well, here they come, don't they? One for me, an' one for you!"

A light wagon, driven rapidly round the corner, drew up at the gate. Elvin Drew jumped down, and helped out his companion, a short, rather thickset girl, with smooth, dark hair, honest eyes, and a sensitive mouth. She came quickly up the path, after an embarrassed word of thanks to the young man.

"He took me in," she began, almost apologetically to Rosa, who surveyed her with some haughtiness. "I was comin' up here to see Dilly, an' he offered me a ride."

Rosa's color and spirits had returned, at the sight of her tangible ally at the gate.

"Well, I guess I must be going," she said, airily. "Elvin won't want to wait. Good-by, Dilly! I'll tell father. Good-by, Molly Drew!"

But Dilly followed her down to the road, where Elvin stood waiting with the reins in his hands. He was a very blond young man, with curly hair, and eyes honest in contour and clear of glance. Perhaps his coloring impressed one with the fact that he should have looked very young; but his face shrunk now behind a subtle veil of keen anxiety, of irritated emotion, which were evidently quite foreign to him. Even a stranger, looking at him, could hardly help suspecting an alien trouble grafted upon a healthy stem. He gave Dilly a pleasant little nod, in the act of turning eagerly to help Rosa into the wagon. But when he would have followed her, Dilly laid a light but imperative hand on his arm.

"Don't you want your fortune told?" she asked, meaningly. "Here's the witch all ready. Ain't it well for me I wa'n't born a hunderd year ago? Shouldn't I ha' sizzled well? An' now, all there is to burn me is God A'mighty's sunshine!"

Elvin laughed lightly.

"I guess I don't need any fortune," he said. "Mine looks pretty fair now. I don't feel as if anybody'd better meddle with it." But he had not withdrawn his arm, and his gaze still dwelt on hers.

"You know suthin' you don't mean to tell," said Dilly, speaking so rapidly that although Rosa bent forward to listen, she caught only a word, here and there. "You think you won't have to tell, but you will. God A'mighty'll make you. You'll be a stranger among your own folks, an' a wanderer on the earth; till you tell. There! go along! Go an' see the punkins an' crazy-quilts!"

She withdrew her hand, and turned away. Elvin, his face suddenly blanched, looked after her, fascinated, while she went quickly up the garden walk. An impatient word from Rosa recalled him to himself, and he got heavily into the wagon and drove on again.

When Dilly reached the steps where her new guest had seated herself, her manner had quite changed. It breathed an open frankness, a sweet and homely warmth which were very engaging. Molly spoke first.

"How pleased he is with her!" she said, dreamily.

"Yes," answered Dilly, "but to-day ain't tomorrer. They're both light-complected. It's jest like patchwork. Put light an' dark together, I say, or you won't git no figger. Here, le's have a mite o' cake! Mis' Tolman's a proper good cook, if her childern **have** all turned out ducks, an' took to the water. Every one on 'em's took back as much as three generations for their noses an' tempers. Strange they had to go so fur!"

She broke the rich brown loaf in the middle, and divided a piece with Molly. Such were the habits calculated to irritate the conventionalities of Tiverton against her. Who ever heard of breaking cake when one could go into the house for a knife! They ate in silence, and the delights of the summer day grew upon Molly as they never did save when she felt the nearness of this queer little woman. Turn which side of her personality she might toward you, Dilly could always bend you to her own train of thought.

"I come down to talk things over," said Molly, at last, brushing the crumbs of cake from her lap. "I've got a chance in the shoe-shop."

"Do tell! Well, ain't that complete? Don't you say one word, now! I know how 'tis. You think how you'll have to give up the birds' singin', an' your goin' into the woods arter groundpine, an' stay cooped up in a boardin'-house to Sudleigh. I know how 'tis! But don't you fret. You come right here an' stay Sundays, an' we'll eat up the woods an' drink up the sky! There! It's better for ye, dear. Some folks are made to live in a holler tree, like me; some ain't. You'll be better on't among folks."

Molly's eyes filled with tears.

"You've been real good to me," she said, simply.

"I wish I'd begun it afore," responded Dilly, with a quick upward lift of her head, and her brightest smile. "You see I didn't know ye very well, for all you'd lived with old Mis' Drew so many year. I 'ain't had much to do with folks. I knew ye hadn't got nobody except her, but I knew, too, ye were contented there as a cricket. But when she died, an' the house burnt down, I begun to wonder what was goin' to become on ye."

Molly sat looking over at the pine woods, her lips compressed, her cheeks slowly reddening. Finally she burst passionately forth,--

"Dilly, I'd like to know why I couldn't have got some rooms an' kep' house for Elvin? His mother's my own aunt!"

"She wa'n't his mother, ye know. She was His stepmother, for all they set so much by one Another. Folks would ha' talked, an' I guess Rosy wouldn't ha' stood that, even afore they were engaged. Rosy may not like corn-fodder herself, any more 'n t'other dog did, but she ain't goin' to see other noses put into't without snappin' at 'em."

"Well, it's all over," said Molly, drearily. "It 'ain't been hard for me stayin' round as I've done, an' sewin' for my board; but it's seemed pretty tough to think of Elvin livin' in that little shanty of Caleb's an' doin' for himself. I never could see why he didn't board somewheres decent."

"Wants to save his six hunderd dollars, to go out West an' start in the furniture business," said Dilly, succinctly. "Come, Molly, what say to walkin' over to Sudleigh Cattle-Show?"

Molly threw aside her listless mood like a garment.

"Will you?" she cried. "Oh, I'd like to! You know I'm sewin' for Mis' Eli Pike; an' they asked me to go, but I knew she'd fill up the seat so I should crowd 'em out of house an' home. Will you, Dilly?"

"You wait till I git suthin' or other to put over my head," said Dilly, rising with cheerful decision. "Here, you gi' me that cake! I'll tie it up in a nice clean piece o' table-cloth, an' then we'll take along a few eggs, so 't we can trade 'em off for bread an' cheese. You jest pull in my sheets, an' shet the winder, while I do it. Like as not there'll be a shower this arternoon."

When the little gate closed behind them, Molly felt eagerly excited, as, if she were setting forth for a year's happy wandering. Dilly knew the ways of the road as well as the wood. She was, as usual, in light marching order, a handkerchief tied over her smooth braids; another, slung on a stick over her shoulder, contained their luncheon and the eggs for barter. All her movements were buoyant and free, like those of a healthy animal let loose in pleasant pastures. She walked so lightly that the eggs in the handkerchief were scarcely stirred.

"See that little swampy patch!" she said, stopping when they had rounded the curve in the road. "A week or two ago, that was all alive with redbud flowers. I dunno the right name on 'em, an' I don't care. Redbirds, I call 'em. I went over there, one day, an' walked along between the hummocks, spush! spush! You won't find a nicer feelin' than that, wherever ye go. Take off your shoes an' stockin's, an' wade into a swamp! Warm, coarse grass atop! Then warm, black mud, an' arter that, a layer all nice an' cold that goes down to Chiny, fur's I know! That was the day I meant to git some thoroughwort over there, to dry, but I looked at the redbird flowers so long I didn't have time, an' I never've been sence."

Molly laughed out, with a pretty, free ripple in her voice.

"You're always sayin' that, Dilly! You never have time for anything but doin' nothin'!"

A bright little sparkle came into Dilly's eyes, and she laughed, too.

"Why, that's what made me give' up nussin' two year ago," she said, happily. "I wa'n't havin' no time at all. I couldn't live my proper life. I al'ays knew I should come to that, so I'd raked an' scraped, an' put into the bank, till I thought I'd got enough to buy me a mite o' flour while I lived, an' a pine coffin arter I died; an' then I jest set up my Ebenezer I'd be as free's a bird. Freer, I guess I be, for they have to scratch pretty hard, come cold weather, an' I bake me a 'tater, an' then go clippin' out over the crust, lookin' at the bare twigs. Oh, it's complete! If I could live this way, I guess a thousand years'd be a mighty small dose for me. Look at that goldenrod, over there by the stump! That's the kind that's got the most smell."

Molly broke one of the curving plumes.

"I don't see as it smells at all," she said, still sniffing delicately.

"Le'me take it! Why, yes, it does, too! Everything smells *some*. Oftentimes it's so faint it's more like a feelin' than a smell. But there! you ain't a witch, as I be!"

"I wish you wouldn't say that!" put in Molly, courageously. "You make people think you are."

"Law, then, let 'em!" said Dilly, with a kindly indulgence. "It don't do them no hurt, an' it gives me more fun'n the county newspaper. They'd ruther I'd say I was a witch'n tell 'em I've got four eyes an' eight ears where they 'ain't but two. I tell ye, there's a good deal missed when ye stay to home makin' pies, an' a good deal ye can learn if ye live out-door. Why, there's Tolman's cows! He dunno why they dry up; but I do. He, sends that little Davie with 'em, that don't have no proper playtime; an' Davie gallops 'em all the way to pastur', so't he can have a minute to fish in the brook. An' then he gallops 'em home ag'in, because he's stole a piece out o' the arternoon. I ketched him down there by the brook, one day, workin' away with a bent pin, an' the next mornin' I laid a fish-hook on the rock, an' hid in the woods to see what he'd say. My! I 'guess Jonah wa'n't more tickled when he set foot on dry land. Here comes the wagons! There's the Poorhouse team fust, an' Sally Flint settin' up straighter 'n a ramrod. An' there's Heman an' Roxy! She don't look a day older'n twenty-five. Proper nice folks, all on 'em, but they make me kind o' home-sick jest because they *be* folks. They do look so sort o' common in their bunnits an' veils, an' I keep thinkin' o' little four-legged creatur's, all fur!" The Tiverton folk saluted them, always cordially, yet each after his kind. They liked Dilly as a prod-uct all their own, but one to be partaken of sparingly, like some wild, intoxicating root.

They loved her better at home, too, than at Sudleigh Fair. It was like a betrayal of their fireside secrets, to see her there in her accustomed garb; so slight a conces-sion to propriety would have lain in her putting on a bonnet and shawl!

As they neared Sudleigh town, the road grew populous with carriages and farm-wagons, "step and step," not all from Tiverton way, but gathered in from the roads converging here. Men were walking up and down the market street, crying their whips, their toy balloons, and a multitude of cheaper gimcracks.

"Forty miles from home! forty miles from home!" called one, more imaginative than the rest. "And no place to lay my head! That's why I'm selling these little whips here to-day, a stranger in a strange land. Buy one! buy one! and the poor pilgrim'll have a supper and a bed! Keep your money in your pocket, and he's a wanderer on the face of the earth!"

Dilly, the fearless in her chosen wilds, took a fold of Molly's dress, and held it tight.

"You s'pose that's so?" she whispered. "Oh, dear! I 'ain't got a mite o' money, on'y these six eggs. Oh, why didn't he stay to home, if he's so possessed to sleep un-der cover? What does anybody leave their home *for*, if they've got one?"

But Molly put up her head, and walked sturdily on.

"Don't you worry," she counselled, in an undertone. "It don't mean any more 'n it does when folks say they're sellin' at a sacrifice. I guess they expect to make enough, take it all together."

Dilly walked on, quite bewildered. She had lost her fine, joyous carriage; her shoulders were bent, and her feet shuffled, in a discouraged fashion, over the un-lovely bricks. Molly kept the lead, with unconscious superiority.

"Le's go into the store now," she said, "an' swap off the eggs. You'll be joggled in this crowd, an' break 'em all to smash. Here, you le' me have your handkerchief! I'll see to it all." She kept the handkerchief in her hand, after their slight "tradin'" had been accomplished; and Dilly, too dispirited to offer a word, walked meekly about after her.

The Fair was held, according to ancient custom, in the town-hall, of which the upper story had long been given over to Sudleigh Academy. Behind the hall lay an enormous field, roped in now, and provided with pens and stalls, where a great as-semblage of live-stock lowed, and grunted, and patiently chewed the cud.

"Le's go in there fust," whispered Dilly. "I sha'n't feel so strange there as I do with folks. I guess if the four-footed creatur's can stan' it, I can. Pretty darlin'!" she added, stopping before a heifer who had ceased eating and was looking about her with a mild and dignified gaze. Dilly eagerly sought out a stick, and began to scratch the delicate head. "Pretty creatur'! Smell o' her breath, Molly! See her nose, all wet, like pastur' grass afore day! Now, if I didn't want to live by myself, I'd like to curl me up in a stall, 'side o' her."

"'Mandy, you an' Kelup come here!" called Aunt Melissa Adams. She loomed very prosperous, over the way, in her new poplin and her lace-trimmed cape. "Jest look at these roosters! They've got spurs on their legs as long's my darnin'-needle. What under the sun makes 'em grow so! An' ain't they the nippin'est little creatur's you ever see?"

"They're fightin'-cocks," answered Caleb, tolerantly.

"Fightin'-cocks? You don't mean to tell me they're trained up for that?"

"Yes, I do!"

"Well, I never heard o' such a thing in a Christian land! never! Whose be they? I'll give him a piece o' my mind, if I live another minute!"

"You better let other folks alone," said Caleb, stolidly.

"'Mandy," returned Aunt Melissa, in a portentous undertone, "be you goin' to stan' by an' see your own aunt spoke to as if she was the dirt under your feet?"

Amanda had once in her life asserted herself at a crucial moment, and she had never seen cause to regret it. Now she "spoke out" again. She made her slender neck very straight and stiff, and her lips set themselves firmly over the words,--

"I guess Caleb won't do you no hurt, Aunt Melissa. He don't want you should make yourself a laughin'-stock, nor I don't either. There's Uncle Hiram, over lookin' at the pigs. I guess he don't see you. Caleb, le's we move on!"

Aunt Melissa stood looking after them, a mass of quivering wrath.

"Well, I must say!" she retorted to the empty air. "If I live, I must say!"

Dilly took her placid companion by the arm, and hurried her on. Human jangling wore sadly upon her; under such maddening onslaught she was not incapable of developing "nerves." They stopped before a stall where another heifer stood, chewing her cud, and looking away into remembered pastures.

"Oh, see!" said Molly, "'Price $500'! Do you b'lieve it?"

"Well, well!" came Mrs. Eli Pike's ruminant voice from the crowd. "I'm glad I don't own that creatur'! I shouldn't sleep nights if I had five hunderd dollars in cow."

"Tain't five hunderd dollars," said Hiram Cole, elbowing his way to the front. "'Tain't p'inted right, that's all. P'int off two ciphers--"

"Five dollars!" snickered a Crane boy, diving through the crowd, and proceeding to stand on his head in a cleared space beyond. "That's wuth less'n Miss Lucindy's hoss!"

Hiram Cole considered again, one lean hand stroking his cheek.

"Five--fifty--" he announced. "Well, I guess *'tis* five hunderd, arter all! Anybody must want to invest, though, to put all their income into perishable cowflesh!"

"You look real tired," whispered Molly. "Le's come inside, an' perhaps we can set down."

The old hall seemed to have donned strange carnival clothes, for a mystic Saturnalia. It was literally swaddled in bedquilts,-- tumbler-quilts, rising-suns, Jacob's-ladders, log-cabins, and the more modern and altogether terrible crazy-quilt. There were square yards of tidies, on wall and table, and furlongs of home-knit lace. Dilly looked at this product of the patient art of woman with a dispirited gaze.

"Seems a kind of a waste of time, don't it?" she said, dreamily, "when things are blowin' outside? I wisht I could see suthin' made once to look as handsome as green buds an' branches. Law, dear, now jest turn your eyes away from them walls, an' see the tables full of apples! an' them piles o' carrots, an' cabbages an' squashes over there! Well, 'tain't so bad if you can look at things the sun's ever shone on, no matter if they be under cover." She wandered up and down the tables, caressing the rounded outlines of the fruit with her loving gaze. The apples, rich and fragrant, were a glory and a joy. There were great pound sweetings, full of the pride of mere bigness; long purple gilly-flowers, craftily hiding their mealy joys under a sad-colored skin; and the Hubbardston, a portly creature quite unspoiled by the prosperity of growth, and holding its lovely scent and flavor like an individual charm. There was the Bald'in, stand-by old and good as bread; and there were all the rest. We know them, we who have courted Pomona in her fair New England orchards.

Near the fancy-work table sat Mrs. Blair, of the Old Ladies' Home, on a stool she had wrenched from an unwilling boy, who declared it belonged up in the Academy, whence he had brought it "to stan' on" while he drove a nail. And though he besought her to rise and let him return it, since he alone must be responsible, the old lady continued sitting in silence. At length she spoke,--

"Here I be, an' here I'm goin' to set till the premiums is tacked on. Them pinballs my neighbor, Mis' Dyer, made with her own hands, an' she's bent double o' rheumatiz. An' I said I'd bring 'em for her, an' I'd set by an' see things done fair an' square."

"There, Mrs. Blair, don't you worry," said Mrs. Mitchell, a director of the Home, putting a hand on the martial and belligerent shoulder, "Don't you mind if she doesn't get a premium. I'll buy the pinballs, and that will do almost as well."

"My! if there ain't goin' to be trouble between Mary Lamson an' Sereno's Hattie, I'll miss my guess!" said a matron, with an appreciative wag of her purplebonneted head. "They've either on 'em canned up more preserves 'n Tiverton an' Sudleigh put together, an' Mary's got I dunno what all among 'em!--squash, an' dandelion, an' punkin with lemon in't. That's steppin' acrost the bounds, *I* say! If she gits a premium for puttin' up gardin-sass, I'll warrant there'll be a to-do. An' Hattie'll make it!"

"I guess there won't be no set-to about such small potaters," said Mrs. Pike, with dignity. Her broad back had been unrecognized by the herald, careless in her haste. "Hattie's ready an' willin' to divide the premium, if't comes to her, an' I guess Mary'd be, put her in the same place."

"My soul an' body!" exclaimed another, trudging up and waving a large palm-leaf fan. "Well, there, Rosanna Pike! Is that you? Excuse me all, if I don't stop to speak round the circle, I'm so put to't with Passon True's carryin's on. You know he's been as mad as hops over Sudleigh Cattle-Show, reg'lar as the year come round, because there's a raffle for a quilt, or suthin'. An' now he's come an' set up a sort of a stall over t'other side the room, an' folks thinks he's tryin' to git up a revival. I dunno when I've seen John so stirred. He says we hadn't ought to be made a laughin'-stock to Sudleigh, Passon or no Passon. An' old Square Lamb says--"

But the fickle crowd waited to hear no more. With one impulse, it surged over to the other side of the hall, where Parson True, standing behind a table brought down from the Academy, was saying solemnly,--

"Let us engage in prayer!"

The whispering ceased; the titters of embarrassment were stilled, and mothers tightened their grasp on little hands, to emphasize the change of scene from light to graver hue. Some of the men looked lowering; one or two strode out of doors. They loved Parson True, but the Cattle-Show was all their own, and they resented even a ministerial innovation. The parson was a slender, wiry man, with keen blue eyes, a serious mouth, and an overtopping forehead, from which the hair was always brushed straight back. He called upon the Lord, with passionate fervor, to "bless this people in all their outgoings and comings-in, and to keep their feet from paths where His blessing could not attend them."

"Is that the raffle, mother?" whispered the smallest Crane boy; and his mother promptly administered a shake, for the correction of misplaced curiosity.

Then Parson True opened his eyes on his somewhat shamefaced flock and their neighbor townsmen, and began to preach. It was good to be there, he told them, only as it was good to be anywhere else, in the spirit of God. Judgment might overtake them there, as it might at home, in house or field. Were they prepared? He bent forward over the table, his slim form trembling with the intensity of gathering passion. He appealed to each one personally with that vibratory quality of address peculiar to him, wherein it seemed that not only his lips but his very soul challenged the souls before him. One after another joined the outer circle, and faces bent forward over the shoulders in front, with that strange, arrested expression inevitably born when, on the flood of sunny weather, we are reminded how deep the darkness is within the grave.

"Let every man say to himself, 'Thou, God, seest me!'" reiterated the parson. "Thou seest into the dark corners of my heart. What dost Thou see, O God? What dost Thou see?"

Elvin and Rosa had drawn near with the others. She smiled a little, and the hard bloom on her cheeks had not wavered. No one looked at them, for every eye dwelt on the preacher; and though Elvin's face changed from the healthy certainty of life and hope to a green pallor of self-recognition, no one noticed. Consequently, the general surprise culminated in a shock when he cried out, in a loud voice, "God be merciful! God be merciful! I ain't fit to be with decent folks! I'd ought to be in jail!" and pushed his way through the crowd until he stood before the parson, facing him with bowed head, as if he found in the little minister the vicegerent of God. He had kept Rosa's hand in a convulsive grasp, and he drew her with him into the eye of the world. She shrank back, whimpering feebly; but no one took note of her. The parson knew exactly what, to do when the soul travailed and cried aloud. He stretched forth his hands, and put them on the young man's shoulders.

"Come, poor sinner, come!" he urged, in a voice of wonderful melting quality. "Come! Here is the throne of grace! Bring your burden, and cast it down."

The words roused Elvin, or possibly the restraining touch. He started back.

"I can't!" he cried out, stridently. "I can't yet! I can't! I can't!"

Still leading Rosa, who was crying now in good earnest, he turned, and pushed his way out of the crowd. But once outside that warm human circuit, Rosa broke loose from him. She tried to speak for his ear alone, but her voice strove petulantly through her sobs:

"Elvin Drew, I should think you'd be ashamed of yourself! You've made me ridiculous before the whole town, and I never'll speak to you again as long as I live. If I hadn't stayed with you every minute, I should think you'd been drinking, and I believe to my soul you have!" She buried her face in her handkerchief, and stumbled over to a table where Laura Pettis was standing, open-eyed with amazement, and the two clasped each other, while Rosa cried on. Elvin only looked about him, in a bewildered fashion, when the warm hand was wrenched away; then, realizing that he was quite alone, his head bent under a deeper dejection. He seemed unable to move from the spot, and stood there quite stupidly, until murmurs of "What's the matter of him?" came from the waiting crowd, and Parson True himself advanced, with hands again outstretched. But Dilly Joyce forestalled the parson. She, too came forward, in her quick way, and took Elvin firmly by the arm.

"Here, dear," she said, caressingly, "you come along out-doors with us!"

Elvin turned, still hanging his head, and the three (for little Molly had come up on the other side, trying to stand very tall to show her championship) walked out of the hall together. Dilly had ever a quick eye for green, growing things, and she remembered a little corner of the enclosure, where one lone elm-tree stood above a bank. Thither she led him, with an assured step; and when they had reached the shadow, she drew him forward, and said, still tenderly,--

"There, dear, you set right down here an' think it over. We'll stay with ye. We'll never forsake ye, will we, Molly?"

Molly, who did not know what it was all about, had no need to know. "Never!" she said, stanchly.

The three sat down there; and first the slow minutes, and then the hours, went by. It had not been long before some one found out where they were, and curious groups began to wander past, always in silence, but eying them intently. Elvin sat with his head bent, looking fixedly at a root of plantain; but Molly confronted the alien faces with a haughty challenging stare, while her cheeks painted themselves ever a deeper red. Dilly leaned happily back against the elm trunk, and dwelt upon the fleece-hung sky; and her black eyes grew still calmer and more content. She looked as if she had learned what things are lovely and of good repute. When the town-clock struck noon, she brought forth their little luncheon, and pressed it upon the others, with a nice hospitality. Elvin shook his head, but Molly ate a trifle, for pride's sake.

"You go an' git him a mite o' water," whispered Dilly, when they had finished. "I would, but I dunno the ways o' this place. It'll taste good to him."

Molly nodded, and hurried away; presently she came back, bearing a tin cup, and Elvin drank, though he did not thank her.

In the early afternoon, Ebenezer Tolman came striding down between the pens in ostentatious indignation. He was a tall, red-faced man, with a large, loose mouth, and blond-gray whiskers, always parted and blowing in the wind. He wore, with manifest pride, the reputation of being a dangerous animal when roused. He had bought a toy whip, at little Davie's earnest solicitation, and, lashing it suggestively against his boot, he began speaking long before he reached the little group. The lagging crowd of listeners paused, breathless, to lose no word.

"Look here, you! don't ye darken my doors ag'in, an' don't ye dast to open your head to one o' my folks! We're done with ye! Do you hear? We're done with ye! Rosy'll ride home with me to-night, an' she'll ride with you no more!"

Elvin said nothing, though his brow contracted suddenly at Rosa's name. Ebenezer was about to speak again; but the little parson came striding swiftly up, his long coat flying behind him, and Tolman, who was a church-member, in good and regular standing, moved on. But the parson was routed, in his turn. Dilly rose, and, as some one afterwards said, "clipped it right up to him."

"Don't you come now, dear," she advised him, in that persuasive voice of hers. "No, don't you come now. He ain't ready. You go away, an' let him set an' think it out." And the parson, why he knew not, turned about, and went humbly back to his preaching in the hall.

The afternoon wore on, and it began to seem as if Elvin would never break from his trance, and never speak. Finally, after watching him a moment with her keen eyes, Dilly touched him lightly on the arm.

"The Tolmans have drove home," she said, quietly. "All on 'em. What if you should git your horse, an' take Molly an' me along?"

Elvin came to his feet with a lurch. He straightened himself.

"I've got to talk to the parson," said he.

"So I thought," answered Dilly, with composure, "but 'tain't no place here. You ask him to ride, an' let Miss Dorcas drive home alone. We four'll stop at my house, an' then you can talk it over."

Elvin obeyed, like a child tired of his own way. When they packed themselves into the wagon,--where Dilly insisted on sitting behind, to make room,--the Tiverton and Sudleigh people stood about in groups, to watch them. Hiram Cole came forward, just as Elvin took up the reins.

"Elvin," said he, in a cautious whisper, with his accustomed gesture of scraping his cheek, "I've got suthin' to say to ye. Don't ye put no money into Dan Forbes's hands. I've had a letter from brother 'Lisha, out in Illinois, an' he says that business Dan wrote to you about--well, there never was none! There ain't a stick o' furniture made there! An' Dan's been cuttin' a dash lately with money he got som'er's or other, an' he's gambled, an' I dunno what all, an' been took up. An' now he's in jail. So don't you send him nothin'. I thought I'd speak."

Elvin looked at him a moment, with a strange little smile dawning about his mouth.

"That's all right," he said, quickly, and drove away.

To Molly, the road home was like a dark passage full of formless fears. She did not even know what had befallen the dear being she loved best; but something dire and tragic had stricken him, and therefore her. The parson was acutely moved for the anguish he had not probed. Only Dilly remained cheerful. When they reached her gate, it was she who took the halter from Elvin's hand, and tied the horse. Then she walked up the path, and flung open her front door.

"Come right into the settin'-room," she said. "I'll git ye some water right out o' the well. My throat's all choked up o' dust."

The cheerful clang of the bucket against the stones, the rumble of the windlass, and then Dilly came in with a brimming bright tin dipper. She offered it first to the parson, and though she refilled it scrupulously for each pair of lips, it seemed a holy loving-cup. They sat there in the darkening room, and Dilly "stepped round" and began to get supper. Molly nervously joined her, and addressed her, once or twice, in a whisper. But Dilly spoke out clearly in, answer, as if rebuking her.

"Le's have a real good time," she said, when she had drawn the table forward and set forth her bread, and apples, and tea. "Passon, draw up! You drink tea, don't ye? I don't, myself. I never could bear to spile good water. But I keep it on hand for them that likes it. Elvin, here! You take this good big apple. It's man's size more 'n woman's, I guess."

Elvin pushed back his chair.

"I ain't goin' to put a mouthful of victuals to my lips till I make up my mind whether I can speak or not," he said, loudly.

"All right," answered Dilly, placidly. "Bless ye! the teapot'll be goin' all night, if ye say so."

Only Dilly and the parson made a meal; and when it was over, Parson True rose, as if his part of the strange drama must at last begin, and fell on his knees.

"Let us pray!"

Molly, too, knelt, and Elvin threw his arms upon the table, and laid his head upon them. But Dilly stood erect. From time to time, she glanced curiously from the parson to the lovely darkened world outside her little square of window, and smiled slightly, tenderly, as if out there she saw the visible God. The parson prayed for "this sick soul, our brother," over and over, in many phrases, and with true and passionate desire. And when the prayer was done, he put his hand on the young man's shoulder, and said, with a yearning persuasiveness,--

"Tell it now, my brother! Jesus is here."

Elvin raised his head, with a sudden fierce gesture toward Dilly.

"She knows," he said. "She can see the past. She'll tell you what I've done."

"I 'ain't got nothin' to tell, dear," answered Dilly, peacefully. "Everything you've done's between you an' God A'mighty. I 'ain't got nothin' to tell!"

Then she went out, and, deftly unharnessing the horse, put him in her little shed, and gave him a feed of oats. The hens had gone to bed without their supper.

"No matter, biddies," she said, conversationally, as she passed their roost. "I'll make it up to you in the mornin'!"

When she entered the house again, Elvin still sat there, staring stolidly into the dusk. The parson was praying, and Molly, by the window, was holding the sill tightly clasped by both hands, as if threatening herself into calm. When the parson rose, he turned to Elvin, less like the pastor than the familiar friend. One forgot his gray hairs in the loving simplicity of his tone.

"My son," he said, tenderly, "tell it all! God is merciful."

But again Dilly put in her voice.

"Don't you push him, Passon! Let him speak or not, jest as he's a mind to. Let God A'mighty do it His way! Don't *you* do it!"

Darkness settled in the room, and the heavenly hunter's-moon rose and dispelled it.

"O God! can I?" broke forth the young man. "O God! if I tell, I'll go through with it. I will, so help me!"

The moving patterns of the vine at the window began to etch themselves waveringly on the floor. Dilly bent, and traced the outline of a leaf with her finger.

"I'll tell!" cried Elvin, in a voice exultant over the prospect of freedom. "I'll tell it all. I wanted money. The girl I meant to have was goin' with somebody else, an'

I'd got to scrape together some money, quick. I burnt down my house an' barn. I got the insurance money. I sent some of it out West, to put into that furniture business, an' Dan Forbes has made way with it. I only kept enough to take Rosa an' me out there. I'll give up that, an' go to jail; an' if the Lord spares my life, when I come out I'll pay it back, principal an' int'rest."

Molly gave one little moan, and buried her face in her hands. The parson and Dilly rose, by one impulse, and went forward to Elvin, who sat upright, trembling from excitement past. Dilly reached him first. She put both her hands on his forehead, and smoothed back his hair.

"Dear heart," she said, in a voice thrilled through by music,--"dear heart! I was abroad that night, watchin' the stars, an' I see it all. I see ye do it. You done it real clever, an' I come nigh hollerin' out to ye, I was so pleased, when I see you was determined to save the livestock. An' that barn-cat, dear, that old black Tom that's ketched my chickens so long!--you 'most broke your neck to save him. But I never should ha' told, dear, never! 'specially sence you got out the creatur's."

"And 'in Christ shall all be made alive!'" said the parson, wiping his eyes, and then beginning to pat Elvin's hand with both his own. "Now, what shall we do? What shall we do? Why not come home with me, and stay over night? My dear wife will be glad to see you. And the morning will bring counsel."

Elvin had regained a fine freedom of carriage, and a decision of tone long lost to him. He was dignified by the exaltation of the moment.

"I've got it all fixed," he said, like a man. "I thought it all out under that elm-tree, today. You drive me over to Sheriff Holmes's, an' he'll tell me what's right to do,--whether I'm to go to the insurance people, or whether I'm to be clapped into jail. He'll know. It's out o' my hands. I'll go an' harness now."

Parson True drew Molly forward from her corner, and held her hand, while he took Elvin's, and motioned Dilly to complete the circle.

"Jesus Christ be with us!" he said, solemnly. "God, our Father, help us to love one another more and more tenderly because of our sins!"

While Elvin was harnessing, a dark figure came swiftly through the moonlight.

"Elvin," whispered Molly, sharply. "O Elvin, I can't bear it! You take what money you've got, an' go as fur as you can. Then you work, an' I'll work, an' we'll pay 'em back. What good will it do, for you to go to jail? Oh, what good will it do!"

"Poor little Molly!" said he. "You do care about me, don't you? I sha'n't forget that, wherever I am."

Molly came forward, and threw her arms about him passionately.

"Go! go!" she whispered, fiercely. "Go now! I'll drive you some'er's an' bring the horse back. Don't wait! I don't want a hat."

Elvin smoothed her hair.

"No," said he, gravely, "you'll see it different, come mornin'. The things of this world ain't everything. Even freedom ain't everything. There's somethin' better. Good-by, Molly. I don't know how long a sentence they give; but when they let me out, I shall come an' tell you what I think of you for standin' by. Parson True!"

The parson came out, and Dilly followed. When the two men were seated in the wagon, she bent forward, and laid her hand on Elvin's, as it held the reins.

"Don't you be afraid," she said, lovingly. "If they shet ye up, you remember there ain't nothin' to be afraid of but wrong-doin', an' that's only a kind of a sickness we al'ays git well of. An' God A'mighty's watchin' over us all the time. An' if you've sp'iled your chance in this life, don't you mind. There's time enough. Plenty o' time, you says to yourself, plenty!"

She drew back, and they drove on. Molly, in heart-sick sobbing, threw herself forward into the little woman's arms, and Dilly held her with an unwearied cherishing.

"There, there, dear!" she said, tenderly. "Ain't it joyful to think he's got his soul out o' prison, where he shet it up? He's all free now. It's jest as if he was born into a new world, to begin all over."

"But, Dilly, I love him so! An' I can't do anything! not a thing! O Dilly, yes! yes! Oh, it's little enough, but I could! I could save my shoe-shop money, an' help him pay his debt, when he's out o' jail."

"Yes," said Dilly, joyously. "An' there's more'n that you can do. You can keep him in your mind, all day long, an' all night long, an' your sperit'll go right through the stone walls, if they put him there, an' cheer him up.

"He won't know how, but so it'll be, dear, so it'll be. Folks don't know why they're uplifted sometimes, when there ain't no cause; but *I* say it's other folks's love. Now you come in, dear, an' we'll make the bed--it's all aired complete--an' then we'll go to sleep, an' see if we can't dream us a nice, pleasant dream,--all about green gardins, an' the folks we love walking in the midst of 'em!"

BANKRUPT

Miss Dorcas True stood in her square front entry, saying good-by to Phoebe Marsh. The entry would have been quite dark from its time-stained woodwork and green paper, except for the twilight glimmer swaying and creeping through the door leading into the garden. Out there were the yellow of coreopsis, and the blue of larkspur, melted into a dim magnificence of color, suffusing all the air; to one who knew what common glory was a-blowing and a-growing there without, the bare seclusion of the house might well seem invaded by it, like a heavenly flood. Phoebe, too, in her pink calico, appeared to spread abroad the richness of her youth and bloom, and radiate a certain light about her where she stood. She was tall, her proportions were ample, and her waist very trim. She had the shoulders and arms of the women of an elder time, whom we classify vaguely now as goddesses. The Tiverton voices argued that she would have been "real handsome if she'd had any sense about doin' her hair;" which was brought down loosely over her ears, in the fashion of her Aunt Phoebe's miniature. Miss Dorcas beside her looked like one of autumn's brown, quiescent stems left standing by the way. She was firmly built, yet all her lines subdued themselves to that meagreness which ever dwells afar from beauty. The deep marks of hard experience had been graven on her forehead, and her dark eyes burned inwardly; the tense, concentrated spark of pain and the glowing of happy fervor seemed as foreign to them as she herself to all the lighter joys and hopes. Her only possibility of beauty lay in an abundance of soft dark hair; but even that had been restricted and coiled into a compact, utilitarian compass. She had laid one nervous hand on Phoebe's arm, and she grasped the arm absently, from time to time, in talking, with unconscious joy in its rounded warmth. She spoke cautiously, so that her voice might not be heard within.

"Then you come over to-morrow, after the close of service, if it's convenient. You can slip right into the kitchen, just as usual. Any news?"

Phoebe, too, lowered her voice, but the full sweetness of its quality thrilled out.

"Mary Frances Giles is going to be married next week. I've been down to see her things. She's real pleased."

"You don't suppose they'll ask father to marry 'em?" Miss Dorcas spoke quite eagerly.

"Oh, no, they can't! It's a real wedding, you know. It's got to be at the house."

"Yes, of course it's got to! I knew that myself, but I couldn't help hoping. Well, goodnight. You come Sunday."

Phoebe lifted her pink skirts about her, and stepped, rustling and stately, down the garden walk. Miss Dorcas drew one deep breath of the outer fragrance, and turned back into the house. A thin voice, enfeebled and husky from old age, rose in the front room, as she entered:

"Dorcas! Dorcas! you had a caller?"

Her father, old Parson True, lay in the great bed opposite the window. A thin little twig of a man, he was still animated, at times, by the power of a strenuous and dauntless spirit. His hair, brushed straight back from the overtopping forehead, had grown snowy white, and the eager, delicate face beneath wore a strange pathos from the very fineness of its nervously netted lines. Not many years after his wife's death, the parson had shown some wandering of the wits; yet his disability, like his loss, had been mercifully veiled from him. He took calmly to his bed, perhaps through sheer lack of interest in life, and it became his happy invention that he was "not feeling well," from one day to another, but that, on the next Sunday, he should rise and preach. He seemed like an unfortunate and uncomplaining child, and the village folk took pride in him as something all their own; a pride enhanced by his habit, in this weak estate, of falling back into the homely ways of speech he had used long ago when he was a boy "on the farm." In his wife's day, he had stood in the pulpit above them, and expounded scriptural lore in academic English; now he lapsed into their own rude phrasing, and seemed to rest content in a tranquil certainty that nothing could be better than Tiverton ways and Tiverton's homely speech.

"Dorcas," he repeated, with all a child's delight in his own cleverness, "you've had somebody here. I heard ye!"

Dorcas folded the sheet back over the quilt, and laid her hand on his hair, with all the tenderness of the strong when they let themselves brood over the weak.

"Only Phoebe, on her way home," she answered, gently. "The doctor visited her school to-day. She thinks he may drop in to see you to-night. I guess he give her to understand so."

The minister chuckled.

"Ain't he a smart one?" he rejoined. "Smart as a trap! Dorcas, I 'ain't finished my sermon. I guess I shall have to preach an old one. You lay me out the one on the salt losin' its savor, an' I'll look it over."

"Yes, father."

The same demand and the same answer, varied but slightly, had been exchanged between them every Saturday night for years. Dorcas replied now without thinking. Her mind had spread its wings and flown out into the sweet stillness of the garden and the world beyond; it even hastened on into the unknown ways of guesswork, seeking for one who should be coming. She strained her ears to hear the beating of hoofs and the rattle of wheels across the little, bridge. The dusk sifted in about the house, faster and faster; a whippoorwill cried from the woods. So she sat until the twilight had vanished, and another of the invisible genii was at hand, saying, "I am Night."

"Dorcas!" called the parson again. He had been asleep, and seemed now to be holding himself back from a broken dream. "Dorcas, has your mother come in yet?"

"No, father."

"Well, you wake me up when you see her down the road; and then you go an' carry her a shawl. I dunno what to make o' that cough!" His voice trailed sleepily off, and Dorcas rose and tiptoed out of the room. She felt the blood in her face; her ears thrilled noisily. The doctor's, wagon, had crossed the bridge; now it was whirling swiftly up the road. She stationed herself in the entry, to lose no step in his familiar progress. The horse came lightly along, beating out a pleasant tune of easy haste. He was drawn up at the gate, and the doctor threw out his weight, and jumped buoyantly to the ground. There was the brief pause of reaching for his medicine-case, and then, with that firm step whose rhythm she knew so well, he was walking up the path. Involuntarily, as Dorcas awaited him, she put her hand to her heart with one of those gestures that seem so melodramatic and are so real; she owned to herself, with a throb of appreciative delight, how the sick must warm at his coming. This new doctor of Tiverton was no younger than Dorcas herself, yet with his erect carriage and merry blue eye she seemed to be not only of another temperament, but another time. It had never struck him that they were contemporaries. Once he had told Phoebe, in a burst of affection and pitying praise, that he should have liked Miss Dorcas for a maiden aunt.

"Good evening," he said, heartily, one foot on the sill. "How's the patient?"

At actual sight of him, her tremor vanished, and she answered very quietly,--

"Father's asleep. I thought you wouldn't want he should be disturbed; so I came out."

The doctor took off his hat, and pushed back his thick, unruly hair.

"Yes, that was right," he said absently, and pinched a spray of southernwood that grew beside the door. "How has he seemed?"

"About as usual."

"You've kept on with the tonic?"

"Yes."

"That's good! Miss Dorcas, look up there. See that moon! See that wisp of an old blanket dragging over her face! Do you mind coming out and walking up and down the road while we talk? I may think of one or two directions to give about your father."

Dorcas stepped forward with the light obedience given to happy tasking. She paused as! quickly.

"Oh!" she exclaimed. "I can't. Father might wake up. I never leave him alone."

"Never mind, then! let's sit right down here on the steps. After all, perhaps it's pleasanter. What a garden! It's like my mother's. I could pick out every leaf in the dark, by the smell. But you're alone, aren't you? I'm not keeping you from any one?"

"Oh, no! I'm all alone, except father."

"Yes. The fact is, I went into your school to-day, and the teacher said she was coming here to-night. She offered to bring you a message, but I said I should come myself. I'm abominably late. I couldn't get here any earlier."

"Oh, yes! Phoebe! She was here over an hour ago. Phoebe's a real comfort to me." She was seated on the step above him, and it seemed very pleasant to her to hear his voice, without encountering also the challenge of his eyes.

"No, is she though?" The doctor suddenly faced round upon her. "Tell me about it!"

Then, quite to her surprise, Dorcas found herself talking under the spell of an interest so eager that it bore her on, entirely without her own guidance.

"Well, you see there's a good many things I keep from father. He never's been himself since mother died. She was the mainstay here. But he thinks the church prospers just the same, and I never've told him the attendance dropped off when they put up that 'Piscopal building over to Sudleigh. You 'ain't lived here long enough to hear much about that, but it's been a real trial to him. The summer boarders built it, and some rich body keeps it up; and our folks think it's complete to go over there and worship, and get up and down, and say their prayers out loud."

The doctor laughed out.

"I've heard about it," said he. "You know what Brad Freeman told Uncle Eli Pike, when they went in to see how the service was managed? Somebody found the places in the prayer-book for them, and Brad was quick-witted, and got on very well; but Eli kept dropping behind. Brad nudged him. 'Read!' he said out loud. 'Read like the devil!' I've heard that story on an average of twice a day since I came to Tiverton. I'm not tired of it yet!"

Miss Dorcas, too, had heard it, and shrunk from its undisguised profanity. Now she laughed responsively.

"I guess they do have queer ways," she owned. "Well, I never let father know any of our folks go over there. He'd be terrible tried. And I've made it my part in our meeting to keep up the young folks' interest as much as I can. I've been careful never to miss my Sunday-school class. They're all girls, nice as new pins, every one of 'em! Phoebe was in it till a little while ago, but now she comes here and sits in the kitchen while I'm gone. I don't want father to know that, for I hope it never'll come into his head he's so helpless; but I should be worried to death to have him left alone. So Phoebe sits there with her book, ready to spring if she should hear anything out o' the way."

The doctor had lapsed into his absent mood, but now he roused himself, with sudden interest.

"That's very good of her, isn't it?" he said "You trust her, don't you?"

"Trust Phoebe! Well, I guess I do! I've known her ever since she went to Number Five, and now she's keeping the school herself. She's a real noble girl!"

"Tell me more!" said the doctor, warmly. "I want to hear it all. You're so new to me here in Tiverton! I want to get acquainted."

Miss Dorcas suddenly felt as if she had been talking a great deal, and an overwhelming shyness fell upon her.

"There isn't much to tell," she hesitated. "I don't know's anything'd happened to me for years, till father had his ill-turn in the spring, and we called you in. He don't seem to realize his sickness was anything much. I've told the neighbors not to dwell on it when they're with him. Phoebe won't; she's got some sense."

"Has she?" said the doctor, still eagerly. "I'm glad of that, for your sake!" He rose to go, but stood a moment near the steps, dallying with a reaching branch of jessamine; it seemed persuading him to stay. He had always a cheery manner, but to-night it was brightened by a dash of something warm and reckless. He had the air of one awaiting good news, in confidence of its coming. Dorcas was alive to the rapt contagion, and her own blood thrilled. She felt young.

"Well!" said he, "well, Miss Dorcas!" He took a step, and then turned back. "Well, Miss Dorcas," he said again, with an embarrassed laugh, "perhaps you'd like to gather in one more church-goer. If I have time tomorrow, I'll drop in to your service, and then I'll come round here, and tell your father I went."

Dorcas rose impulsively. She could have stretched out her hands to him, in the warmth of her gratitude.

"Oh, if you would! Oh, how pleased he'd be!"

"All right!" Now he turned away with decision. "Thank you, Miss Dorcas, for staying out. It's a beautiful evening. I never knew such a June. Good-night!" He strode down the walk, and gave a quick word to his horse, who responded in whinnying welcome. An instant's delay, another word, and they were gone.

Dorcas stood listening to the scatter of hoofs down the dusty road and over the hollow ledge. She sank back on the sill, and, step by step, tried to retrace the lovely arabesque the hour had made. At last, she had some groping sense of the full beauty of living, when friendship says to its mate, "Tell me about yourself!" and the frozen fountain wells out, every drop cheered and warmed, as it falls, in the sunshine of sympathy. She saw in him that perfection of life lying in strength, which he undoubtedly had, and beauty, of which he had little or much according as one chose to think well of him. To her aching sense, he was a very perfect creature, gifted with, infinite capacities for help and comfort.

But the footfalls ceased, and the garden darkened by delicate yet swift degrees; a cloud had gone over the moon, fleecy, silver-edged, but still a cloud. The waning of the light seemed to her significant; she feared lest some bitter change might befall the moment; and went in, bolting the door behind her. Once within her own little bedroom, she loosened her hair, and moved about aimlessly, for a time, careless of sleep, because it seemed so far. Then a sudden resolve nerved her, and she stole back again to the front door, and opened it. The night was blossoming there, glowing now, abundant. It was so rich, so full! The moonlight here, and star upon star above, hidden not by clouds but by the light! Need she waste this one night out of all her unregarded life? She stepped forth among the flower-beds, stooping, in a passionate fervor, to the blossoms she could reach; but, coming back to the southernwood, she took it in her arms. She laid her face upon it, and crushed the soft leaves against her cheeks. It made all the world smell of its own balm and dew. The fragrance and beauty of the time passed into her soul, and awakened corners there all unused to such sweet incense. She was drunken with the wine that is not of grapes. She could not have found words for the passion that possessed her, though she hugged it to her heart like another self; but it was elemental, springing from founts deeper than those of life and death. God made it, and, like all His making, it was divine. She sat there, the southernwood still gathered into her arms, and at last emotion stilled itself, and passed into thought; a wild temptation rose, and with its first whisper drove a hot flush into her cheeks, and branded it there. Love! she had never named the name in its first natal significance. She had scarcely read it; for romance, even in books, had passed her by. But love! she knew it as the insect knows how to spread his new sun-dried wings in the air for which he was create. Sitting there, in a happy drowse, she thought it all out. She was old, plain, unsought; the man she exalted was the flower of his kind. He would never look on her as if she might touch the hem of wifehood's mantle; so there would be no shame in choosing him. Just to herself, she might name the Great Name. He would not know. Only her own soul would know, and God who gave it, and sent it forth fitted with delicate, reaching tentacles to touch the rock set there to wound them. She began to feel blindly that God was not alone the keeper of eternal Sabbaths, but the germinant heat at the heart of the world. If she were a young girl, like Phoebe, there would be shame. Even a thought of him would be a stretching forth her hand to touch him, saying, "Look at me! I am here!" but for her it was quite different. It would be like a dream, some grandmother dreamed in the sun, of rosy youth and the things that never came to pass. No one would be harmed, and the sleeper would have garnered one hour's joy before she took up her march again on the lonesomest road of all,-- so lonesome, although it leads us, home! Thus she thought, half sleeping, until the night-dews clung in drops upon her hair; then she went in to bed, still wrapped about with the drapery of her dreams.

Next morning, when Dorcas carried in her father's breakfast, she walked with a springing step, and spoke in a voice so full and fresh it made her newly glad.

"It's a nice day, father! There'll be lots of folks out to meeting."

"That's a good girl!" This was his commendation, from hour to hour; it made up the litany of his gratitude for what she had been to him. "But I dunno's I feel quite up to preachin' to-day, Dorcas!"

"That'll be all right, father. We'll get somebody."

"You bring me out my sermon-box after breakfast, an' I'll pick out one," said he, happily. "Deacon Tolman can read it."

But, alas! Deacon Tolman had been dead this many a year!

A little later, the parson sat up in bed, shuffling his manuscript about with nervous hands, and Dorcas, in the kitchen, stood washing her breakfast dishes. That eager interest in living still possessed her. She began humming, in a timid monotone. Her voice had the clearness of truth, with little sweetness; and she was too conscious of its inadequacy to use it in public, save under the compelling force of conscience. Hitherto, she had only sung in Sunday-school, moved, as in everything, by the pathetic desire of "doing her part;" but this morning seemed to her one for lifting the voice, though not in Sunday phrasing. After a little thought, she began thinly and sweetly,--

"Early one morning, just as the sun was rising,
I heard a maid sing in the valley below:
'O don't deceive me! O never leave me
How could you use a poor maiden so?'"

A gruff voice from the, doorway broke harshly in upon a measure.

"Yes! yes! Well! well! Tunin' up a larrady, ain't ye?"

Dorcas knew who it was, without turning round,--a dark, squat woman, broad all over; broad in the hips, the waist, the face, and stamped with the race-mark of high cheekbones. Her thick, straight black hair was cut "tin-basin style;" she wore men's boots, and her petticoats were nearly up to her knees.

"Good morning, Nancy!" called Dorcas, blithely, wringing out her dishcloth. "Come right in, and sit down."

Nance Pete (in other words, Nancy the wife of Pete, whose surname was unknown) clumped into the room, and took a chair by the hearth. She drew forth a short black pipe, looked into it discontentedly, and then sat putting her thumb in and out of the bowl.

"You 'ain't got a mite o' terbacker about ye? Hey what?" she asked.

Dorcas had many a time been shocked at the same demand. This morning, something humorous about it struck her, and she laughed.

"You know I haven't, Nancy Pete! Did you mend that hole in your skirt, as I told you?"

Nance laboriously drew a back breadth of her coarse plaid skirt round to the front, and displayed it, without a word. A three-cornered tear of the kind known as a barn-door had been treated by tying a white string well outside it, and gathering up the cloth, like a bag. Dorcas's sense of fitness forbade her to see anything humorous in so original a device. She stood before the woman in all the moral excellence of a censor fastidiously clad.

"O Nancy Pete!" she exclaimed. "How could you?"

Nance put her cold pipe in her mouth, and began sucking at the unresponsive stem.

"You 'ain't got a bite of anything t' eat, have ye?" she asked, indifferently.

Dorcas went to the pantry, and brought forth pie, doughnuts and cheese, and a dish of cold beans. The coffee-pot was waiting on the stove. One would have said the visitor had been expected. Nance rose and tramped over to the table. But Dorcas stood firmly in the way.

"No, Nancy, no! You wait a minute! Are you going to meeting to-day?"

"I 'ain't had a meal o' victuals for a week!" remarked Nance, addressing no one in particular.

"Nancy, are you going to meeting?"

"Whose seat be I goin' to set in?" inquired Nance, rebelliously, yet with a certain air of capitulation.

"You can sit in mine. Haven't you sat there for the last five years? Now, Nancy, don't hinder me!"

"Plague take it, then! I'll go!"

At this expected climax, Dorcas stood aside, and allowed her visitor to serve herself with beans. When Nance's first hunger had been satisfied, she began a rambling monologue, of an accustomed sort to which Dorcas never listened.

"I went down to peek into the Poorhouse winders, this mornin'. There they all sut, like rats in a trap. 'Got ye, 'ain't they?' says I. Old Sal Flint she looked up, an' if there'd been a butcher-knife handy, I guess she'd ha' throwed it. 'It's that Injun!' says she to Mis' Giles. 'Don't you take no notice!' 'I dunno's I'm an Injun,' says I, 'I dunno how much Injun I be. I can't look so fur back as that. I dunno's there's any more Injun in me than there is devil in you!' I says. An' then the overseer he come out, an' driv' me off. 'You won't git me in there,' says I to him, 'not so long's I've got my teeth to chaw sassafras, an' my claws to dig me a holler in the ground!' But when I come along, he passed me on the road, an' old Sal Flint sut up by him on the seat, like a bump on a log. I guess he was carryin' her over to that Pope-o'-Rome meetin' they've got over to Sudleigh."

Dorcas turned about, in anxious interest.

"Oh, I wonder if he was! How *can* folks give up their own meeting for that?"

Nance pushed her chair back from the table.

"Want to see all kinds, I s'pose," she said, slyly. "Guess I'll try it myself, another Sunday!"

"Anybody to home?" came a very high and wheezy voice from the doorway. Dorcas knew that also, and so did Nance Pete.

"It's that old haddock't lives up on the mountain," said the latter, composedly, searching in her pocket, and then pulling out a stray bit of tobacco and pressing it tenderly into her pipe.

An old man, dressed in a suit of very antique butternut clothes, stood at the sill, holding forward a bunch of pennyroyal. He was weazened and dry; his cheeks were parchment color, and he bore the look of an active yet extreme old age. He was totally deaf. Dorcas advanced toward him, taking a bright five-cent piece from her pocket. She held it out to him, and he, in turn, extended the pennyroyal; but before taking it, she went through a solemn pantomime. She made a feint of accepting the herb, and then pointed to him and to the road.

"Yes, yes!" said the old man, irritably. "Bless ye! of course I'm goin' to meetin'. I'll set by myself, though! Yes, I will! Las' Sunday, I set with Jont Marshall, an' every time I sung a note, he dug into me with his elbow, till I thought I should ha' fell out the pew-door. My voice is jest as good as ever 'twas, an' sixty-five year ago come spring, I begun to set in the seats."

The coin and pennyroyal changed ownership, and he tottered away, chattering to himself in his senile fashion.

"Look here, you!" he shouted back, his hand on the gate. "Heerd anything o' that new doctor round here? Well, he's been a-pokin' into my ears, an' I guess he'd ha' cured me, if anybody could. You know I don't hear so well's I used to. He went a-peekin' an' a-pryin' round my ears, as if he'd found a hornet's nest. I dunno what he see there; I know he shook his head. I guess we shouldn't ha' got no such a man to settle down here if he wa'n't so asthmy he couldn't git along where he was. That's the reason he come, they say. He's a bright one!"

Dorcas left her sweeping, and ran out after him. For the moment, she forgot his hopeless durance in fleshly walls.

"Did he look at 'em?" she cried. "Did he? Tell me what he said!"

"Why, of course I don't hear no better yit!" answered old Simeon, testily, turning to stump away, "but that ain't no sign I sha'n't! He's a beauty! I set up now, when he goes by, so's I can hear him when he rides back. I put a quilt down in the fore-yard, an' when the ground trimbles a mite, I git up to see if it's his hoss. Once I laid there till 'leven. He's a beauty, he is!"

He went quavering down the road, and Dorcas ran back to the house, elated afresh. An unregarded old man could give him the poor treasure of his affection, quite unasked. Why should not she?

Nance was just taking her unceremonious leave. Her pockets bulged with doughnuts, and she had wrapped half a pie in the Sudleigh "Star," surreptitiously filched from the woodbox.

"Well, I guess I'll be gittin' along towards meetin'," she said, in a tone of unconcern, calculated to allay suspicion. "I'm in hopes to git a mite o' terbacker out o' Hiram Cole, if he's settin' lookin' at his pigs, where he is 'most every Sunday. I'll have a smoke afore I go in."

"Don't you be late!"

"I'm a-goin' in late, or not at all!" answered Nance, contradictorily. "My bunnit ain't trimmed on the congregation side, an' I want to give 'em a chance to see it all round. I'm a-goin' up the aisle complete!"

Dorcas finished her work, and, having tidied her father's room, sat down by his bedside for the simple rites that made their Sabbath holy. With the first clanging stroke of the old bell, not half a mile away, they fell into silence, waiting reverently through the necessary pause for allowing the congregation to become seated. Then they went through the service together, from hymn and prayer to the sermon. The parson had his manuscript ready, and he began reading it, in the pulpit-voice of his prime. At that moment, some of his old vigor came back to him, and he uttered the conventional phrases of his church with conscious power; though so little a man, he had always a sonorous delivery. After a page or two, his hands began to tremble, and his voice sank.

"You read a spell, Dorcas," he whispered, in pathetic apology. "I'll rest me a minute." So Dorcas read, and he listened. Presently he fell asleep, and she still went on, speaking the words mechanically, and busy with her own tumultuous thoughts. Amazement possessed her that the world could be so full of joy to which she had long been deaf. She could hear the oriole singing in the elm; his song was almost articulate. The trees waved a little, in a friendly fashion, through the open windows; friendly in the unspoken kinship of green things to our thought, yet remote in their own seclusion. One tall, delicate locust, gowned in summer's finest gear, stirred idly at the top, as if through an inward motion, untroubled by the wind. Dorcas's mind sought out the doctor, listening to the sermon in her bare little church, and she felt quite content. She had entered the first court of love, where a spiritual possession is enough, and asks no alms of bodily nearness. When she came to the end of the sermon, her hands fell in her lap, and she gave herself up without reserve to the idle delight of satisfied dreaming. The silence pressed upon her father, and he opened his eyes wide with the startled look of one who comprehends at once the requirements of time and place. Then, in all solemnity, he put forth his hands; and Dorcas, bending her head, received the benediction for the congregation he would never meet again. She roused herself to bring in his beef-tea, and at the moment of carrying away the tray, a step sounded on the walk. She knew who it was, and smiled happily. The lighter foot keeping pace beside it, she did not hear.

"Dorcas," said her father, "git your bunnit. It's time for Sunday-school."

"Yes, father."

The expected knock came at the door. She went forward, tying on her bonnet, and her cheeks were pink. The doctor stood on the doorstone, and Phoebe was with him. He smiled at Dorcas, and put out his hand. This, according to Tiverton customs, was a warm demonstration at so meaningless a moment; it seemed a part of his happy friendliness. It was Phoebe who spoke.

"I'll stay outside while the doctor goes in. I can sit down here on the step. Your father needn't know I am here any more than usual. I told the doctor not to talk, coming up the walk."

The doctor smiled at her. Phoebe looked like a rose in her Sunday white, and the elder woman felt a sudden joy in her, untouched by envy of her youth and bloom. Phoebe only seemed a part of the beautiful new laws to which the world was freshly tuned, Dorcas coveted nothing; she envied nobody. She herself possessed all, in usurping her one rich kingdom.

"All right," she said. "The doctor can step in now, and see father. I'll hurry back, as soon as Sunday-school is over." She walked away, glancing happily at the flowers on either side of the garden-path. She wanted to touch all their leaves, because, last night, he had praised them.

Returning, when her hour was over, she walked very fast; her heart was waking into hunger, and she feared he might be gone. But he was there, sitting on the steps beside Phoebe, and when the gate swung open, they did not hear. Phoebe's eyes were dropped, and she was poking her parasol into the moss-encrusted path;

the doctor was looking into her face, and speaking quite eagerly. He heard Dorcas first, and sprang up. His eyes were so bright and forceful in the momentary gleam of meeting hers, that she looked aside, and tried to rule her quickening breath.

"Miss Dorcas," said he, "I'm telling this young lady she mustn't forget to eat her dinner at school. I find she quite ignores it, if she has sums to do, or blots to erase. Why, it's shocking."

"Of course she must eat her dinner!" said Dorcas, tenderly. "Why, yes, of course! Phoebe, do as he tells you. He knows."

Phoebe blushed vividly.

"Does he?" she answered, laughing. "Well, I'll see. Good-by, Miss Dorcas. I'll come in for Friday night meeting, if I don't before. Good-by."

"I'll walk along with you," said the doctor. "If you'll let me," he added, humbly.

Phoebe turned away with a little toss of her head, and he turned, too, breaking a sprig of southernwood. Dorcas was glad to treasure the last sight of him putting to his lips the fragrant herb she had bruised for his sake. It seemed to carry over into daylight the joy of the richer night; it was like seeing the silken thread on which her pearls were strung. She called to them impetuously,--

"Pick all the flowers you want to, both of you!" Then she went in, but she said aloud to herself, "They're all for you--" and she whispered his name.

"Dorcas," said her father, "the doctor's been here quite a spell. He says there was a real full meetin.' Even Nancy Pete, Dorcas! I feel as if my ministration had been abundantly blessed."

Then, in that strangest summer in Dorcas's life, time seemed to stand still. The happiest of all experiences had befallen her; not a succession of joys, but a permanent delight in one unchanging mood. The evening of his coming had been the first day; and the evening and the morning had ever since been the same in glory. He came often, sometimes with Phoebe, sometimes alone; and, being one of the men on whom women especially lean, Dorcas soon found herself telling him all the poor trials of her colorless life. Nothing was too small for his notice. He liked her homely talk of the garden and the church, and once gave up an hour to spading a plot where she wanted a new round bed. Dorcas had meant to put lilies there, but she remembered he loved ladies'-delights; so she gathered them all together from the nooks and corners of the garden, and set them there, a sweet, old-fashioned company. "That's for thoughts!" She took to wearing flowers now, not for the delight of him who loved them, but merely as a part of her secret litany of worship. She slept deeply at night, and woke with calm content, to speak one name in the way that forms a prayer. He was her one possession; all else might be taken away from her, but the feeling inhabiting her heart must live, like the heart itself.

By the time September had yellowed all the fields, there came a week when Phoebe's aunt, down at the Hollow, was known to be very ill; so Phoebe no longer came to care for the parson through the Sunday-school hour. But the doctor appeared, instead.

"I'm Phoebe," he said, laughing, when Dorcas met him at the door. "She can't come; so I told her I'd take her place."

These were the little familiar deeds which gilded his name among the people. Dorcas had been growing used to them. But on the' next Sunday morning, when she was hurrying about her kitchen, making early preparations for the cold mid-day meal, a daring thought assailed her. Phoebe might come to-day, and if the doctor also dropped in, she would ask them both to dinner. There was no reason for inviting him alone; besides, it was happier to sit by, leaving him to some one else. Then the two would talk, and she, with no responsibility, could listen and look, and hug her secret joy.

"I ain't a-goin' to meetin' to-day!" came Nance Pete's voice from the door. She stood there, smoking prosperously, and took out her pipe, with a jaunty motion, at the words. "I stopped at Kelup Rivers', on the way over, an' they gi'n me a good breakfast, an' last week, that young doctor gi'n me a whole paper o' fine-cut. I ain't a-goin' to meetin'! I'm goin' to se' down under the old elm, an' have a real good smoke."

"O Nancy!" Dorcas had no dreams so happy that such an avalanche could not sweep them aside. "Now, do! Why, you don't want me to think you go to church just because I save you some breakfast!"

Nance turned away, and put up her chin to watch a wreath of smoke.

"I dunno why I don't," said she. "The world's nothin' but buy an' sell. You know it, an' I know it!' 'Tain't no use coverin' on't up. You heerd the news? That old fool of a Sim Barker's dead. The doctor, sut up all night with him, an' I guess now he's layin' on him out. I wouldn't ha' done it! I'd ha' wropped him up in his old coat, an' glad to git rid on him! Well, he won't cheat ye out o' no more five-cent pieces, to squander in terbacker. You might save 'em up for me, now he's done for!" Nance went stalking away to the gate, flaunting a visible air of fine, free enjoyment, the product of tobacco and a bright morning. Dorcas watched her, annoyed, and yet quite helpless; she was outwitted, and she knew it. Perhaps she sorrowed less deeply over the loss to her pensioner's immortal soul, thus taking holiday from spiritual discipline, than the serious problem involved in subtracting one from the congregation. Would a Sunday-school picnic constitute a bribe worth mentioning? Perhaps not, so far as Nance was concerned; but her own class might like it, and on that young blood she depended, to vivify the church.

A bit of pink came flashing along the country road. It was Phoebe, walking very fast.

"Dear heart!" said Dorcas, aloud to herself, as the girl came hurriedly up the path. She was no longer a pretty girl, a nice girl, as the commendation went. Her face had gained an exalted lift; she was beautiful. She took Miss Dorcas by the arms, and laughed the laugh that knows itself in the right, and so will not be shy.

"Miss Dorcas," she said, "I've got to tell you right out, or I can't do it at all. What should you say if I told you I was married?--to the doctor?"

Dorcas looked at her as if she did not hear.

"It's begun to get round," went on Phoebe, "and I wanted to give you the word myself. You see, auntie was sick, and when he was there so much, she grew to depend on him, and one day, when we'd been engaged a week, she said, why shouldn't we be married, and he come right to the house to live? He's only boarding, you know. And nothing to do but it must be done right off, and so I--I said 'yes! And we were married, Thursday. Auntie's better, and O Miss Dorcas! I think we're going to have a real good time together." She threw her arms about Dorcas, and put down her shining brown head upon them.

Dorcas tried to answer. When she did speak, her voice sounded thin and faint, and she wondered confusedly if Phoebe could hear.

"I didn't know--" she said. "I didn't know--"

"Why, no, of course not!" returned Phoebe, brightly. "Nobody did. You'd have been the first, but I didn't want the engagement talked about till auntie was better.

Oh, I believe that's his horse's step! I'll run out, and ride home with him. You come, too, Miss Dorcas, and just say a word!"

Dorcas loosened the girl's arms about her, and, bending to the bright head, kissed it twice. Phoebe, grown careless in her joy, ran down the walk to stop the approaching wagon; and when she looked round, Dorcas had shut the door and gone in. She waited a moment for her to reappear, and then, remembering the doctor had had no breakfast, she stepped into the wagon, and they drove happily away.

Dorcas went to her bedroom, touching the walls, on the way, with her groping hands. She sat down on the floor there, and rested her head against a chair. Once only did she rouse herself, and that was to go into the kitchen and set away the great bowl of *blanc-mange* she had been making for dinner. She had not strained it all, and the sea-weed was drying on the sieve. Then she went back into the bedroom, and pulled down the green slat curtains with a shaking hand. Twice her father called her to bring his sermons, but she only answered, "Yes, father!" in dull acquiescence, and did not move. She was benumbed, sunken in a gulf of shame, too faint and cold to save herself by struggling. Her poor innocent little fictions made themselves into lurid writings on her brain. She had called him hers while another woman held his vows, and she was degraded. Her soul was wrecked as truly as if the whole world knew it, and could cry to her "Shame!" and "Shame!" The church-bells clanged out their judgment of her. A new thought awakened her to a new despair. She was not fit to teach in Sunday-school any more. Her girls, her innocent, sweet girls! There was contagion in her very breath. They must be saved from it; else when they were old women like her, some sudden vice of tainted blood might rise up in them, no one would know why, and breed disease and shame. She started to her feet. Her knees trembling under her, she ran out of the house, and hid herself behind the great lilac-bush by the gate.

Deacon Caleb Rivers came jogging past, late for church, but driving none the less moderately. His placid-faced wife sat beside him; and Dorcas, stepping out to stop them, wondered, with a wild pang of perplexity over the things of this world, if 'Mandy Rivers had ever known the feeling of death in the soul. Caleb pulled up.

"I can't come to Sunday-school, to-day," called Dorcas, stridently. "You tell them to give Phoebe my class. And ask her if she'll keep it. I sha'n't teach any more."

"Ain't your father so well?" asked Mrs. Rivers, sympathetically, bending forward and smoothing her mitts. Dorcas caught at the reason.

"I sha'n't leave him any more," she said. "You tell 'em so. You fix it."

Caleb drove on, and she went back into the house, shrinking under the brightness of the air which seemed to quiver so before her eyes. She went into her father's room, where he was awake and wondering.

"Seems to me I heard the bells," he said, in his gentle fashion. "Or have we had the 'hymns, an' got to the sermon?"

Dorcas fell on her knees by the bedside.

"Father," she began, with difficulty, her cheek laid on the bedclothes beside his hand, "there was a sermon about women that are lost. What was that?"

"Why, yes," answered the parson, rousing to an active joy in his work. "'Neither do I condemn thee!' That was it. You git it, Dorcas! We must remember such poor creatur's; though, Lord be praised! there ain't many round here. We must remember an' pray for 'em."

But Dorcas did not rise.

"Is there any hope for them, father?" she asked, her voice muffled. "Can they be saved?"

"Why, don't you remember the poor creatur' that come here an' asked that very question because she heard I said the Lord was pitiful? Her baby was born out in the medder, an' died the next day; an' she got up out of her sickbed at the Poorhouse, an' come totterin' up here, to ask if there was any use in her sayin', 'Lord, be merciful to me, a sinner!' An' your mother took her in, an' laid her down on this very bed, an' she died here. An' your mother hil' her in her arms when she died. You ask her if she didn't!" The effort of continuous talking wearied him, and presently he dozed off. Once he woke, and Dorcas was still on her knees, her head abased. "Dorcas!" he said, and she answered, "Yes, father!" without raising it; and he slept again. The bell struck, for the end of service. The parson was awake. He stretched out his hand, and it trembled a moment and then fell on his daughter's lowly head.

"The grace of our Lord Jesus Christ--" the parson said, and went clearly on to the solemn close.

"Father," said Dorcas. "Father!" She seemed to be crying to One afar. "Say the other verse, too. What He told the woman."

His hand still on her head, the parson repeated, with a wistful tenderness stretching back over the past,--

"'Neither do I condemn thee; go, and sin no more.'"

NANCY BOYD'S LAST SERMON

It was the lonesome time of the year: not November, that accomplishment of a gracious death, but the moment before the conscious spring, when water-courses have not yet stirred in awakening, and buds are only dreamed of by trees still asleep but for the sweet trouble within their wood; when the air finds as yet no response to the thrill beginning to creep where roots lie blind in the dark; when life is at the one dull, flat instant before culmination and movement. I had gone down post-haste to my well-beloved Tiverton, in response to the news sent me by a dear countrywoman, that Nancy Boyd, whom I had not seen since my long absence in Europe, was dying of "galloping consumption." Nancy wanted to bid me good-by. Hiram Cole met me, lean-jawed, dust-colored, wrinkled as of old, with the overalls necessitated by his "sleddin'" at least four inches too short. Not the Pyramids themselves were such potent evidence that time may stand still, withal, as this lank, stooping figure, line for line exactly what it had been five years before. Hiram helped me into the pung, took his place beside me, and threw a conversational "huddup" to the rakish-looking sorrel colt. We dashed sluing away down the country road, and then I turned to look at my old friend. He was steadfastly gazing at the landscape ahead, the while he passed one wiry hand over his face, to smooth out its broadening smile. He was glad to see me, but his private code of decorum forbade the betrayal of any such "shaller" emotion.

"Well, Hiram," I began, "Tiverton looks exactly the same, doesn't it? And poor Nancy, how is she?"

"Nancy's pretty low," said Hiram, drawing his mitten over the hand that had been used to iron out his smile, and giving critical attention to the colt's off hind-leg. "She hil' her own all winter, but now, come spring, she's breakin' up mighty fast. They don't cal'late she'll live more'n a day or two."

"Her poor husband! How will he get along without her!"

Hiram turned upon me with vehemence.

"Why, don't you know?" said he. "'Ain't nobody told ye? She 'ain't got no hus-band."

"What? Is the Cap'n dead?"

"Dead? Bless ye, he's divorced from Nancy, an' married another woman, two year ago come this May!"

I was amazed, and Hiram looked at me with the undisguised triumph of one who has news to sell, be it good or bad.

"But Nancy has written me!" I said. "She told me the neighborhood gossip; why didn't she tell me that?"

"Pride, I s'pose, pride," said Hiram. "You can't be sure how misery'll strike folks. It's like a September gale; the best o' barns'll blow down, an' some rickety shanty'll stan' the strain. But there! Nancy's had more to bear from the way she took her troubles than from the troubles themselves. Ye see, 'twas this way. Cap'n Jim had his own reasons for wantin' to git rid of her, an' I guess there was a time when he treated her pretty bad. I guess he as good's turned her out o' house an' home, an' when he sued for divorce for desertion, she never said a word; an' he got it, an' up an' married, as soon as the law'd allow, Nancy never opened her head, all through it. She jest settled down, with a bed an' a chair or two, in that little house she owned down by Wilier Brook, an' took in tailorin' an' mendin'. One spell, she bound shoes. The whole town was with her till she begun carryin' on like a crazed creatur', as she did arterwards."

My heart sank. Poor Nancy! if she had really incurred the public scorn, it must have been through dire extremity.

"Ye see," Hiram continued, "folks were sort o' tried with her from the begin-nin'. You know what a good outfit she had from her mother's side,--bureaus, an' beddin', an' everything complete? Well, she left it all right there in the house, for Jim to use, an' when he brought his new woman home, there the things set jest the same, an' he never said a word. I don't deny he ought to done different, but then, if Nancy wouldn't look out for her own interests, you can't blame him so much, now can ye? But the capsheaf come about a year ago, when Nancy had a smart little sum o' money left her,--nigh onto a hunderd dollars. Jim he'd got into debt, an' his oxen died, an' one thing an' another, he was all wore out, an' had rheumatic fever; an' if you'll b'lieve it, Nancy she went over an' done the work, an' let his wife nuss him. She wouldn't step foot into the bedroom, they said; she never see Jim once, but there she was, slavin' over the wash-tub and ironin'-board,--an' as for that money, I guess it went for doctor's stuff an' what all, for Jim bought a new yoke of oxen in the spring."

"But the man! the other wife! how could they?"

"Oh, Jim's wife's a pretty tough-hided creatur', an' as for him, I al'ays thought the way Nancy behaved took him kind o' by surprise, an' he had to give her her head, an' let her act her pleasure. But it made a sight o' town talk. Some say Nancy ain't quite bright to carry on so, an' the women-folks seem to think she's a good deal to blame, one way or another. Anyhow, she's had a hard row to hoe. Here we be, an' there's Hannah at the foreroom winder. You won't think o' goin' over to Nancy's till arter supper, will ye?"

When I sat alone beside Nancy's bed, that night, I had several sides of her sad story in mind, but none of them lessened the dreariness of the tragedy. Before my brief acquaintance with her, Nancy was widely known as a travelling-preacher, one who had "the power." She must have been a strangely attractive creature, in those early days, alert, intense, gifted with such a magnetic reaching into another life that it might well set her aside from the commoner phases of a common day, and crowned, as with flame, by an unceasing aspiration for the highest. At thirty, she married a dashing sailor, marked by the sea, even to the rings in his ears; and when I knew them, they were solidly comfortable and happy, in a way very reassuring to one who could understand Nancy's temperament; for she was one of those who, at every step, are flung aside from the world's sharp corners, bruised and bleeding.

As to the storm and shipwreck of her life, I learned no particulars essentially new. Evidently her husband had suddenly run amuck, either from the monotony of his inland days, or from the strange passion he had conceived for a woman who was Nancy's opposite.

That night, I sat in the poor, bare little room, beside the billowing feather-bed where Nancy lay propped upon pillows, and gazing with bright, glad eyes into my face, one thin little hand clutching mine with the grasp of a soul who holds desperately to life. And yet Nancy was not clinging to life itself; she only seemed to be, because she clung to love.

"I'm proper glad to see ye," she kept saying, "proper glad."

We were quite alone. The fire burned cheerily in the kitchen stove, and a cheap little clock over the mantel ticked unmercifully fast; it seemed in haste for Nancy to be gone. The curtains were drawn, lest the thrifty window-plants should be frostbitten, and several tumblers of jelly on the oilcloth-covered table bore witness that the neighbors had put aside their moral scruples and their social delicacy, and were giving of their best, albeit to one whose ways were not their ways. But Nancy herself was the centre and light of the room,--so frail, so clean, with her plain nightcap and coarse white nightgown, and the small checked shawl folded primly over her shoulders. Thin as she was, she looked scarcely older than when I had seen her, five years ago; yet since then she had walked through a blacker valley than the one before her.

"Now don't you git all nerved up when I cough," she said, lying back exhausted after a paroxysm. "I've got used to it; it don't trouble me no more'n a mosquiter. I want to have a real good night now, talkin' over old times."

"You must try to sleep," I said. "The doctor will blame me, if I let you talk."

"No, he won't," said Nancy, shrewdly. "He knows I 'ain't got much time afore me, an' I guess he wouldn't deny me the good on't. That's why I sent for ye, dear; I 'ain't had anybody I could speak out to in five year, an' I wanted to speak out, afore I died. Do you remember how you used to come over an' eat cold b'iled dish for supper, that last summer you was down here?"

"Oh, don't I, Nancy! there never was anything like it. Such cold potatoes--"

"B'iled in the pot-liquor!" she whispered, a knowing gleam in her blue eyes. "That's the way; on'y everybody don't know. An' do you remember the year we had greens way into the fall, an' I wouldn't tell you what they was? Well, I will, now; there was chickweed, an' pusley, an' mustard, an' Aaron's-rod, an' I dunno what all."

"Not Aaron's-rod, Nancy! it never would have been so good!"

"It's truth an' fact! I b'iled Aaron's-rod, an' you eat it. That was the year Mis' Blaisdell was mad because you had so many meals over to my house, an' said it was the last time she'd take summer boarders an' have the neighbors feed 'em."

"They were good old days, Nancy!"

"I guess they were! yes, indeed, I guess so! Now, dear, I s'pose you've heard what I've been through, sence you went away?"

I put the thin hand to my cheek.

"Yes," I said, "I have heard."

"Well, now, I want to tell you the way it 'pears to me. You'll hear the neighbors' side, an' arter I'm gone, they'll tell you I was under-witted or bold. They've been proper good to me sence I've been sick, but law! what do they know about it, goin' to bed at nine o'clock, an' gittin' up to feed the chickens an' ride to meetin' with their husbands? No more'n the dead! An' so I want to tell ye my story, myself. Now, don't you mind my coughing dear! It don't hurt, to speak of, an' I feel better arter it.

"Well, I dunno where to begin. The long an' short of it was, dear, James he got kind o' uneasy on land, an' then he was tried with me, an' then he told me, one night, when he spoke out, that he didn't care about me as he used to, an' he never should, an' we couldn't live no longer under the same roof. He was goin' off the next day to sea, or to the devil, he said, so he needn't go crazy seein' Mary Ann Worthen's face lookin' at him all the time. It ain't any use tryin' to tell how I felt. Some troubles ain't no more 'n a dull pain, an' some are like cuts an' gashes. You can feel your heart drop, drop, like water off the eaves. Mine dropped for a good while arter that. Well, you see I'd been through the fust stages of it. I'd been eat up by jealousy, an' I'd slaved like a dog to git him back; but now it had got beyond such folderol. He was in terrible trouble, an' I'd got to git him out. An' I guess 'twas then that I begun to feel as if I was his mother, instid of his wife. 'Jim,' says I, (somehow I have to Say 'James,' now we're separated!) 'don't you fret. I'll go off an' leave ye, an' you can get clear o' me accordin' to law, if you want to. I'm sure you can. I sha'n't care.' He turned an' looked at me, as if I was crazed or he was himself, 'You won't care?' he says. 'No,' says I, 'I sha'n't care.' I said it real easy, for 'twas true. Somehow, I'd got beyond carin'. My heart dropped blood, but I couldn't bear to have him in trouble. 'They al'ays told me I was cut out for an old maid," I says, 'an' I guess I be. Housekeepin' 's a chore, anyway. You let all the stuff set right here jest as we've had it, an' ask Cap'n Fuller to come an' bring his chist; an' I'll settle down in the Willer Brook house an' make button-holes. It's real pretty work.' You see, the reason I was so high for it was 't I knew if he went to sea, he'd git in with a swearin', drinkin' set, as he did afore, an' in them days such carryin's-on were dretful to me. If I'd known he'd marry, I dunno what course I should ha' took; for nothin' could ha' made that seem right to me, arter all had come and gone. But I jest thought how James was a dretful handy man about the house, an' I knew he set by Cap'n Fuller. The Cap'n 'ain't no real home, you know, an' I thought they'd admire to bach it together."

"Did you ever wonder whether you had done right? Did you ever think it would have been better for him to keep his promises to you? For him to be unhappy?"

A shade of trouble crossed her face.

"I guess I did!" she owned. "At fust, I was so anxious to git out o' his way, I never thought of anything else; but when I got settled down here, an' had all my time for spec'latin' on things, I was a good deal put to 't whether I'd done the best anybody could. But I didn't reason much, in them days; I jest felt. All was, I couldn't bear to have James tied to me when he'd got so's to hate me. Well, then he married--"

"Was she a good woman?"

"Good enough, yes; a leetle mite coarse-grained, but well-meanin' all through. Well, now, you know the neighbors blamed me for lettin' her have my things. Why, bless you, I didn't need 'em! An' Jim had used 'em so many years, he'd ha' missed 'em if they'd been took away. Then he never was forehanded, an' how could he ha' furnished a house all over ag'in, I'd like to know? The neighbors never understood. The amount of it was, they never was put in jest such a place, any of 'em."

"O Nancy, Nancy!" I said, "you cared for just one thing, and it was gone. You didn't care for the tables and chairs that were left behind!"

Two tears came, and dimmed her bright blue eyes. Her firm, delicate mouth quivered.

"Yes," she said, "you see how 'twas. I knew you would. Well, arter he was married, there was a spell when 'twas pretty tough. Sometimes I couldn't hardly help goin' over there by night an' peekin' into the winder, an' seein' how they got along. I went jest twice. The fust time was late in the fall, an' she was preservin' pears by lamplight. I looked into the kitchin winder jest as she was bendin' over the stove, tryin' the syrup, an' he was holdin' the light for her to see. I dunno what she said, but 'twas suthin' that made 'em both laugh out, an' then they turned an' looked at one another, proper pleased. I dunno why, but it took right hold o' me, an' I started runnin' an' I never stopped till I got in, here an' onto my own bed. I thought 'twould ha' been massiful if death had took me that night, but I'm glad it didn't, dear, I'm glad it didn't! I shouldn't ha' seen ye, if it had, an' there's a good many things I shouldn't ha' had time to study out. You jest put a mite o' cayenne pepper in that cup, an' turn some hot water on it. It kind o' warms me up."

After a moment's rest, she began again.

"The next time I peeked was the last, for that night they'd had some words, an' they both set up straight as a mack'rel, an' wouldn't speak to one another. That hurt me most of anything. I never've got over the feelin' that I was James's mother, an' that night I felt sort o' bruised all through, as if some stranger'd been hurtin' him. So I never went spyin' on 'em no more. I felt as if I couldn't stan' it. But when I went to help her with the work, that time he was sick, I guess the neighbors thought I hadn't any sense of how a right-feelin' woman ought to act. I guess they thought I was sort o' coarse an' low, an' didn't realize what I'd, been through. Dear, don't you never believe it. The feelin' that's between husband an' wife's like a live creatur', an' when he told me that night that he didn't prize me no more, he wounded it; an' when he married the other woman, he killed it dead. If he'd ha' come back to me then, an' swore he was the same man I married, I could ha' died for him, jest as I would this minute, but he never should ha' touched me. But suthin' had riz up in the place o' the feelin' I had fust, so't I never could ha' helped doin' for him, any more'n if he'd been my own child."

"'In the resurrection, they neither marry nor are given in marriage!'"

"I guess that's it," said Nancy. "On'y you have to live through a good deal afore you understand it. Well, now, dear, I'm nearin' the end. There's one thing that's come to me while I've been livin' through this, that I 'ain't never heard anybody mention; an' I want you to remember it, so's you can tell folks that are in great trouble, the way I've been. I've been thinkin' on't out that there's jest so much of everything in the world,--so much gold, so much silver, so many di'monds. You can't make no more nor no less. All you can do is to pass 'em about from hand to hand, so't sometimes here'll be somebody that's rich, an' then it'll slip away from him, an' he'll be poor. Now, accordin' to my lights, it's jes' so with love. There's jest so much, an' when it's took away from you, an' passed over to somebody else, it's alive, it's there, same as ever it was. So 't you ain't goin' to say it's all holler an' empty, this world. You're goin' to say, 'Well, it's som'er's, if 'tain't with me!'"

Nancy had straightened herself, without the support of her pillows. Her eyes were bright. A faint flush had come upon her cheeks. A doctor would have told me that my devoted friendship had not saved me from being a wretched nurse.

"My home was broke up," she went on, "but there's a nice, pretty house there jest the same. There's a contented couple livin' in it, an' what if the wife ain't me? It ain't no matter. P'r'aps it's a lot better that somebody else should have it, somebody that couldn't git along alone; an' not me, that can see the rights o' things. Jest so much love, dear--don't you forget that--no matter where 'tis! An' James could take his love away from me, but the Lord A'mighty himself can't take mine from him. An' so 'tis, the world over. You can al'ays love folks, an' do for 'em, even if your doin' 's only breakin' your heart an' givin' 'em up. An' do you s'pose there's any sp'ere o' life where I sha'n't be allowed to do somethin' for James? I guess not, dear, I guess not, even if it's only keepin' away from him."

Nancy lived three days, in a state of delighted content with us and our poor ministrations; and only once did we approach the subject of that solemn night. As the end drew near, I became more and more anxious to know if she had a wish unfulfilled, and at length I ventured to ask her softly, when we were alone,--

"Would you like to see him?"

Her bright eyes looked at me, in a startled way.

"No, dear, no," she said, evidently surprised that I could ask it. "Bless you, no!"

STROLLERS IN TIVERTON

In Tiverton, when reminiscences are in order, we go back to one very rich year; then the circus and strolling players came to town, and the usual camp-meeting was followed by an epidemic of scarlet fever, which might have stood forth as the judgment of heaven, save that the newly converted were stricken first and undoubtedly fared hardest. Hiram Cole said it was because they'd "got all their nerve-juice used up, hollerin' hallelujah." But that I know not. This theory of nerve-juice, was a favorite one with Hiram: he contended that it had a powerful hand in determining the results of presidential elections; and, indeed, in swaying the balance of power among the nations of the earth.

Even in the early spring, there had been several cases of fever at Sudleigh; and so, when the circus made application for a license to take possession of the town, according to olden custom, the public authorities very wisely refused. Tiverton, however, was wroth at this arbitrary restriction. For more years than I can say, she had driven over to Sudleigh "to see the caravan;" and now, through some crack-brained theory of contagion, the caravan was to be barred out. We never really believed that the town-fathers had taken their highhanded measure on account of scarlet fever. We saw in it some occult political significance, and referred ominously to the butter we carried there on Saturdays, and to the possibility that, if they cast us off, a separation might affect them far more seriously than it would us. But to our loud-voiced delight, the caravan, finding that it was to be within hailing distance, and unwilling to pass on without further tribute, extended the sceptre to Tiverton herself; and Brad Freeman joyfully discussed the project of making a circus ground of his old race-course, which, he declared, he had purposed planting with tobacco. We never knew whether to believe this or not, though we had many times previously gone over Brad's calculation, by which he figured that he could sell at least three tons of fine-cut from one summer's produce. To that specious logic, we always listened with unwilling admiration; but when we could shake off the glamour inseparable from a problem made to come out right, we were accustomed to turn to one another, demanding with cold scepticism, "Where'd he git his seed?"

In spite of the loss of this potential crop, however, Brad was magnanimously willing to let his field; and Tiverton held her head high, in the prospect of having a circus of her own. We intimated that it would undoubtedly be fair weather, owing to our superior moral desert as compared with that of Sudleigh, which was annually afflicted with what had long been known as "circus-weather." For Sudleigh had sinned, and Nature was thenceforth deputed to pay her back, in good old Hebrew style. One circus-day--before the war, as I believe--Sudleigh fenced up the spring in a corner of her grounds, and with a foolish thrift sold ice-water to the crowd, at a penny a glass. Tiverton was furious, and so, apparently, were the just heavens; for every circus-day thereafter it rained, in a fashion calculated to urge any forehanded Noah into immediate action. We of Tiverton never allowed our neighbor to forget her criminal lapse. When, on circus-afternoon, we met one of the rival township, dripping as ourselves, we said, with all the cheerfulness of conscious innocence,--

"Water enough for everybody, to-day! Guess ye won't have to peddle none out!"

"Seems to be comin' down pretty fast! You better build a platfoam over that spring! Go hard with ye if't overflowed!"

Strange to say, Sudleigh seemed to regard these time-licensed remarks with little favor; she even intimated that they smacked of the past, and were wearisome in her nostrils. But not for that did we halt in their distribution. Moreover, we flaunted our domestic loyalty by partaking of no Sudleigh fluid within the grounds. We carried tea, coffee, lemonade, milk, an ambitious variety of drinks, in order that even our children might be spared the public disgrace of tasting Sudleigh water; and it was a part of our excellent fooling to invite every Sudleighian to drink with us. Even the virtues, however, spare their votaries no pang; and in every family, this unbending fealty resulted in the individual members' betaking themselves to the pump or well, immediately on getting home, even before attempting to unharness. About five o'clock, on circus-afternoon, there would be a general rumbling of buckets and creaking of sweeps, while a chorus rose to heaven, "My! I was 'most choked!"

But our *fete*-day dawned bright and speckless. We rose before three o'clock, every man, woman and child of us, to see the procession come into town. It would leave the railway at Sudleigh, and we had a faint hope of its forming in regulation style, and sweeping into Tiverton, a blaze of glittering chariots surmounted by queens of beauty, of lazy beasts of the desert sulking in their cages, and dainty-stepping horses, ridden by bold amazons. For a time, the expectation kept us bright and hopeful, although most of us had only taken a "cold bite" before starting; but as the eastern saffron pencilled one line of light and the bird chorus swelled in piercing glory, we grew cross and all unbefitting the smiling morn. Only Dilly Joyce looked sunshiny as ever, for she had no domestic cares to beckon her; she and Nance Pete, who was in luck that day, having a full pipe. Dilly had nestled into a rock, curved in the form of a chair, and lay watching the eastern sky, a faint smile of pleasure parting her lips when the saffron hardened into gold.

"Nice, dear, ain't it?" she said, as I paused a moment near her, "I al'ays liked the side o' the road. But it's kind o' disturbin' to have so much talk. I dunno's you can help it, though, where there's so many people. Most o' the time, I'm better on't to home, but I did want to see an elephant near to!"

The sky broadened into light, and the birds jeered at us, poor, draggled folk who lived in boxes and were embarrassed by the morn. The men grew nervous, for milking-time was near, and in imagination I have no doubt they heard the lowing of reproachful kine.

"Well, 'tain't no use," said Eli Pike, rising from the stone-wall, and stretching himself, with decision. "I've got to 'tend to them cows, whether or no!" And he strolled away on the country-road, without a look behind. Most of the other men, as in honor bound, followed him; and the women, with loud-voiced protest against an obvious necessity, trailed after them, to strain the milk. Only we who formed the gypsy element were left behind.

"I call it a real shame!" announced Mrs. Pike, gathering her summer shawl about her shoulders, and stepping away with an offended dignity such as no delinquent elephant could have faced. "I warrant ye, they wouldn't ha' treated Sudleigh so. They wouldn't ha' dared!"

"I dunno's Sudleigh's any more looked up to'n we be," said Caleb Rivers, who had been so tardy in bestirring himself that he formed a part of the women's corps. "I guess, if the truth was known, Tiverton covers more land'n Sudleigh does, on'y Sudleigh's all humped up together into a quart bowl. I guess there's countries that 'ain't heard o' Sudleigh, an' wouldn't stan' much in fear if they had!"

And so Tiverton dispersed, unamiably, and with its public pride hurt to the quick. I tried to take pattern by Dilly Joyce, and steal from nature a little of the wonderful filial enjoyment which came to her unsought. When Dilly watched the sky, I did, also; when she brightened at sound of a bird hitherto silent, I tried to set down his notes in my memory; and when she closed her eyes, and shut out the world, to think it over, I did the same. But the result was different. Probably Dilly opened hers again upon the lovely earth, but I drifted off into dreamland, and only awoke, two hours after, to find the scenes marvellously changed. It was bright, steady morning, the morning come to stay. Tiverton had performed its dairy rites, and returned again, enlivened by a cup of tea; and oh, incredible joy! there was a grunting and panting, a swaying of mighty flanks. The circus was approaching, from Sudleigh way. Instantly I was alert and on my feet, for it would have been impossible to miss the contagion of the general joy. I knew how we felt, not as individuals, but as Tivertonians alone. We were tolerant potentates, waiting, in gracious majesty, to receive a deputation from the farther East. It grieves me much to stop here and confess, with a necessary honesty, that this was but a sorry circus, gauged by the conventional standards; else, I suppose, it had never come to Tiverton at all. The circus-folk had evidently dressed for travelling, not for us. The chariots, some of them still hooded in canvas, were very small and tarnished. There were but three elephants, two camels, and a most meagre display of those alluring cages made to afford even the careless eye a sudden, quickening glimpse of restless, tawny form, or slothful hulk within. Yet why depreciate the raw material whereof Fancy has power divine to build her altogether perfect heights? Here was the plain, homely setting of our plainer lives, and right into the midst of it had come the East. The elephants affected us most; we probably thought little about the immemorial mystery, the vague, occult tradition wrapped in that mouse-colored hide; but even to our dense Western imagination such quickening suggestion was vividly apparent. We knew our world; usually it seemed to us the only one, even when we looked at the stars. But at least one other had been created, and before us appeared its visible sign,--my lord the elephant! There he was, swaying along, conscious philosopher, conscious might, yet holding his omniscience in the background, and keeping a wary eye out for the peanuts with which we simple country souls had not provided ourselves. There was one curious thing about it all. We had seen the circus at Sudleigh, as I have said, yet the fact of entertaining it within our borders made it seem exactly as if we had never laid eyes upon it before. This was our caravan, and God Almighty had created the elephant for us. Dilly Joyce slipped her hand quickly in mine and pressed it hard. She was quite pale. Yet it was she who acted upon the first practical thought. She recovered herself before my lord went by, took a ginger cookie from her pocket, and put it into Davie Tolman's hand.

"Here," she said, pushing him forward, "you go an' offer it to him. He'll take it. See'f he don't!"

Davie accepted the mission with joy, and persisted in it until he found himself close beside that swaying bulk, and saw the long trunk curved enticingly toward him. Then he uttered one explosive howl, and fell back on the very toes of us who were pressing forward to partake, by right of sympathy, in the little drama.

"Lordy Massy, keep still!" cried out Nance Pete; and she snatched him up bodily, and held him out to the elephant. I believe my own pang at that moment to have been general. I forgot that elephants are not carnivorous, and shuddered back, under the expectation of seeing Davie devoured, hide and hair. But Nance had the address to stiffen the little arm, and my lord took the cookie, still clutched in the despairing hand, and passed on. Then Davie wiped his eyes, after peeping stealthily about to see whether any one was disposed to jeer at him, and took such courage that he posed, ever after, as the hero of the day.

The procession had nearly passed us when we saw a sight calculated to animate us anew with a justifiable pride. Sudleigh itself, its young men and maidens, old men and children, was following the circus into our town. It would not have a circus of its own, forsooth, but it would share in ours! We, as by one consent, assumed an air of dignified self-importance. We were the hosts of the day; we bowed graciously to such of our guests as we knew, and, with a mild tolerance, looked over the heads of those who were unfamiliar. Yet nothing checked our happy companionship with the caravan; still we followed by the side of the procession, through tangles of blackberry vine, and over ditch and stubble. Some of the boys mounted the walls, and ran wildly, dislodging stones as they went, and earning no reproof from the fathers who, on any other day, would have been alive to a future mowing and the clashing of scythe and rock. There was, moreover, an impression abroad that our progress could by no means be considered devoid of danger.

"S'pose that fellar should rise up, an' wrench off them bars!" suggested Heman Blaisdell, pointing out one cage where a great creature, gaudy in stripes, paced back and forth, throwing us an occasional look of scorn and great despite. "I wouldn't give much for my chances! Nor for anybody else's!"

"My soul an' body!" ejaculated a woman. "I hope they don't forgit to lock them cages up! Folks git awful careless when they do a thing every day! I forgot to shet up the hins last week, an' that was the night the skunk got in."

"I'm glad Brad brought his gun," said another, in the tone of one who would have crossed herself had there been a saint to help. And thereafter we kept so thickly about Brad, walking with his long free stride, that his progress became impeded, and he almost fell over us. Suddenly, from the front, a man's voice rose in an imperative cry,--

"Turn round! turn round!"

Quite evidently the mandate was addressed to us, and we turned in a mass, fleeing back into Sudleigh's very arms. For a moment, it was like Sparta and Persia striving in the Pass; then Sudleigh turned also, such as were on foot, and fled with us. We pressed up the bank, as soon as we could collect our errant wits; some of us, with a sense of coming calamity, mounted the very wall, and there we had a moment to look about us. The caravan was keeping steadily on, like fate and taxes, and facing it stood a carryall attached to a frightened horse. On the front seat, erect in her accustomed majesty, sat Aunt Melissa Adams; and Uncle Hiram, ever a humble charioteer, was by her side. They, too, had driven out to see the circus, but alas! it had not struck them that they might meet it midway, with no volition of drawing up at the side of the road and allowing it to pass. The old horse, hardened to the vicissitudes of many farming seasons, had necessarily no acquaintance with the wild beasts of the Orient; no past experience, tucked away in his wise old head, could explain them in the very least. He plunged and reared; he snorted with fear, and Aunt Melissa began to emit shrieks of such volume and quality that the mangy lion, composing himself to sleep in his cage, rose, and sent forth a cry that Tiverton will long remember. We did not stop to explain our forebodings, but we were sure that, in some mysterious way, Aunt Melissa was doomed, and that she had brought her misfortune on herself. A second Daniel, she had no special integrity to stand her in need. And still the circus advanced, and the horse snorted and backed. He was a gaunt old beast, but in his terror, one moment of beauty dignified him beyond belief. His head was high, his eyes were starting.

"Turn round!" cried the men, but Uncle Hiram was paralyzed, and the reins lay supine in his hands, while he screamed a wheezy "Whoa!" Then Brad Freeman, as usual in cases outside precedent, became the good angel of Tiverton. He forced his gun on the person nearest at hand--who proved to be Nance Pete--and dashed forward. Seizing the frightened horse by the head, he cramped the wheel scientifically, and turned him round. Then he gave him a smack on the flank, and the carryall went reeling and swaying back into Tiverton, the *avant-courrier* of the circus. You should have heard Aunt Melissa's account of that ride, an epic moment which she treasured, in awe, to the day of her death. According to her, it asked no odds from the wild huntsman, or the Gabriel hounds. Well, we cowards came down from the wall, assuring each other, with voices still shaking a little, that we knew it was nothing, after all, and that nobody but Aunt Melissa would make such a fuss. How she did holler! we said, with conscious pride in our own self-possession when brought into unexpectedly close relations with wild beasts; and we trudged happily along through the dust stirred by alien trampling, back to Tiverton Street, and down into Brad Freeman's field. It would hardly be possible to describe our joy in watching the operation of tent-raising, nor our pride in Brad Freeman, when he assumed the character of host, and not only made the circus-folk free of the ground they had hired, but hurried here and there, helping with such address and muscular vigor that we felt defrauded in never having known how accomplished he really was. The strollers recognized his type, in no time; they were joking with him and clapping him on the back before the first tent had been unrolled. Now, none of us had ever seen a circus performer, save in the ring; and I think we were disappointed, for a moment, at finding we had in our midst no spangled angels in rosy tights, no athletes standing on their heads by choice, and quite preferring the landscape upside down, but a set of shabbily dressed, rather jaded men and women, who were, for all the world, just like ourselves, save that they walked more gracefully, and spoke in softer voice. But when the report went round that the cook was getting breakfast ready--out of doors, too!--we were more than compensated for the loss of such tinsel joys. Chattering and eager, we ran over to the dining-tent, and there, close beside it, found the little kitchen, its ovens smoking hot, and a man outside, aproned and capped, cutting up chops and steaks, with careless deftness, and laying them in the great iron pans, preparatory to broiling.

"By all 't's good an' bad!" swore Tom McNeil, a universal and sweeping oath he much affected, "they've got a whole sheep an' a side o' beef! Well, it's high livin', an' no mistake!"

We who considered a few pies a baking, watched this wholesale cookery in bewildered fascination. A savory smell arose to heaven. I never was so hungry in my life, and I believe all Tiverton would own to the same craving. Perhaps some wild instinct sprang up in us with the scent of meat in out-door air, but at any rate, we became much exhilarated, and our attention was only turned from the beguiling chops by Mrs. Wilson's saying, in a low tone, to her husband,--

"Lothrop, if there ain't Lucindy, an' that Molly McNeil with her! What's Lucindy got? My sake alive! you might ha' known she'd do suthin' to make anybody wish they'd stayed to home. If you can git near her, you keep a tight holt on her, or she'll be jumpin' through a hoop!"

I turned, with the rest. Yes, there was Miss Lucindy, tripping happily across the level field. Molly McNeil hastened beside her, and between them they carried a large clothes-basket, overflowing with flaming orange-red; a basket heaped with sunset, not the dawn! They were very near me when I guessed what it was; so near that I could see the happy smile on Lucindy's parted lips, and note how high the rose flush had risen in her delicate cheek, with happiness and haste.

"Stortions!" broke out a voice near me, in virile scorn,--Nance Pete's,--"stortions! Jes' like her! Better picked 'em a mess o' pease!"

It was, indeed, a basket of red nasturtiums, and the sun had touched them into a glory like his own. For one brief moment, we were ashamed of Lucindy's "shallerness" and irrelevancy; but the circus people interpreted her better. They rose from box and hamper where they had been listlessly awaiting their tardy breakfast, and crowded forward to meet her. They knew, through the comradeship of all Bohemia, exactly what she meant.

"My!" said Miss Lucindy, smiling full at them as they came,--her old, set smile had been touched, within a year, by something glad and free,--"set 'em down now, Molly. My! are you the folks? Well, I thought you'd seem different, somehow, but anyway, we brought you over a few blooms. We thought you couldn't have much time, movin' round so, to work in your gardins, especially the things you have to sow every year. Yes, dear, yes! Take a good handful. Here's a little mignonette I put in the bottom, so't everybody could have a sprig. Yes, there's enough for the men, too. Why, yes, help yourself! Law, dear, why don't you take off your veil? Hot as this is!" for the bearded lady, closely masked in black *barege*, had come forward and hungrily stretched out a great hand for her share.

We never knew how it all happened, but during this clamor of happy voices, the chops were cooked and the coffee boiled; the circus people turned about, and trooped into the tent where the tables were set, and they took Miss Lucindy with them. Yes, they did! Molly McNeil stayed contentedly outside; for though she had brought her share of the treasure, quite evidently she considered herself a friendly helper, not a partner in the scheme. But Miss Lucindy was the queen of the carnival. We heard one girl say to another, as our eccentric townswoman swept past us, in the eager crowd, "Oh, the dear old thing!" We saw a sad-eyed girl bend forward, lift a string of Miss Lucindy's apron (which, we felt, should have been left behind in the kitchen) and give it a hearty kiss. Later, when, by little groups, we peeped into the dining-tent, we saw Miss Lucindy sitting there at the table, between two women who evidently thought her the very nicest person that had ever crossed their wandering track. There she was, an untouched roll and chop on her plate, a cup of coffee by her side. She was not talking. She only smiled happily at those who talked to her, and her eyes shone very bright. We were ashamed; I confess it. For was not Sudleigh, also, there to see?

"Oh, my soul!" exclaimed Mrs. Wilson, in fretful undertone. "I wish the old Judge was here!"

Her husband turned and looked at her, and she quailed; not with fear of him, but at the vision of the outraged truth.

"Well, no," she added, weakly, "I dunno's I wish anything so bad as that, but I do declare I think there ought to be somebody to keep a tight grip on Lucindy!"

Who shall deem himself worthy to write the chronicle of that glorious day?

There were so many incidents not set down in the logical drama; so many side-shows of circumstance! We watched all the mysterious preparations for the afternoon performance, so far as we were allowed, with the keenness of the wise, who recognize a special wonder and will not let it pass unproved. We surrounded Miss Lucindy, when she came away from her breakfast party, and begged for an exact account of all her entertainers had said; but she could tell us nothing. She only reiterated, with eyes sparkling anew, that they were "proper nice folks, proper nice! and she must go home and get Ellen. If she'd known they were just like other folks she'd have brought Ellen this morning; but she'd been afraid there'd be talk that little girls better not hear."

At noon, we sat about in the shade of the trees along the wall, and ate delicious cold food from the butter-boxes and baskets our men-folks had brought over during the forenoon lull; and we assiduously offered Sudleigh a drink, whenever it passed the counter where barrels of free spring-water had been set. And then, at the first possible moment, we paid our fee, and went inside the tent to see the animals. That scrubby menagerie had not gained in dignity from its transference to canvas walls. The enclosure was very hot and stuffy; there was a smell of dust and straw. The lion stretched himself, from time to time, and gave an angry roar for savage, long-lost joys. One bear, surely new to the business, kept walking up and down, up and down, moaning, in an abandon of homesickness. Brad Freeman stood before the cage when I was there.

"Say, Brad," said the Crane boy, slipping his arm into the hunter's, in a good-fellowship sure to be reciprocated. "Davie Tolman said you's goin' to fetch over your fox, an' sell him to the circus. Be you?"

"My Lord!" answered Brad, very violently for him, the ever-tolerant. "No! I'm goin' to let him go. ***Look at that!***" And while the Crane boy, unconcerned, yet puzzled, gave his full attention to the bear, Brad passed on.

There was a wolf, I remember, darting about his cage, slinking, furtive, ever on a futile prowl. He especially engaged the interest of Tom McNeil, who said admiringly, as I, too, looked through the bars, "Ain't he a prompt little cuss?" I felt that with Tom it was the fascination of opposites; he never could understand superlative energy.

Just as we were trooping into the larger tent (there were no three rings, I beg to say, maliciously calculated to distract the attention! One, of a goodly size, was quite enough for us!) a little voice piped up, "The snake's got loose!" How we surged and panted, and fought one another for our sacred lives! In vain were we urged to stand still; we strove the more. And when a bit of rope perversely and maliciously coiled itself round Rosa Tolman's ankle, she gave a shriek so loud and despairing that it undid us anew. If Sheriff Holmes had not come forward and sworn at us, I believe we should have trampled one another out of existence; but he seemed so palpably the embodiment of authority, and his oath the oath undoubtedly selected by legislature for that very occasion, that we paused, and on the passionate asseveration of a circus man that the snake was safely in his cage, consented to be calm. But Aunt Melissa Adams, unstrung by her earlier experience, would trust no doubtful circumstance. She plodded back into the animal-tent, assured herself, with her own eyes, of the snake's presence at his own hearthstone, and came back satisfied, just as the clown entered the ring. The performance needs no bush. We had palmleaf fans offered us, pop-corn, and pink lemonade. We sweltered under the blazing canvas, laughed at the clown's musty fooling, which deserved rather the reverence due old age, and wondered between whiles if there would be a shower, and if tent-poles were ever struck. Then it was all over, and we trailed out, in great bodily discomfort and spiritual joy, to witness, quite unlooked for, the most vivid drama of the day. Young Dana Marden was there, he and his wife who lived down in Tiverton Hollow. Dana was a nephew of Josh, of hapless memory, and "folks said" that, like Josh, he had "all the Marden setness, once git him riled." But Mary Worthen had not been in the least afraid of that when she married him. Before their engagement, some one had casually mentioned Dana's having inherited "setness" for his patrimony.

"I know it," she said, "and if I had anything to do with him, I'd break him of it, or I'd break his neck!"

Tiverton had been very considerate in never repeating that speech to Dana; and his wife, in all their five years of married life, had not fulfilled her threat. As we were making ready to leave the grounds, that day, and those who had horses were "tacklin up," we became aware that Dana, a handsome, solid, fresh-colored fellow, sat in his wagon with pretty Mary beside him, and that they evidently had no intention of moving on. Of course we approached, to find out what the trouble might be.

"We can send word to have Tom Bunker milk the cows," said Dana, with distinct emphasis, "an' we can stay for the evenin' performance. Or we can go now. Only, you've got to say which!"

"I don't want to say," returned Mary, placidly, "because I don't know which you'd rather have. You just tell me *so* much!"

A frown contracted his brow; he looked a middle-aged man. When he spoke, his voice grated.

"You tell which, or we'll set here all night, an' I don't speak another word to you till you do!"

But Mary said nothing.

"My soul!" whispered Mrs. Rivers to me. "She's got herself into it now, jest as they say Lyddy Ann Marden done, with Josh. She'll have to back down!"

Several more of those aimless on-lookers, ever ready for the making of crowds, surged forward. The wagon was blocking the way. We realised with shame that Sudleigh, too, was here, to say nothing of sister towns less irritating to our pride. It was Uncle Eli Pike who stepped into the breach.

"Here, Dana!" he called, and, as we were glad to remember, all the aliens in the crowd could hear, "I guess that hoss o' yourn's gittin' a mite balky. I'll lead him a step, if you say so." And without a word of assent from Dana, he guided the horse out of the grounds, and started him on the road. We watched the divided couple, on their common way. Dana was driving, it is true; but we knew, with a heavy certainty, that he was not speaking to his wife. He was a Marden, and nothing would make him speak.

This slight but very significant episode sent us home in a soberer mind than any of us had anticipated, after the gaudy triumphs of the day. We could not quell our curiosity over the upshot of it all, and that night, after the chores were done, we sat in the darkness, interspersing our comments on the spangled butterflies of horse and hoop with an awed question, now and then, while the minute-hand sped, "S'pose they've spoke yit?"

Alas! the prevailing voice was still against it; and when we went to market, and met there the people from the Hollow (who were somewhat more bucolic than we), they passed about the open secret. Dana did not speak to his wife. Again we knew he never would. The summer waned; the cows were turned into the shack, and the most "forehanded" among us began to cut boughs for banking up the house, and set afoot other preparations for winter's cold. Still Dana had not spoken. But the effect on Mary was inexplicable to us all. We knew she loved him deeply, and that the habits of their relationship were very tender; we expected her to sink and fail under the burden of this sudden exile of the heart, just as Lyddy Ann had done, so many years ago. But Mary held her head high, and kept her color. She even "went abroad" more than usual; ostentatiously so, we thought, for she would come over to Tiverton to pass the afternoon, after the good, old-fashioned style, with women whom she knew but slightly. And, most incredible of all, though Dana would not speak to her, she spoke to him! Once, in driving past, I heard her clear voice (it seemed now a dauntless voice!) calling,--

"Dana, dinner's ready!" Dana dropped the board he was carrying, and went in, a fierce yet dogged look upon his face, as if it needed hourly schooling to mirror his hard heart. Then the agent of the Sudleigh "Star," who was canvassing for a new domestic paper, had also his story to tell. He went to the Mardens', and Mary, who admitted him, put down her name, and then called blithely into the kitchen,--

"Dana, I'm all out o' change. Will you hand me a dollar 'n' a quarter?"

Dana, flushed red and overwhelmed by a pitiable embarrassment, came to the door and gave the money; and Mary, with that proud unconsciousness which made us wonder anew every time we saw it in her, thanked him, and dismissed the visitor, as if nothing were wrong. The couple went as usual to church and sociable. Certain lines deepened in Dana's face, but Mary grew every day more light-heartedly cheerful. Yet the one-sided silence lived, with the terrible tenacity of evil.

So the days went on until midwinter snows began to blow, and then we learned, with a thrill of pride, that the International Dramatic Company proposed coming to our own little hall, for a two weeks' engagement. Some said Sudleigh Opera House was too large for it, and too expensive; but we, the wiser heads, were grandly aware that, with unusual acumen, the drama had at last recognized the true emporium of taste. We resolved that this discriminating company should not repent its choice. A week before the great first night, magnificent posters in red and blue set before us, in very choice English, the dramatic performances, "Shakespearean and otherwise," destined to take place among us. The leading parts were to be assumed by Mr. and Mrs. Van Rensellaer Wilde, "two of the foremost artists in the stellar world, supported by an adequate company."

The announcement ended with the insinuating alliteration, "Popular prices prevail." The very first night, we were at the door, an excited crowd, absolutely before it was open; but early as we went, the hospitable pianist held the field before us; the hall resounded with his jocund banging at the very moment when the pioneer among us set foot within. I have never seen anywhere, either on benefit or farewell night, a cordiality to be compared with that which presided over our own theatre in Tiverton Hall. Mr. Van Rensellaer Wilde himself stood within the doorway, to greet us as we came; a personable man, with the smooth, individual face of his profession, a moist and beery eye, a catholic smile, tolerant enough to include the just and the unjust, a rusty, old-fashioned stock, and the very ancientest brown Prince Albert coat still in reputable existence,--a strange historical epitome of brushings and spongings, of camphor exile and patient patching. Quite evidently he was not among the prosperous, even in his stellar world. But not for that would he repine. This present planet was an admirable plot of ground, and here he stood, cheerfully ready to induct us, the Puritan-born, into the fictitious joys thereof. And popular prices prevailed; the floor of the hall itself confirmed it. It was divided, by chalk-lines, into three sections. Enter the first division, and a legend at your feet indicated the ten-cent territory. Advance a little, and "twenty-five cents" met the eye; and presently, approaching the platform, you were in the seats of the scornful, thirty-five cents each. The latter, by common consent, were eschewed by the very first comers, not alone for reasons of thrift, but because we thought they ought to be left for old folks, "a leetle mite hard o' hearin'," or the unfortunates who were "not so fur-sighted" as we. So we seated ourselves in delight already begun, for was not Mr. Gad Greenfield performing one of the "orchestral pieces" which the programme had led us to expect? The piano was an antique, accustomed to serve as victim at Sudleigh's dancing-school and sociables. I have never heard its condition described, on its return to Sudleigh; I only know that, from some eccentric partiality, Gad Greenfield's music was all *fortissimo*. Sally Flint, brought thither by the much-enduring overseer, for the sake of domestic peace, seemed to be the only one who did not regard Gad's performance with unquestioning awe. She was heard to say aloud, in a penetrating voice,--

"My soul an' body! what a racket!"

Whereupon she deliberately pulled some wool from the tassel of her chinchilla cloud, and stuffed a little wad into each ear. We were sorry for the overseer, thus put to shame by his untutored charge, and delicately looked away, after making sure Sally had "r'ared as high" as she proposed doing. She was the overseer's cross; no one could help him bear it.

And now the curtain went up,--though not on the play, let me tell you! On slighter joys, a fillip to the taste. A juggler, "all complete" in black small-clothes and white kid gloves, stood there ready to burn up our handkerchiefs, change our watches into rabbits, and make omelets in our best go-to-meeting hats. I cannot remember all the wonderful things he did (everything, I believe, judging from the roseate glow left in my mind, everything that juggler ever achieved short of the Hindoo marvel of cutting up maidens and splicing them together again, or planting the magic tree); I only know we were too crafty to help him, and though he again and again implored a volunteer from the audience to come and play the willing victim, we clung to our settees the more, so that Gad of the piano was obliged to fill the gap. And when the curtain came down, and went up again on a drawing-room, with a red plush chair in it, and a lady dressed in a long-tailed white satin gown, where were we? In Tiverton? Nay, in the great world of fashion and of crime. I remember very little now about the order of the plays; very little of their names and drift. I only know we were swept triumphantly through the widest range ever imagined since the "pastoral-comical, historical- pastoral," of old Polonius. And in all, fat, middle-aged Wilde was the dashing hero, the deep-dyed villain; and his wife, middle-aged as he, and far, oh, far more corpulent! played the lovely heroine, the blooming victim, the queen of hearts. And she was truly beautiful to us, that blowsy dame, through the beguiling witchery of her art. The smarting tears came into our eyes when, in "Caste," she staggered back, despairing, lost in grief, unable to arm her soldier for the march. Melodrama was her joy, and as we watched her lumbering about the stage in a white muslin dress, with the artificial springiness of a youth that would never return, we could have risen as one man, to snatch her from the toils of villany. She was a cool piece, that swiftly descending star! She had a way of deliberately stepping outside the scenes and letting down her thin black hair, before the tragic moment; then would she bound back again, and tear every passion to tatters, in good old-fashioned style. In "The Octoroon" especially she tore our hearts with it, so that it almost began to seem as if political issues were imminent. For between the acts, men bent forward to their neighbors, and put their heads together, recalling abolition times; and one poor, harmless old farmer from Sudleigh way was glared at in a fashion to which he had once been painfully accustomed, while murmurs of "Copperhead! Yes, Copperhead all through the war!" must have penetrated where he sat. But he was securely locked up in his fortress of deaf old age, and met the hostile glances benignly, quite unconscious of their meaning. In one particular, we felt, for a time, that we had been deceived. The Shakespearean drama had not been touched on as we had been led to expect; but at last, in the middle of the second week, we were rejoiced by the announcement that "Othello" would that night be appropriately set forth. The Moor of Venice! He would never have recognized himself--his great creator would never have guessed his identity--as presented by Mr. Van Rensellaer Wilde. I give you my word for that! From beginning to end of the performance, Tiverton groped about, in a haze of perplexity, rendered ever the more dense by the fact that none of the actors knew their parts. I am inclined to think they had enriched their announcement by this allusion to the Shakespearean drama in a moment of wild ambition, as we gladly commit ourselves to issues far-off and vague; and then, with a chivalrous determination to vindicate their written word; they had embarked on a troublous sea for which they had "neither mast nor sail, nor chart nor rudder." So they went bobbing about in a tub, and we, with a like paucity of equipment, essayed to follow them.

Othello himself was a veiled mystery in our eyes.

"Ain't he colored?" whispered Mrs. Wilson to me; and while I hesitated, seeking to frame an answer both terse and true, she continued, although he was at that moment impressing the Senate with his great apology, "Is he free?"

I assured her on that point, and she settled down to a troubled study of the part, only to run hopelessly aground when Desdemona, in her stiff white satin gown, announced her intention of cleaving to the robust blackamoor, in spite of fate and father. That seemed a praiseworthy action, "taken by and large," but we could not altogether applaud it. "Abolition," as we were, the deed wounded some race prejudice in us, and Mrs. Hiram Cole voiced the general sentiment when she remarked audibly,--

"One color's as good as another, come Judgment Day, but let 'em marry among themselves, *I* say!"

The poverty of the scenery had something to do with our dulness in following the dramatic thread, for how should we know that our own little stage, disguised by a slender tree-growth, was the island of Cyprus, and that Desdemona, tripping through a doorway, in the same satin gown, had just arrived from a long and perilous voyage? "The riches of the ship" had "come on shore," but for all we knew, it had been in the next room, taking a nap, all the while. In the crucial scene between Cassio and Iago, we got the impression that one was as drunk as the other, and that Cassio acted the better man of the two, chiefly because of his grandiloquent apostrophe relative to the thieving of brains. We approved of that, and looked meaningly round at old Cap'n Fuller, who was at that time taking more hard cider than we considered good for him. But when the final catastrophe came, we, having missed the logical sequence, were totally unprepared. Mr. Wilde, with a blackamoor fury irresistibly funny to one who has seen a city coal-man cursing another for not moving on, smothered his shrieking spouse in a pillow brought over for that purpose from the Blaisdells', where most of the actors were boarding. We were not inclined to endure this quietly. The more phlegmatic among us moved uneasily in our seats, and one or two men, excitable beyond the ordinary, sprang up, with an oath. Mrs. Wilson dragged her husband down again.

"For massy sake, do set still!" she urged. "He 'ain't killed her. Don't you see them toes a-twitchin'?"

No, Mrs. Wilde was not dead, as her weary appearance in the afterpiece attested; but she had been cruelly abused, and the murmurs, here and there, as we left the hall, went far to show that Othello had done well in voluntarily paying the debt of nature, and that Emilia thought none too ill of him.

"Ought to ha' been strong up, by good rights," growled Tiverton. "you can't find a jury 't would acquit *him*!"

Night after night, we conscientiously sat out the aforesaid afterpiece, innocently supposed to be our due because it had formed a part of the initial performance. However long our weary strollers might delay it, in the empty hope of our going home content, there we waited until the curtain went up. It was a dreary piece of business, varied by horse-play considered "kind o' rough" by even the more boisterous among us. Sometimes it was given, minstrel-wise, in the time-honored panoply of burnt cork; again, poor weary souls! they lacked even the spirit to blacken themselves, and clinging to the same dialogue, played boldly in Caucasian fairness, with the pathetically futile disguise of a Teuton accent. And last of all, Mr. Wilde would appear before the curtain, and "in behalf of Mrs. Wilde, self and company" thank us movingly for our kind attention, and announce the next night's bill.

The last half hour was my chosen time for leaning back against the wall, and allowing thought and glance to dwell lovingly on Tiverton faces. O worn and rugged features of the elder generation to whose kinship we are born! What solution, even of Time, the all-potent, shall wash your meaning from the heart? An absolute lack of self-consciousness had quite transformed the gaze they bent upon the stage. A veil had been swept aside, and the true soul shone forth; that soul which ever dwells apart, either from the dignity of its estate or, being wrought of fibre more delicate than air, because it fears recoil and hurt. There were Roxy and her husband, he too well content with life as it is, to be greatly moved by its counterfeit; she sparkling back some artless reply to the challenge of feeble romance and wingless wit. There was Uncle Eli, a little dazed by these strange doings, the hand on his knee shaking, from time to time, under the stimulus of unshared thought. There was Miss Lucindy, with Ellen and all the McNeils, a care-free, happy phalanx, smiling joyously at everything set before them, with that spontaneous rapture so good to see. One night, Nance Pete appeared, and established herself, with great importance, in the first row of the ten-cent seats; but she fell asleep, and snored with embarrassing volume and precision. She never came again, and announced indifferently, to all who cared to hear, that when she "wanted to see a passel o' monkeys, she'd go to the circus, an' done with it." There, too, one night when Comedy burlesqued her own rapt self, was Dana Marden; but he came alone. Mary had a cold, we heard, and "thought she'd better stay in." Dana sat through the foolish play, unmoved. His brow loomed heavy, like Tragedy's own mask, and it grew ever blacker while the scene went on. Hiram Cole whispered me,--

"He'll kill himself afore he's done with it. He's gone in for the whole hog, but he 'ain't growed to it, as Old Josh had. The Marden blood run emptin's afore it got to him."

The last night came of all our blissful interlude, and on that night, by some stroke of fate, the bill was "Oliver Twist." Of that performance let naught be spoken, save in reverence. For, by divine leading it might seem, and not their own good wit, those poor players had been briefly touched by the one true fire. Shakespeare had beckoned them, and they had passed him by; Comedy and Tragedy had been their innocent sport. How funny their tragedy had been, how sad their comedy, Momus only might tell. But to-night some gleaming wave from a greater sea had lifted them, and borne them on. Still they played, jarringly, for that was their untutored wont. Their speech roared, loud defiance to grammar's idle saws, their costumes were absurd remnants of an antique past; but a certain, rude, and homely dignity had transfigured them, and enveloped, too, this poor drama which, after all, goes very deep, down to the springs of life and love. There was a dirty and wicked abomination of a Fagin. Wilde himself played Sykes, and we of Tiverton, who know little about the formless monster dwelling under the garnished pavement of every great city, and rising, once in a century or so, to send red riot and ruin through the streets,--even we could read the story of his word and glance. Unconsciously to ourselves, we guessed at Whitechapel and the East End "tough," and shuddered under the knowledge of evil. Mrs. Wilde, her heavy face many a shade sincerer than when she walked in dirty white satin, was Nancy; and in her death, culminated the grand moment of Tiverton's looking the drama in the face, and seeing it for what it is,-- the living sister of life itself. Sykes really killed her alarmingly well. Round the stage he dragged her, bruised and speechless, with such cruel realism that we women crouched and shivered; and when she staggered to her knees, and told her pitiful lie for the brute she loved, the general shudder of worship and horror thrilled us into a mighty reverence for the tie stronger than death and hell, binding the woman to the man, and lifting Love triumphant on his cross of pain. With Nancy's final sigh, another swept through the hall, like breath among the trees, and, drawn by what thread I know not, I looked about me, and all unwittingly was present at another great last act. Dana Marden and his wife were in front of me, not three seats away. Mary was very pale, and sat quite motionless, looking down into her lap; but Dana bent forward, gripping the seat in front of him with white and straining hands. His face, drawn and knotted, was a mirror of such anguish as few of us imagine; we only learn its power when it steals upon us in the dark, and our souls wrestle with it for awful mastery. He seemed to be suffering an extremity of physical pain. After that, I gave little heed to the stage. I was only conscious that the curtain had gone down, and that Mr. Wilde was thanking us for our kind attention, and expressing a flattering hope that another year would find him again in our midst. We did not want the farce, that night, even as our rightful due. We got up, and filed out in silence. I was just behind Dana and Mary; so near that I could have touched him when, halfway, down the hall, he put out a clumsy hand and drew her shawl closer about her shoulders. Then he set his face straight forward again, but not before I had noticed how the lips were twitching still, in that dumb protest against the fetters of his birth. Again he turned to her, as suddenly as if a blow had forced his face about. I heard his voice, abrupt, explosive, full of the harshness so near at hand to wait on agony,--

"You got your rubbers on?"

Mary started a little, and a tremor like that of cold, went over her; but she kept her head firmly erect.

"Yes, Dana," she said, clearly, just as she had spoken to him all those months, "I've got 'em on."

Before eleven o'clock, the next morning, the news had spread all over joyful Tiverton. Dana had spoken at last! But Mary! Within a week, she took to her bed, quite overmastered by a lingering fever. She "came out all right," as we say among ourselves, though after Dana had suffered such agonies of tenderness over her as few save mothers can know, or those who have injured their beloved. But she has never since been quite so dauntless, quite so full of the joy of life. As Hiram Cole again remarked, it is a serious thing to draw too heavily on the nerve-juice.

The Codes Of Hammurabi And Moses
W. W. Davies

QTY

The discovery of the Hammurabi Code is one of the greatest achievements of archaeology, and is of paramount interest, not only to the student of the Bible, but also to all those interested in ancient history...

Religion   **ISBN:** *1-59462-338-4*   **Pages:132**

MSRP $12.95

The Theory of Moral Sentiments
Adam Smith

QTY

This work from 1749. contains original theories of conscience amd moral judgment and it is the foundation for systemof morals.

Philosophy **ISBN:** *1-59462-777-0*   **Pages:536**

MSRP $19.95

Jessica's First Prayer
Hesba Stretton

QTY

In a screened and secluded corner of one of the many railway-bridges which span the streets of London there could be seen a few years ago, from five o'clock every morning until half past eight, a tidily set-out coffee-stall, consisting of a trestle and board, upon which stood two large tin cans, with a small fire of charcoal burning under each so as to keep the coffee boiling during the early hours of the morning when the work-people were thronging into the city on their way to their daily toil...

Childrens   **ISBN:** *1-59462-373-2*

Pages:84

MSRP $9.95

My Life and Work
Henry Ford

QTY

Henry Ford revolutionized the world with his implementation of mass production for the Model T automobile. Gain valuable business insight into his life and work with his own auto-biography... "We have only started on our development of our country we have not as yet, with all our talk of wonderful progress, done more than scratch the surface. The progress has been wonderful enough but..."

Biographies/   **ISBN:** *1-59462-198-5*

Pages:300

MSRP $21.95

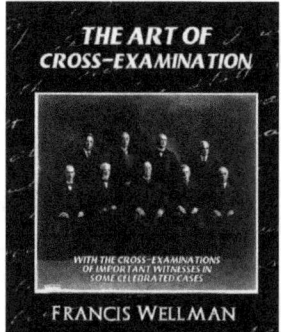

The Art of Cross-Examination
Francis Wellman

QTY

I presume it is the experience of every author, after his first book is published upon an important subject, to be almost overwhelmed with a wealth of ideas and illustrations which could readily have been included in his book, and which to his own mind, at least, seem to make a second edition inevitable. Such certainly was the case with me; and when the first edition had reached its sixth impression in five months, I rejoiced to learn that it seemed to my publishers that the book had met with a sufficiently favorable reception to justify a second and considerably enlarged edition. ..

Pages:412

Reference   ISBN: *1-59462-647-2*   *MSRP $19.95*

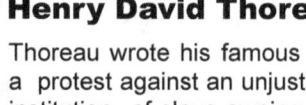

On the Duty of Civil Disobedience
Henry David Thoreau

QTY

Thoreau wrote his famous essay, On the Duty of Civil Disobedience, as a protest against an unjust but popular war and the immoral but popular institution of slave-owning. He did more than write—he declined to pay his taxes, and was hauled off to gaol in consequence. Who can say how much this refusal of his hastened the end of the war and of slavery ?

Law   ISBN: *1-59462-747-9*   **Pages:48**

MSRP $7.45

Dream Psychology Psychoanalysis for Beginners
Sigmund Freud

QTY

Sigmund Freud, born Sigismund Schlomo Freud (May 6, 1856 - September 23, 1939), was a Jewish-Austrian neurologist and psychiatrist who co-founded the psychoanalytic school of psychology. Freud is best known for his theories of the unconscious mind, especially involving the mechanism of repression; his redefinition of sexual desire as mobile and directed towards a wide variety of objects; and his therapeutic techniques, especially his understanding of transference in the therapeutic relationship and the presumed value of dreams as sources of insight into unconscious desires.

Pages:196

Psychology   ISBN: *1-59462-905-6*   *MSRP $15.45*

The Miracle of Right Thought
Orison Swett Marden

QTY

Believe with all of your heart that you will do what you were made to do. When the mind has once formed the habit of holding cheerful, happy, prosperous pictures, it will not be easy to form the opposite habit. It does not matter how improbable or how far away this realization may see, or how dark the prospects may be, if we visualize them as best we can, as vividly as possible, hold tenaciously to them and vigorously struggle to attain them, they will gradually become actualized, realized in the life. But a desire, a longing without endeavor, a yearning abandoned or held indifferently will vanish without realization.

Pages:360

Self Help   ISBN: *1-59462-644-8*   *MSRP $25.45*

www.**bookjungle**.com *email: sales@bookjungle.com fax: 630-214-0564 mail: Book Jungle PO Box 2226 Champaign, IL 61825*

QTY

The Rosicrucian Cosmo-Conception Mystic Christianity by *Max Heindel*   ISBN: *1-59462-188-8*   **$38.95**
The Rosicrucian Cosmo-conception is not dogmatic, neither does it appeal to any other authority than the reason of the student. It is: not controversial, but is: sent forth in, the hope that it may help to clear...   *New Age/Religion Pages 646*

Abandonment To Divine Providence by *Jean-Pierre de Caussade*   ISBN: *1-59462-228-0*   **$25.95**
"The Rev. Jean Pierre de Caussade was one of the most remarkable spiritual writers of the Society of Jesus in France in the 18th Century. His death took place at Toulouse in 1751. His works have gone through many editions and have been republished...   *Inspirational/Religion Pages 400*

Mental Chemistry by *Charles Haanel*   ISBN: *1-59462-192-6*   **$23.95**
Mental Chemistry allows the change of material conditions by combining and appropriately utilizing the power of the mind. Much like applied chemistry creates something new and unique out of careful combinations of chemicals the mastery of mental chemistry...   *New Age Pages 354*

The Letters of Robert Browning and Elizabeth Barret Barrett 1845-1846 vol II   ISBN: *1-59462-193-4*   **$35.95**
by *Robert Browning and Elizabeth Barrett*   *Biographies Pages 596*

Gleanings In Genesis (volume I) by *Arthur W. Pink*   ISBN: *1-59462-130-6*   **$27.45**
Appropriately has Genesis been termed "the seed plot of the Bible" for in it we have, in germ form, almost all of the great doctrines which are afterwards fully developed in the books of Scripture which follow...   *Religion/Inspirational Pages 420*

The Master Key by *L. W. de Laurence*   ISBN: *1-59462-001-6*   **$30.95**
In no branch of human knowledge has there been a more lively increase of the spirit of research during the past few years than in the study of Psychology, Concentration and Mental Discipline. The requests for authentic lessons in Thought Control, Mental Discipline and...   *New Age/Business Pages 422*

The Lesser Key Of Solomon Goetia by *L. W. de Laurence*   ISBN: *1-59462-092-X*   **$9.95**
This translation of the first book of the "Lernegton" which is now for the first time made accessible to students of Talismanic Magic was done, after careful collation and edition, from numerous Ancient Manuscripts in Hebrew, Latin, and French...   *New Age/Occult Pages 92*

Rubaiyat Of Omar Khayyam by *Edward Fitzgerald*   ISBN:*1-59462-332-5*   **$13.95**
Edward Fitzgerald, whom the world has already learned, in spite of his own efforts to remain within the shadow of anonymity, to look upon as one of the rarest poets of the century, was born at Bredfield, in Suffolk, on the 31st of March, 1809. He was the third son of John Purcell...   *Music Pages 172*

Ancient Law by *Henry Maine*   ISBN: *1-59462-128-4*   **$29.95**
The chief object of the following pages is to indicate some of the earliest ideas of mankind, as they are reflected in Ancient Law, and to point out the relation of those ideas to modern thought.   *Religiom/History Pages 452*

Far-Away Stories by *William J. Locke*   ISBN: *1-59462-129-2*   **$19.45**
"Good wine needs no bush, but a collection of mixed vintages does. And this book is just such a collection. Some of the stories I do not want to remain buried for ever in the museum files of dead magazine-numbers an author's not unpardonable vanity..."   *Fiction Pages 272*

Life of David Crockett by *David Crockett*   ISBN: *1-59462-250-7*   **$27.45**
"Colonel David Crockett was one of the most remarkable men of the times in which he lived. Born in humble life, but gifted with a strong will, an indomitable courage, and unremitting perseverance...   *Biographies/New Age Pages 424*

Lip-Reading by *Edward Nitchie*   ISBN: *1-59462-206-X*   **$25.95**
Edward B. Nitchie, founder of the New York School for the Hard of Hearing, now the Nitchie School of Lip-Reading, Inc, wrote "LIP-READING Principles and Practice". The development and perfecting of this meritorious work on lip-reading was an undertaking...   *How-to Pages 400*

A Handbook of Suggestive Therapeutics, Applied Hypnotism, Psychic Science   ISBN: *1-59462-214-0*   **$24.95**
by *Henry Munro*   *Health/New Age/Health/Self-help Pages 376*

A Doll's House: and Two Other Plays by *Henrik Ibsen*   ISBN: *1-59462-112-8*   **$19.95**
Henrik Ibsen created this classic when in revolutionary 1848 Rome. Introducing some striking concepts in playwriting for the realist genre, this play has been studied the world over.   *Fiction/Classics/Plays 308*

The Light of Asia by *sir Edwin Arnold*   ISBN: *1-59462-204-3*   **$13.95**
In this poetic masterpiece, Edwin Arnold describes the life and teachings of Buddha. The man who was to become known as Buddha to the world was born as Prince Gautama of India but he rejected the worldly riches and abandoned the reigns of power when...   *Religion/History/Biographies Pages 170*

The Complete Works of Guy de Maupassant by *Guy de Maupassant*   ISBN: *1-59462-157-8*   **$16.95**
"For days and days, nights and nights, I had dreamed of that first kiss which was to consecrate our engagement, and I knew not on what spot I should put my lips..."   *Fiction/Classics Pages 240*

The Art of Cross-Examination by *Francis L. Wellman*   ISBN: *1-59462-309-0*   **$26.95**
Written by a renowned trial lawyer, Wellman imparts his experience and uses case studies to explain how to use psychology to extract desired information through questioning.   *How-to/Science/Reference Pages 408*

Answered or Unanswered? by *Louisa Vaughan*   ISBN: *1-59462-248-5*   **$10.95**
Miracles of Faith in China   *Religion Pages 112*

The Edinburgh Lectures on Mental Science (1909) by *Thomas*   ISBN: *1-59462-008-3*   **$11.95**
This book contains the substance of a course of lectures recently given by the writer in the Queen Street Hail, Edinburgh. Its purpose is to indicate the Natural Principles governing the relation between Mental Action and Material Conditions...   *New Age/Psychology Pages 148*

Ayesha by *H. Rider Haggard*   ISBN: *1-59462-301-5*   **$24.95**
Verily and indeed it is the unexpected that happens! Probably if there was one person upon the earth from whom the Editor of this, and of a certain previous history, did not expect to hear again...   *Classics Pages 380*

Ayala's Angel by *Anthony Trollope*   ISBN: *1-59462-352-X*   **$29.95**
The two girls were both pretty, but Lucy who was twenty-one who supposed to be simple and comparatively unattractive, whereas Ayala was credited, as her Bombwhat romantic name might show, with poetic charm and a taste for romance. Ayala when her father died was nineteen...   *Fiction Pages 484*

The American Commonwealth by *James Bryce*   ISBN: *1-59462-286-8*   **$34.45**
An interpretation of American democratic political theory. It examines political mechanics and society from the perspective of Scotsman James Bryce   *Politics Pages 572*

Stories of the Pilgrims by *Margaret P. Pumphrey*   ISBN: *1-59462-116-0*   **$17.95**
This book explores pilgrims religious oppression in England as well as their escape to Holland and eventual crossing to America on the Mayflower, and their early days in New England...   *History Pages 268*

QTY

The Fasting Cure *by Sinclair Upton*   ISBN: *1-59462-222-1*   **$13.95**
In the Cosmopolitan Magazine for May, 1910, and in the Contemporary Review (London) for April, 1910, I published an article dealing with my experi-
ences in fasting. I have written a great many magazine articles, but never one which attracted so much attention... New Age/Self Help/Health Pages 164

Hebrew Astrology *by Sepharial*   ISBN: *1-59462-308-2*   **$13.45**
In these days of advanced thinking it is a matter of common observation that we have left many of the old landmarks behind and that we are now pressing
forward to greater heights and to a wider horizon than that which represented the mind-content of our progenitors... Astrology Pages 144

Thought Vibration or The Law of Attraction in the Thought World   ISBN: *1-59462-127-6*   **$12.95**

by William Walker Atkinson   Psychology/Religion Pages 144

Optimism *by Helen Keller*   ISBN: *1-59462-108-X*   **$15.95**
Helen Keller was blind, deaf, and mute since 19 months old, yet famously learned how to overcome these handicaps, communicate with the world, and
spread her lectures promoting optimism. An inspiring read for everyone... Biographies/Inspirational Pages 84

Sara Crewe *by Frances Burnett*   ISBN: *1-59462-360-0*   **$9.45**
In the first place, Miss Minchin lived in London. Her home was a large, dull, tall one, in a large, dull square, where all the houses were alike, and all the
sparrows were alike, and where all the door-knockers made the same heavy sound... Childrens/Classic Pages 88

The Autobiography of Benjamin Franklin *by Benjamin Franklin*   ISBN: *1-59462-135-7*   **$24.95**
The Autobiography of Benjamin Franklin has probably been more extensively read than any other American historical work, and no other book of its kind
has had such ups and downs of fortune. Franklin lived for many years in England, where he was agent... Biographies/History Pages 332

Name	
Email	
Telephone	
Address	
City, State ZIP	

☐ **Credit Card**   ☐ **Check / Money Order**

Credit Card Number	
Expiration Date	
Signature	

Please Mail to: *Book Jungle*
PO Box 2226
Champaign, IL 61825
or Fax to: *630-214-0564*

ORDERING INFORMATION

web: *www.bookjungle.com*
email: *sales@bookjungle.com*
fax: *630-214-0564*
mail: *Book Jungle PO Box 2226 Champaign, IL 61825*
or PayPal *to sales@bookjungle.com*

Please contact us for bulk discounts

DIRECT-ORDER TERMS

**20% Discount if You Order
Two or More Books**
Free Domestic Shipping!
Accepted: Master Card, Visa,
Discover, American Express

QTY

The Fasting Cure *by Sinclair Upton*   ISBN: *1-59462-222-1*   **$13.95**
*In the Cosmopolitan Magazine for May, 1910, and in the Contemporary Review (London) for April, 1910, I published an article dealing with my experi-
ences in fasting. I have written a great many magazine articles, but never one which attracted so much attention... New Age/Self Help/Health Pages 164*

Hebrew Astrology *by Sepharial*   ISBN: *1-59462-308-2*   **$13.45**
*In these days of advanced thinking it is a matter of common observation that we have left many of the old landmarks behind and that we are now pressing
forward to greater heights and to a wider horizon than that which represented the mind-content of our progenitors...   Astrology Pages 144*

Thought Vibration or The Law of Attraction in the Thought World   ISBN: *1-59462-127-6*   **$12.95**

by William Walker Atkinson   *Psychology/Religion Pages 144*

Optimism *by Helen Keller*   ISBN: *1-59462-108-X*   **$15.95**
*Helen Keller was blind, deaf, and mute since 19 months old, yet famously learned how to overcome these handicaps, communicate with the world, and
spread her lectures promoting optimism. An inspiring read for everyone...   Biographies/Inspirational Pages 84*

Sara Crewe *by Frances Burnett*   ISBN: *1-59462-360-0*   **$9.45**
*In the first place, Miss Minchin lived in London. Her home was a large, dull, tall one, in a large, dull square, where all the houses were alike, and all the
sparrows were alike, and where all the door-knockers made the same heavy sound...   Childrens/Classic Pages 88*

The Autobiography of Benjamin Franklin *by Benjamin Franklin*   ISBN: *1-59462-135-7*   **$24.95**
*The Autobiography of Benjamin Franklin has probably been more extensively read than any other American historical work, and no other book of its kind
has had such ups and downs of fortune. Franklin lived for many years in England, where he was agent...   Biographies/History Pages 332*

Name	
Email	
Telephone	
Address	
City, State ZIP	

☐ **Credit Card**   ☐ **Check / Money Order**

Credit Card Number	
Expiration Date	
Signature	

Please Mail to: Book Jungle
PO Box 2226
Champaign, IL 61825
or Fax to: 630-214-0564

ORDERING INFORMATION

web*: www.bookjungle.com*
email*: sales@bookjungle.com*
fax*: 630-214-0564*
mail*: Book Jungle PO Box 2226 Champaign, IL 61825*
or PayPal *to sales@bookjungle.com*

Please contact us for bulk discounts

DIRECT-ORDER TERMS

**20% Discount if You Order
Two or More Books**
Free Domestic Shipping!
Accepted: Master Card, Visa,
Discover, American Express

www.ingramcontent.com/pod-product-compliance
Lightning Source LLC
Chambersburg PA
CBHW080730020726
47503CB00010B/2860